W9-BYK-626

"I've got a suspect. It's only a matter of time before I charge him."

Sheriff Fielder's mouth stretched into a thin smile as he continued. "Lucky for us he's right here in town. Someone you know, as a matter of fact."

No shock for Will there. At the time of Frannie's disappearance he'd known almost everyone in town.

"Someone you knew *real* well. Jed Louis," Fielder said with obvious relish. "He's guilty as sin, and I expect to bring him in any day now."

Jed? What kind of crap was this? Will's expression didn't change, but inside he wanted to smash his fist into something. How much worse could things get?

"I don't believe Jed did it."

"That's your problem, Ranger McClain. Even you won't be able to deny the facts when you see them."

Great. What a homecoming. His foster brother was the prime suspect in the murder of their foster mother.

Dear Reader,

When K.N. Casper, Roz Denny Fox and I were asked to write a trilogy set in Texas, we wanted to explore a nontraditional Texas setting. Rather than the plains or prairies, or the rolling hills of central Texas, we chose Caddo Lake, the only natural lake in Texas, found on the Texas-Louisiana border. Caddo Lake is an eerie, mysterious, beautiful lake full of cypress stands and legends galore. What more fitting place to explore a mystery and bring a foster family back together could you think of?

When we drove through the town of Uncertain, we knew we'd found the perfect setting. Although Uncertain is a real town, none of the characters or businesses exist anywhere other than our imaginations.

Come explore mysterious Caddo Lake with us....

Sincerely,

Eve Gaddy

P.S. I love to hear from readers. Write me at P.O. Box 131701, Tyler, TX 75713-1704. Or e-mail egaddy@tcainternet.com and visit my Web site at www.sff.net/people/Eve.Gaddy.

A Man of His Word
Eve Gaddy

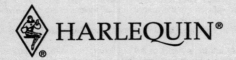

HARLEQUIN®

TORONTO • NEW YORK • LONDON
AMSTERDAM • PARIS • SYDNEY • HAMBURG
STOCKHOLM • ATHENS • TOKYO • MILAN • MADRID
PRAGUE • WARSAW • BUDAPEST • AUCKLAND

If you purchased this book without a cover you should be aware
that this book is stolen property. It was reported as "unsold and
destroyed" to the publisher, and neither the author nor the
publisher has received any payment for this "stripped book."

ISBN 0-373-70990-0

A MAN OF HIS WORD

Copyright © 2001 by Eve Gaddy.

All rights reserved. Except for use in any review, the reproduction or
utilization of this work in whole or in part in any form by any electronic,
mechanical or other means, now known or hereafter invented, including
xerography, photocopying and recording, or in any information storage
or retrieval system, is forbidden without the written permission of the
publisher, Harlequin Enterprises Limited, 225 Duncan Mill Road,
Don Mills, Ontario, Canada M3B 3K9.

All characters in this book have no existence outside the imagination of
the author and have no relation whatsoever to anyone bearing the same
name or names. They are not even distantly inspired by any individual
known or unknown to the author, and all incidents are pure invention.

This edition published by arrangement with Harlequin Books S.A.

® and TM are trademarks of the publisher. Trademarks indicated with
® are registered in the United States Patent and Trademark Office, the
Canadian Trade Marks Office and in other countries.

Visit us at www.eHarlequin.com

Printed in U.S.A.

This book is for Roz Denny Fox and K.N. Casper,
my fellow trilogy writers. Thanks, you two,
for making the experience a great one. I had a blast!
Also, I have to put in another word (or twelve) for
Rosalyn Alsobrook, who not only told us about the town of
Uncertain, but who critiqued my book. Thanks, Roz, for
everything. I also want to thank Deputy David Nelson for
his help with my many questions about law enforcement.

CHAPTER ONE

HE FOUND IT in the freezer, wrapped in newspaper. Not a very original hiding place for a murder weapon, but Lenny the Leech had never been long on brains. It didn't take any special training to know that.

Texas Ranger Will McClain smiled as he pulled on thin latex gloves and peeled aside the newspaper to reveal a 9mm automatic. "Beautiful," he said to his partner. "Same caliber as the gun that killed Stringer. Want to bet the marks on the casings match?"

"That's a sucker bet," Rafe Wagner said. "Let's bag it and get out of here." He offered Will a paper bag. "The stench is killing me. There must be a year's worth of garbage in this dump."

Will nodded, stuffed the weapon inside the evidence bag and handed it to Wagner to log. As he folded the newspaper to fit into another bag, a headline caught his eye. He stopped in midmotion, staring at the yellowed clipping. Wagner's voice continued from a distance, but Will couldn't distinguish the words.

"What?" Will gazed at Wagner blankly.

"I said hurry up," he repeated.

Will shook his head, still unable to concentrate.

"Hey, McClain, you okay?"

With an effort, Will focused his attention on his

partner. "Yeah, I'm fine. You go ahead. There's something I need to take care of here. I'll catch up in a minute."

As Wagner left, Will took a seat at the chrome-and-black Formica-topped table. A closer inspection of the table proved the color to be the result of the same grunge that covered the rest of the apartment. Careful not to contaminate the newspaper with oils or fluids from the tabletop, he stretched the paper out to read it. Evidence, just like the gun, but Will didn't intend to bag it until he'd read the article below the gut-draining headline.

Mystery Bones Discovered Near
East Texas Lake Identified

Uncertain, Texas. The mystery of Frannie Granger's disappearance may finally be solved. The forty-seven-year-old Harrison County woman vanished nineteen years ago this May. Her remains were recently found close to an Indian burial ground near Caddo Lake. She is believed to have been murdered. On March 28 of this year, upon the discovery of human remains obviously not those of a Caddo Indian of the early nineteenth century, archaeologist Theresa Lang turned the skeleton over to the authorities for identification. This week, dental records proved the bones to be those of Frannie Granger, a widow who was housekeeper for various local residents and who provided foster care for unadoptable children in her own home in Uncertain.

Granger was well liked in the community, and her sudden disappearance caused quite a stir. Sheriff Logan Fielder could not be reached for comment. The question remains, who murdered Frannie Granger, and why?

Will's stomach tightened as his gaze shifted to find the date. Two months old, damn it. And it was only by chance he'd seen it at all.

The printed lines blurred, wavered. He shifted back, twenty-three years into the past. He'd been thirteen years old. Brash, cocky, a troublemaker nobody wanted, headed to juvie hall after one last-ditch attempt by social services to provide the home he needed.

He hadn't wanted it. If he could have managed, he'd have gone back to the streets, or so he told himself. But he'd been too scared to hit the streets again, because even back then he'd known where he'd end up.

Remembering his youthful bravado, Will half smiled. The last thing he'd wanted was to be sent to another foster home. Another family who took him in for the money and booted him out the minute he gave them too much trouble. And he always did.

Then along came Frannie Granger. The woman who had saved his life.

His foster mother hadn't simply disappeared all those years before. Frannie Granger had been murdered.

THE SHERIFF'S OFFICE and jail in Uncertain, Texas, didn't run to comfort, Tessa Lang decided. Not for the prisoners and certainly not for anyone unfortunate enough to have business with Sheriff Logan Fielder, she thought resentfully. Housed in a drab one-story beige brick building in the center of town, it lacked both charm and personality.

In the reception area, a small room with grayish walls and not a picture to be seen, Tessa shifted in the hard orange plastic chair in a vain attempt to find relief from the ridges digging into her back. For the tenth time, she checked her watch and swore silently. Forty-five minutes until class started. She couldn't afford to wait much longer. She glanced at Deputy Kyle Masters, the room's only other occupant, and debated asking him yet again when the sheriff would see her.

Masters sat with his feet on his desk, leafing through the local newspaper. As if he'd read her thoughts, he glanced up and spoke. "Sheriff's likely to be a while. Sure you don't want to talk to me instead?" He added a grin.

No doubt he thought it was charming, but Tessa didn't. A deputy did her no good. He knew that as well as she did. "Yes, I'm sure," she said shortly, hoping Kyle wouldn't ask her for a date again. He seemed like a nice enough man, but Tessa had no interest in dating anything but items uncovered at an archaeological site.

It must be the new haircut, she thought, momentarily distracted from her purpose. She smoothed her now shoulder length red hair. Or maybe it was the sleeveless ice-blue summer dress she'd bought a couple of days ago. Ever since her friend and colleague Ellen

Hampton had convinced her that her appearance needed drastic updating, strange things had happened to her. Three men—two of them total strangers—had asked her out in the past few weeks. A record unequaled in Tessa's experience. Men didn't date her. Normally men didn't even notice her.

Of course, Ellen's exact advice hadn't been that polite, Tessa remembered, smiling. "Tessa, come out of the fifties and join the new millennium," she'd said. "Lose the uptight hair and boring clothes. For Pete's sake, you're an archaeologist, not a mummy."

Who would have thought a different haircut and a few new outfits would have such an effect? Tessa squirmed a bit in her chair, unsure whether she liked the new attention or not. Part of her felt flattered, but a bigger part felt like an imposter—as if she wore the Emperor's new clothes and eventually everyone around would realize it and die laughing.

Thinking about her new look didn't solve her dilemma though. Nothing did. Her problems had all started with the discovery of Frannie Granger's bones, which had prompted Fielder to shut down her dig indefinitely. Rather than spend the time doing absolutely nothing but feel her blood pressure climb, Tessa had asked around and found the local college desperately needed a professor of archaeology, their previous one having unexpectedly died. She took the job and, a bit to her surprise, found she loved it. She wondered what her mother, a distinguished archaeological scholar, would say about her only offspring teaching at what she would undoubtedly label a backwater country college.

Odder even than enjoying teaching was the fact that, for the first time in her life, she had made friends. Real friends. Ellen had been first to extend a welcome, but the other professors and most of the townspeople had followed closely behind. They'd all been amazingly nice.

Everyone except Jed Louis, the man she'd had to take to court before she could gain access to his land. No, Jed didn't like her much, especially after she'd found a murder victim's remains on his land. His foster mother's remains, yet.

Tessa scowled again, glancing at the eternally closed door to the sheriff's office. Fielder hadn't been in any hurry to allow Tessa back on Jed's land, either. The land that lay idle in the elements while the sheriff took his sweet time over a twenty-year-old murder.

Once again, Tessa cursed the day she'd discovered the very twentieth century remains among the broken pottery shards near the nineteenth century Caddo Indian burial mound. Why did the blasted body have to show up in the middle of her dig? And why in the hell couldn't she have at least resumed excavation on another part of the site? She wasn't a novice, she would have been careful not to approach the cordoned-off area, or allow any of her crew to, either.

But Fielder wouldn't even let her set foot on the place. Tessa felt sympathy for the murdered woman, who from all accounts had been very nice, but enough was enough. It was either gain access to the site soon, or kiss her grant money, her thesis and her promising career goodbye. She shuddered, thinking of her mother's reaction to that.

She was just about to leave a pithy message for the blasted lawman when his office door opened. Fielder slouched against the frame, still in no hurry. His gritty-eyed gaze flicked over her with disinterest. His craggy face wore his habitual scowl. In his early sixties, with dark hair liberally shot with gray, he didn't have an ounce of spare flesh on him, contributing to the image Tessa imagined he enjoyed maintaining. Lean, mean, and tough as an old fence post. Sometimes that snake-eyed expression of his gave her the creeps, but right now she was too ticked off to let it faze her.

Finally he nodded. "Ms. Lang."

He drawled her name out. Tessa didn't make the mistake of thinking he meant any respect.

"Well, what can I do for you?" He stood aside and motioned her in.

As if he didn't know. They'd played out this same scenario about a hundred times in the past few weeks. "Sheriff Fielder, you know why I'm here. Surely you've had time by now to gather all the evidence you need."

Fielder settled into his chair, leaving Tessa to perch uncomfortably on yet another hard plastic piece of misery.

"Well, now, that depends. You're mighty anxious to gain access to the murder site, aren't you, Ms. Lang?"

Duh, she thought, barely stopping herself from rolling her eyes. "Yes sir. As I've told you—" a zillion times, she thought darkly ''—it's very important to my thesis that I be allowed to finish the dig started in that area.'' Choking on the need for amiability, or at least civility, she itched to wipe the smirk off his face. Too bad she couldn't think of a way to do it.

Fielder pursed his lips and shuffled through some papers on his desk. ''Then this must be your lucky day, Ms. Lang. I'm about convinced we've got all the evidence to be gained from the site. I've decided to allow you to resume your dig.''

''Like hell she will.'' A deep male voice came from behind her.

Tessa's head whipped around. A stranger filled the office doorway. A very large, very intimidating stranger. From her vantage point, seated in a low-slung chair, Tessa thought he stood about seven feet tall. Mid-thirties, she guessed, with a fallen-angel face she bet earned him more than his share of female attention. Including hers, she realized, with a touch of irritation. Pale blond hair fell to the open collar of a baby-blue button-down dress shirt, the sleeves rolled up to expose tanned, powerful forearms. Washed-out denim clung to long, lean, muscled legs. Scuffed cowboy boots added at least an inch or two to an already impressive stature.

But his eyes were his most arresting feature. Gray-green and sharp with authority, they passed right over her and zeroed in on the sheriff like a laser beam.

Tessa tore her startled gaze away from the commanding vision to glance at Fielder. His mouth opened and closed. No sound emerged, but his face reddened and his harsh features looked even more unaccommodating than usual. Suddenly she felt sorry for Deputy Masters. She doubted the sheriff appreciated his letting the stranger through.

"Who the hell are you?" Fielder asked.

The man strode into the room to stand in front of him. Tessa sucked in her breath at the power he brought along with him.

"Will McClain." Pausing a beat, he reached into the back pocket of his jeans and pulled out a leather case. He flipped it open and added, "Texas Ranger."

If possible, the sheriff's face darkened even more. "McClain?" His brows drew together until they met over the bridge of his nose, then flattened again. "Not—my God, you couldn't be. Not the McClain—"

"The very same," he said, his voice laced with amusement. "Small world, isn't it?"

Tessa shivered at the diabolic smile he offered Fielder, glad she wasn't on the receiving end of it. Still, she had to find out what was going on. Gathering her wits, which seemed to have fled with the Ranger's entrance, she turned to Fielder and spoke briskly. "Excuse me, but what's happening here? I thought you were in charge of the investigation?"

Ignoring her, Fielder rose jerkily, staring at the Ranger in revulsion and—she could have sworn—a hint of fear. "What kind of bullshit is this? Show me that badge again."

McClain shrugged and flipped it to him. Fielder inspected it, his face paling as he did so. He glanced at the Ranger, then back at the badge. After a long pause, he handed it back and said heavily, "I don't believe this."

"Believe it," McClain said, his voice silky, dark.

Fielder shook his head, as if trying to clear it. "What are you doing here?"

"If you'll recall, the Rangers never signed off on this case." He pocketed his badge and nailed the sheriff with another hard smile. "I have orders to finish it."

"Finish it?" He drew himself up and glared, throwing off his momentary lapse with vigor. "I've practically got it sewed up. I didn't ask for the Rangers, and no piece of—" He hesitated, eyeing McClain's stony face. "No Texas Ranger is going to come in and lay claim to a case I've already figured out. I don't need your damned interference."

The Ranger looked almost amused now. "Yeah? I'll be sure and tell my captain you said so. In the meantime, fill me in on what you've got."

Fielder's jaw tightened. He and McClain stared at each other while Tessa grew more puzzled and irritated, and damn it, curious, by the moment.

Turning to Tessa, Fielder said, "Ms. Lang. I'll have to get back to you on that other matter."

Tessa sprang to her feet to gape incredulously at him. "You must be joking! I need access to the burial area, and you just promised it to me." She waved a hand at the man beside her, realizing that though he was big in comparison to her five foot three, he wasn't quite the giant she'd originally thought him. "Everything was fine until he came in. Are you just going to let him order you around?'' From what she knew of Fielder, she couldn't imagine it.

''This is a murder investigation,'' McClain said. ''And that site is pertinent to the investigation.''

''No joke,'' Tessa snapped, her gaze transferring to him. It irked her even more that he towered over her like a massive redwood. ''Since I'm the one who discovered the bones, I think I'm aware of that.''

''Then you should also be aware we can't allow you to disturb the site any further.'' His gaze assessed her dispassionately, his eyes a cool, cynical gray. ''Not until I'm assured all the evidence pertaining to the murder has been collected and logged.''

''But Sheriff Fielder just said—'' she began furiously.

''The subject is closed, Ms. Lang. We'll let you know when the situation changes. Until then, you'd best stay away from that area.''

She couldn't believe what she was hearing. Hands on hips, she jutted out her chin. ''This is an outrage! If you think I'm just going to go meekly away—''

''File a complaint,'' McClain told her, taking her arm to propel her out of the room. Totally ignoring her sputtered protests, he added, ''I'm sure the deputy will be happy to assist you.''

Their gazes locked for a brief moment, and a reluctant smile twisted his mouth. Then he shut the door in her face.

Tessa stared at the closed door, unable to believe what had just happened. ''You wait, Ranger Mc-

Clain,'' she threatened, regaining her power of speech. ''You haven't seen the last of me.''

WILL HAD A MOMENTARY REGRET for pissing off the archaeologist so royally. Another time that strawberry-blond hair, pouty mouth and curvy little body might have interested him. But he wasn't in Uncertain to find a woman, not unless that woman happened to be a murderer. Not about to be distracted, he promptly dismissed the redhead and turned his attention to Sheriff Logan Fielder. The old bastard hadn't changed much.

''Where do you get off—'' Fielder began, striding around the desk as if he intended to punch him.

Will almost wished he'd try it, except the resulting fight would just waste time and energy. ''I've told you my orders, Sheriff. I'm here to investigate Frannie Granger's murder. Accept it, and let's get down to business.''

''I can't believe the punk I used to haul in to my jail is a Texas Ranger.''

''Deal with it.'' Will smiled, enjoying the older man's anger. Knowing it would jerk his chain even more, he pulled up a chair and settled comfortably into it. ''Fill me in.''

Fielder's jaw worked for a long moment. He shrugged, dropping his gaze, and sat back down. ''There's nothing to fill in. I've got a suspect, and it's only a matter of time before I'll be able to charge him.''

''Who is the suspect?''

His mouth stretched into a thin smile as his gaze

met Will's. "Lucky for us he's right here in town. Someone you know, as a matter of fact."

Will simply looked at him, raising an eyebrow. No shock there. At the time of Frannie's disappearance he'd known almost everyone in town.

"Someone you knew *real* well. Jed Louis," Fielder said with obvious relish. "He's guilty as sin, and I expect to bring him in any day now."

Jed? What kind of crap was this? Will's expression didn't change, but inside he wanted to smash his fist into something—preferably Fielder's face. Damn it, how much worse could things get?

"Why?"

Fielder smirked, holding up a hand to tick off reasons on his fingers. "Motive. Means. Opportunity." He propped his forearms on the desk and added, "I've got him cold."

Will drew in a breath, forcing himself to remain calm. "I don't believe Jed did it."

"That's your problem, *Ranger* McClain. Even you won't be able to deny the facts when you see them."

"Show me."

"I'll get the records and the evidence together this afternoon. You'll have them tomorrow."

"I'd better," he said, observing with some satisfaction the smile fading from Fielder's mouth.

Great. What a homecoming. His foster brother was the prime suspect in the murder of their foster mother.

CHAPTER TWO

WILL STRODE out of the sheriff's office, anger fueling his steps. Damn it, how could Jed be the prime suspect? Will might not have seen Jed in nearly twenty years, but he remembered him well. And the boy he'd known couldn't have killed Frannie.

Not deliberately.

Hand on his truck's door handle, Will halted at the unwelcome thought. No, Jed wouldn't have killed Frannie on purpose...but what about an accident?

"Mr. McClain!" a voice with a Southern lilt demanded imperiously.

The redhead, wearing a cool blue sleeveless dress, the kind that made a man grateful for the East Texas humidity, hurried across the parking lot toward him.

"Mr. McClain, I want a word with you."

Theresa Lang, he thought. The archaeologist who'd discovered Frannie's remains. Still ticked, obviously. "It's Ranger McClain. And I'm in a hurry." He meant to find Jed and hear what he had to say. See if he knew Fielder suspected him, though Will imagined he did. *Subtle* wasn't Fielder's middle name.

"That's just too bad. If you think you can brush me aside like some kind of insect, think again. I canceled my class because of you and I intend to discuss this matter now. I've been put off long enough.'' She shoved him back with a surprisingly firm hand, and placed herself between him and the truck's door. ''We're going to talk,'' she said grimly. ''Unless you mean to remove me by force.'' Her chin angled up, thrust forward aggressively.

Will hid a smile. She appeared even tinier in contrast to the huge black truck. Small but feisty, he thought. Might as well deal with her now. He probably needed more time to think matters through before he saw Jed anyway. ''Oh, I wouldn't dream of it.'' He crossed his arms and leaned back against the front quarter panel of the truck, turning his head to give her his undivided attention. ''What's on your mind?''

''My career.''

Will waited but she didn't say any more. ''What about your career?''

''You're killing it. You and Sheriff Fielder.''

''By not allowing you access to the murder site, I presume.''

''That's right.'' She nodded sharply. ''I have a grant. A time limit. If I'm not able to resume my dig soon, then my career is as good as over.''

''That would prevent you from teaching?''

She scowled. ''I'm not a teacher.''

''You said you canceled a class. I assumed that meant you were a teacher.''

''It's temporary.'' She shrugged irritably. ''I had to do something while I waited for that terminally slow sheriff to make up his mind.'' Her blue eyes held a martial light, brightening and intensifying the color.

"The point is, if I'm going to finish my thesis I need access to that site."

He found her earnestness appealing. Too bad he had to disappoint her. "Obviously this is important to you. I can respect that."

"Can you?" She lifted a regal eyebrow as if she didn't believe any such thing. "Then let me back on that land."

Pretty, he thought. The summer sun glinted off her hair, red with hints of gold. Gorgeous eyes, sea-blue and haunting. Her skin looked as soft and creamy as a magnolia blossom, and the slight scattering of freckles across the bridge of her nose gave her an added bit of character. Very pretty, but then he'd always been partial to redheads. She looked much better suited to lounging on a veranda, or better yet, in a dimly lit bedroom, than digging for fossils and broken pottery under the brutal East Texas sun.

"Can't do it," he said regretfully. "Not yet."

"This is my entire career we're talking about!" She smacked her fist against the truck door, wincing when it connected. "Not some minor matter you can dismiss like last week's news."

"And what do you call murder?"

"At the moment, I call it extremely frustrating."

Will smiled. "Yeah, I'll agree to that."

"Isn't there anything I can do to change your mind? I'll be careful, I swear it. The sheriff's had men out there for weeks now, going over everything. Surely he's found all the evidence by now. And if I did find anything, anything at all relevant to your investigation,

I'd turn it over immediately.'' Eyes desperate, she added a final word. "Please."

Will shook his head. "Sorry. I'm trying to find a murderer and I can't allow an archaeologist wanting to play around with clay pots to compromise the investigation."

She sucked in a breath, plainly struggling with her temper.

He supposed he could have phrased that better, but he shrugged mentally. She might as well hear the truth now as later.

"Burial mounds," she corrected. "Caddo Indian burial mounds that are disintegrating as we speak." She bit off each word, her eyes flashing fire. "Pots are only a small part of it. And I'm not playing."

He straightened and gazed down at her. "Neither am I, Ms. Lang. I'm talking murder."

"And I'm talking about my livelihood, my future, my career."

"Over one dig? Over a delay?"

"A delay that means the artifacts and what's left of the mounds themselves are being exposed to the elements. No one would let me shut down properly, they just threw me off the land. Any further delay means I won't be able to finish my thesis. Over two years of work will have been for nothing." She fisted her hands at her side. "*Two years,* for nothing."

He considered her thoughtfully. "It's that important to you?"

"Of course it is. Isn't your career important to you?"

Only the most important thing in his life. And finding Frannie's murderer would be the best thing he'd ever done with that career. Still, Theresa Lang had a point, and a right to be upset at having her livelihood threatened. There might be a way to let her access at least some of the land in question. "Okay, I'll think about it."

"Gee, thanks," she said sarcastically, shoving thick red hair back from her face in a quick, agitated gesture.

He frowned. He'd listened to her, hadn't he? What did she expect—instant gratification? He'd just gotten into town, for crying out loud. "Let me review the case and I'll get back to you."

She sent him a scathing look. "I've heard that before. Weeks ago. From Sheriff Fielder."

"I'm not Fielder," he said, not blaming her for her contempt of the sheriff. "I'll be in touch in the next day or two."

"I won't simply go away, you know. I'll be back if you don't contact me."

Having seen her and talked to her, he didn't doubt that. "Don't worry, Ms. Lang. I keep my word."

"You'd better, Ranger McClain." She moved aside, allowing him to open his door.

"Call me Will." He flashed her a friendly smile, but he didn't think it impressed her. "I have a feeling we're going to be seeing a lot of each other."

"I can hardly wait, *Will,*" she said, her sugar magnolia voice dripping with bitter sarcasm. "You can call me Tessa, as long as you call soon and with the right answer.'' She spun on her heel and marched off, but even her angry stride couldn't disguise the subtle swing of her hips.

Will watched her go with a reluctant smile. He would do what he could to help her professionally. Partly because it was the right thing to do. But also because the earnest Tessa Lang intrigued him. He wouldn't mind a bit getting to know her on a personal level.

WILL FOUND OUT EASILY where Jed lived, simply by asking about him at the local convenience store. Nobody recognized Will, not surprising since he'd grown up and filled out a lot in the past nineteen years. But he remembered many of the locals. Especially ones like old Mrs. Whitney, who still owned the Kit and Caboodle Cottages. She would be glad to rent him a room, he suspected. He had a feeling this whole affair might take longer than he'd bargained on.

A couple of miles south of Uncertain he pulled over to the side of the road and got out to see Jed's place. Though Frannie's land stood next door, the house well hidden, he deliberately didn't look at it. There would be time enough later to deal with the memories that would bring.

No, he preferred to focus on Jed. And the prime property he owned. Beaumarais, he called it. Impressive, Will admitted, taking in the stately white antebellum mansion and the beautifully manicured lawn surrounding it. The land that stretched for acres was just as carefully maintained, with a scattering of horses grazing in the fields. Percherons, Will thought, watching the enormous beasts with their beautiful foals. Jed had always liked the big breed.

Built on a hill overlooking the town, the huge house stood two and half stories tall, with a red tile roof and narrow dormer windows. Massive chimneys flanked the house at either end, while a columned porch ran along the entire front. Whatever Jed had done with his life, he'd obviously succeeded in at least one aspect.

Will had seen the place before, of course, always from a distance. He didn't think it had been this well maintained in old Walter's time. Jed had always referred to it as his future inheritance from his slimeball uncle. Will hadn't quite believed it would happen. Looked like he'd been wrong.

Will climbed back into his truck and drove slowly up the long driveway lined with flowering crepe myrtle in shades of pink, white and crimson. Nineteen years had passed since he'd last seen Jed and Emmy. He'd thought about searching for his foster siblings several times over the years. Something always stopped him.

At first he'd been too busy trying to stay one step ahead of the system, not to mention just plain surviving, to look for anything beyond where his next meal was coming from. Later, after he became a cop, he could have attempted to find them. But he never had. He closed his eyes, knowing why. When he'd left Uncertain at seventeen, he'd closed the door on that part of his past. Frannie was gone, and with her, the only security, the only family he'd ever known. He'd made the decision to go on with his life. He figured Jed and Emmy had, too.

Obviously, they hadn't looked for him, either. And that bothered him. More than he wanted to admit.

What if Jed didn't recognize him? Or worse, had forgotten him? Maybe what had meant so much to him hadn't meant all that much to either of the others. Could be he'd made too much of the bond he'd believed the three foster kids had shared.

He got out of the truck and gazed at the front door. He wouldn't put it off. He owed it to Frannie to find out the truth about her death, and that meant starting with Jed.

He rang the doorbell and waited, resisting the urge to tug on his collar. He was grown now, not some lonely kid looking up to an older brother figure. *Get a grip, McClain,* he told himself. *So what if he doesn't remember you? You've lived through worse.*

A tidy black woman in a neat gray-and-white uniform answered the door. "Can I help you?"

"Jed Louis, please."

"I'll see if he's available." She surveyed him with shrewd, inquisitive eyes. "Can I tell him who's calling?"

"Tell him..." Will hesitated, decided to go for surprise. "Tell him it's an old friend."

She inclined her head, then led him to a room off the main entryway. An anteroom, he supposed they called it, or maybe a parlor. Will glanced around, taking in the Victorian antiques scattered throughout the small room, the delicate, ornate peach couch with two fiddleback chairs beside it. A marble-topped table with a beautifully carved wooden base stood off to the side, holding a Tiffany lamp and more doodads Will assumed were antiques. Cold and formal and nothing at all like the Jed he thought he'd known.

He remembered the day so clearly. A couple of months after Frannie had dragged him home with her, he'd been suspended from school. No surprise, he'd been fighting again. But that time had been different. Because that time he hadn't fought alone. Jed had stood with him, and gained a black eye and bloody nose for his trouble. And Will knew right then he'd found a true brother.

A brother who now stood one step away from being formally charged with murder.

Will was still deciding if he dared sit on the couch or if he'd do better in one of the chairs when he heard footsteps come to a halt behind him. He turned around slowly to see a tall, lanky, black-haired man in stonewashed jeans and a black T-shirt standing in the doorway. Neither spoke a word as they stared at each other.

Jed's puzzled expression gave way to a wide smile. ''Will? My God, it *is* you.'' In a flash he was across the room and had enveloped Will in a hearty bear hug. They pounded each other's backs and asked each other questions neither heard. The rush of emotion shocked him, seemed almost alien to him. Will didn't consider himself an emotional man. Given his life, and his profession, he couldn't afford to be. It had been a long time since he'd let himself care for anyone the way he had for Jed and Emmy. And Frannie.

Finally Jed drew back, and said, "I can't believe you're here. Emmy and I have been wishing—"

"Emmy?" Will interrupted. "Emmy's here, too? In Uncertain?"

Jed nodded, his eyes brightening again. "Yes. Not at this exact moment, though. She's on her honeymoon. She married Riley, just a few days ago."

"Riley Gray Wolf?" Riley had been a friend of Will's, as well as being sweet on Emmy. "So, he and Emmy got together after all." Frannie, he remembered, swallowing a chuckle, hadn't approved of that relationship. She'd thought Emmy way too young to be serious about anyone. Especially Riley.

"Yes, they sure did. He went by Riley Gray for a long time, but he changed it back to Gray Wolf just recently."

"Hard to believe." Will shook his head. "Riley and little Emmy, married."

"She's all grown-up now," Jed said with a smile. "I married a little while ago, too. Gwyn's gone out but she'll be back soon. I want you to stay to meet her."

"I'm looking forward to it," Will said, wondering what sort of woman Jed had married. Maybe she was the one who liked all the fancy junk, because he still didn't think it suited Jed. "Some digs you've got here. I guess the inheritance from the rich uncle came through after all."

"Only out of necessity. There wasn't anyone else he could leave it to," Jed replied, frowning.

Will gestured at the room. "Still. You've prospered."

"I've been fortunate. Life's treated me well."

Yeah, unless he ended up charged with murder, Will thought. "I always knew you'd make it. You were primed to succeed."

He shrugged it off. "Let's go in the library, where it's comfortable."

Relieved, Will grinned. "I didn't think this was your type of room."

Jed shook his head ruefully as they walked down the hall. "June always puts people she's not sure about in there." He cut Will a sideways glance and smiled. "She must think you're a suspicious character. She says the anteroom intimidates those up to no good."

Will laughed as he followed Jed into the library. He let out a low, thoughtful whistle as he looked around. "This is great."

"I like it," Jed said, motioning him to take a seat. "It's one of my favorite rooms."

Thousands of books lined the shelves of the wood-paneled library. A fireplace took up one wall, filled for the summer with baskets of flowers. French doors opened onto a colorful garden and lawn running down to a lake surrounded by mossy cypress. In front of the elegant glass doors stood a neat walnut desk that gleamed with a rich brown sparkle. Burgundy leather chairs, comfortably worn, and an expensive-looking Oriental rug completed the picture. Comfort, class, elegance. Money.

Will drew up one of the chairs, thanking God it

wasn't one of those matchbox things that looked like it would break if a man sat on it.

"What brings you back, Will?" Jed took the other chair, gazing at him intently. "It's not just coincidence, is it? You heard about Frannie."

"A few days ago," Will confirmed. "Read it in an old newspaper. I came as soon as I could."

Jed's gaze, cool and flat, met his. "They believe she was murdered."

"I know." He laced his fingers together, resting his hands on his stomach. "I just came from Fielder's office."

"Fielder?" He gave a humorless laugh. "Bet you didn't get much information from him."

"You'd be surprised," Will said grimly.

Jed shot him a thoughtful glance, then said, "Let me get us something to drink. A beer?"

"Thanks, but I'll pass on the beer for now." Straightening in his seat, he added, "I wouldn't mind a glass of iced tea, though."

Jed left the room, returning in a few moments, saying, "June will bring it out. Do you still drink your tea with a truckload of sugar?" He relaxed in the leather chair, long legs stretched out before him.

Will smiled. "Absolutely. Tea's no good unless it's clinging-to-the-spoon sweet."

While they waited, Will stood, too restless to sit for long. He took a spin around the room, then turned to consider his foster brother. "Tell me something, Jed. Why does Fielder like you for Frannie's murder?"

"Like me? You mean suspect me?"

"Yeah. Why the hell are you his prime suspect?"

Jed didn't seem shocked. He sighed and rubbed a hand over his face. "It's a long story."

"I've got time."

"I can't believe he told you about that. You weren't one of his favorite people, any more than I was. Or am."

"He didn't have a choice," Will said, pulling out his badge. He flipped it to Jed, watched him open the case and study it.

Jed looked up, his expression surprised. "You're a Texas Ranger?"

"Yeah." He watched Jed's eyes as he said it. "And Frannie's murder is my case."

CHAPTER THREE

WILL SPENT THE THREE DAYS following his reunion with Jed in Dallas, giving a deposition on another case. When he returned to Uncertain, Fielder had gathered the majority of the case files together, though a few were unaccountably missing. Still, what Will was able to read didn't look good.

Seated at the deputy's desk, he considered the papers in front of him with a sense of foreboding. The threat to Jed was very real. Circumstantial evidence, but damning.

He tossed the manila folder aside and closed his eyes, then rubbed his temples in a vain attempt to keep his brewing headache at bay. He needed to see the murder site for himself, but his unexpected journey out of town had delayed him. The sheriff hadn't been particularly enthused about his surveying the site, but Will didn't let that bother him. The old man wasn't happy about anything Will did.

Hearing the door open, he glanced up. A woman stepped inside. Blond, pretty, slight. Early thirties, he judged. She didn't speak, but her lips curved in a knowing smile as she walked toward him. Will's eyes widened as he realized who she was. He pushed his chair back and got to his feet. "Emmy?"

Her smile deepened. She rushed forward and flung her arms around him, words tumbling out of her. "I knew you'd come. I told Jed you would." Another enthusiastic hug. "Riley and I got back in town last night. Jed just told me he'd seen you, and where I might find you. So I came down here as soon as I could."

Will returned the hug, then held her away from him so he could look at her. Older, of course, but she was the same Emmy he remembered. Sweet, affectionate. Talkative. Right now her mouth ran a mile a minute. He grinned. "You sure grew up pretty, squirt."

She laughed. "Still have that way with words, don't you? Oh, Will, it's so good to see you. If only Mom Fran…" Her voice trailed off. She blinked rapidly and cleared her throat. "Look at you, a Texas Ranger. Mom Fran would have been so proud."

A surge of grief rose inside Will. Uncomfortable with the emotion Emmy's words brought, he caught her hand and touched her ring. "How about you, all grown-up, and married, too. Are you happy?"

"Ecstatic. Riley is—" She sighed, her expression starry-eyed. "He's wonderful. And he has a daughter. A beautiful, four-year-old daughter. Did you know? So now I'm a mother, too."

"Jed told me when I saw him. He says you're a natural."

Emmy laughed. "I don't know about that, but she's a darling." Then she added, "Everything would be perfect if it weren't for this insane idea that the sheriff has about Jed being a suspect. You're ready to set things right, aren't you, Will?''

Damn, he hated to shatter her confidence in him. If only it were that easy. For Emmy, it was. He shoved a hand through his hair and wondered how to explain things to her. Her loyalty didn't allow her to question Jed. His didn't allow him not to. ''It's not that simple.''

''What do you mean?'' She turned wide, startled eyes to him. ''Why not?''

Will glanced around, aware that Fielder was in his office and that ethics didn't allow him to discuss the case in detail with Emmy—or anyone else, for that matter. ''Let's go grab a bite to eat. We can talk there.''

''All right, but I can't imagine—''

''We'll talk over lunch,'' he repeated, taking her arm as they left.

THE CATFISH CORNER still served the best fried catfish in East Texas. It didn't look a whole lot different than it had nineteen years ago, when they used to come in for special occasions. Dark wooden chairs clustered around sturdy tables topped with red-and-white-checked tablecloths. Huge ferns hung in the windows, a wide bank of them running the length of the back wall. The view of the moss-covered lake with its stands of tall cypress trees was one of the best around.

The same family still ran the place, Will realized when Emmy greeted the hostess, Zelma Lou Ferguson.

''Are you sure you know what you're doing,

Emmy?'' Will heard Zelma ask in a loud whisper. ''Why, you haven't been back from your honeymoon for a day and here you are out with another man!'' She cast an experienced eye over Will, making him feel a bit like a catfish hooked on her line.

Emmy's laughter rang out clearly. ''I doubt Riley's too worried, Zelma. This is Will.''

''Will?'' She stared at him as she offered them the menus. ''Will McClain? I heard you were back in town. Hear you're a Texas Ranger, too.''

''That's right,'' Will said, bracing himself for the inevitable questions.

''Excuse me a minute. Mary Jane, you hurry up and bring some hush puppies and condiments over here,'' she shouted to a waitress. Her eyes brightened with interest as she turned back to Will and Emmy. ''You're here about Frannie Granger's murder, aren't you? Is it true—''

''We're in kind of a hurry, Zelma,'' Emmy interrupted. ''Will has to get back to work.''

Thank you, Emmy, he thought. Not that it slowed Zelma down much. Will remembered that when they'd been in school together her mouth had never been shut. Obviously, she intended to stay and gossip. Luckily another customer came in just then, sparing them further probing. Will had lived in the big city so long, he'd forgotten the speed of the small-town grapevine. Or the intensity of the inhabitants' interest in anything newsworthy. Murder filled the bill in more ways than one.

"Are you married, Will?" Emmy asked after they ordered.

"Nope. Never been down that road." He'd had relationships, of course, but the women had never been able to deal with his passion for his career. And there'd never been anyone important enough to give her the attention and time he should.

Still, vague feelings of dissatisfaction with his life seemed to have intensified recently. He wanted kids someday. Kids who wouldn't have to wonder who their old man was and whether their mother would feed them or be flying so high she'd forget they existed. Kids who could depend on both parents to be there, to provide a home for them, to love them. Of course, before anything like that happened, he needed to find the right woman.

"What have you been doing for the last nineteen years?" Emmy asked, interrupting his reverie.

He smiled at her. Trust Emmy to get to the point. "Law enforcement, most of the time. I went into it when I turned eighteen." He didn't like to remember the year before that, what he'd done in order to stay out of the foster care system. He shook off the memories and turned the question back to Emmy. "What about you? What have you been up to since we all split up?"

"After they took me that day—Lord, Will, they wouldn't even let me say goodbye to you and Jed. Took me right out of school and put me in another foster home." She sighed heavily. "It didn't last.

None of them did. It just wasn't the same after having Mom Fran.''

''No, it wouldn't have been,'' he agreed, remembering all the homes he'd gone through before Frannie. ''I split before social services could find me. Thank God, they never did.'' Again he brushed the unwelcome memories aside. ''But since you've grown up, what have you been doing?''

''Do you want the short version or the long one?''

He smiled. ''The short one for now. Later we'll catch up more.''

''Most recently I was a blackjack dealer on a riverboat. But I've been a waitress, a housekeeper—'' She stopped and laughed. ''You'd be surprised at all the things I've done.'' They talked some more, hitting the highlights until the waitress set their food before them.

Will took a bite of hush puppy, savoring the taste. ''What brought you back to Uncertain, Emmy?''

''Partly what finally brought you back here, I imagine. Frannie.'' She cut a catfish filet with her fork and took a bite, her gaze distant. ''I read the article about the bones being found, and knew I had to come back. I had decided to look for my birth mother anyway, so it seemed logical to seek some answers here.''

''I always wondered if you'd try to discover your birth parents. Did you find your mother?''

''No.'' Regret flickered in her eyes. ''I've put the search on hold. We—Riley and I received some threatening letters during the search. Rather than risk Riley and Alanna getting hurt, I just gave up. I'm trying to get on with life with my husband and child. The past doesn't seem as important now."

"Except for Frannie," Will said.

Her gaze met his. "Yes, except for Frannie. And what about Jed? Is he really a suspect?"

He set his fork down. "Emmy, I can't talk about it. It's an open case and—"

She interrupted impatiently. "I'm not asking for state secrets. Is Jed a suspect? Surely you can answer that."

He hesitated. "Let's just say you wouldn't like the answer."

"Well, do something." She made a stabbing motion with her fork. "You can't let the sheriff arrest Jed."

"I may not have any choice."

"You don't seriously think Jed—" She broke off. Her eyes widened with horror. "You can't think Jed did it."

His hand curled into a fist on his thigh. Emmy was the last person in the world he wanted to discuss this with. He lowered his voice, not wanting anyone else to overhear. "Do you remember that day? Remember the argument? I've never seen Jed that angry. Or Frannie, either."

Emmy also lowered her voice but spoke intensely. "I don't care how angry he was, Jed would never have hurt Frannie. I can't believe you'd think for a minute—"

Will cut her off. "I don't want to think it. But I can't get that fight out of my mind." Jed had been furious at Frannie for denying him the chance to go to Juilliard to study classical music. And none of his arguments had swayed her. That day, the day Frannie disappeared, they'd had their worst fight yet, culminating with Jed leaving in a rage and Frannie rushing after him. "You remember, don't you, Emmy? You told the sheriff about it."

Her eyes clouded and she frowned. "He wormed it out of me. I was thirteen, I didn't know what else to do. I thought he'd throw me in jail if I didn't answer him."

"Don't beat yourself up about it. He heard it from me, too, when he questioned me at school the next day. And eventually, Jed admitted to it." It still infuriated him to remember how easily Fielder had extracted that information from him.

Emmy frowned. "But if he's using those conversations against Jed...that's not evidence! My God, Will, we were just a couple of kids."

"Maybe so, but the fact remains he knows about the argument. And I can tell you one thing. None of this helps Jed's case."

None of the evidence Will had seen so far helped Jed's case. It only made things blacker. He was going to have to question Jed. Officially. And hope he could find something Fielder had missed to help prove his innocence.

AT JED'S LAWYER'S REQUEST, the questioning took place in Riley Gray Wolf's law office. Dexter Thorndyke, Jed's attorney, was as good as they came, a point definitely in Jed's favor. Thorndyke, or Thorny as some people called him, had been an assistant D.A. in New Orleans before he'd switched to defense law. He was smart, cagey, and the best attorney Will could think of for Jed to have in his corner. Rumor had it his services didn't come cheap. Rumor also held that Jed's wife Gwyn was loaded.

Frankly, Will didn't care how Jed and Gwyn afforded Thorndyke, he was just glad Jed had him.

Fielder was also present, though Will let him know he was running this particular show. Still, Will didn't expect miracles, and could only hope the sheriff wouldn't make matters worse.

"I appreciate your willingness to talk to us again," he said to Jed as they all took their seats around the oval wood table in Riley's conference room. "I realize you've been over this with Sheriff Fielder, but I hoped we might shed some light on exactly what happened."

Jed wasn't happy about being interviewed again. Not that Will blamed him. He wasn't real happy about having to question him.

"Okay, let's get started." Will pulled out the notes from Fielder's interrogation, though he knew them well by now. "In your statement to Sheriff Fielder on April 10 of this year, you say that the last time you saw Frannie Granger was the morning of her disappearance." He studied Jed across the table. "Can you tell me about that day?"

Jed's jaw tightened, but he spoke readily enough. "Frannie and I argued that morning. About where I was going to college. I left the house and she followed me out. We talked a bit longer, then Frannie said she had to get to work.''

"According to witnesses," Fielder put in, "it wasn't just a simple argument. They were both spitting mad and yelling and Louis here was cussing up a storm. And he didn't tell us about the fight voluntarily at first. It was only after I reminded him I had several statements about it that he admitted to it.''

"It was nearly twenty years ago," Jed said, sparing the sheriff an angry glance. "I didn't remember the exact sequence of events.''

"I don't believe my client needs to answer any more questions about that particular point, Sheriff,'' Thorndyke said, his Louisiana drawl pronounced. "He's already been over that with you several times.''

Will warned Fielder off with a frown. Returning to Jed, he asked, "Where did you go after you left Frannie? Did you go to school?''

"No. I was angry, so I skipped school and went fishing. Look, Will, I told Fielder all this the first time he questioned me. Besides, you know it, too.''

"I'm aware of that. Just making sure I have everything correct.'' He looked down at the paper he held and asked another question—one Fielder had asked, apparently, but the answer wasn't documented. "Did anyone see you go out in your boat?''

Hands clasped on the table in front of him, Jed frowned in concentration. After a moment he said, "The clerk at Bubba's. I had to get gas.''

"Do you remember who the clerk was?''

"Sure. He worked there a couple of years. It was Rob Boulder. But he left town years ago."

"We'll try to locate him. Did anyone else see you?"

"Not that I'm aware of."

Now for the big question. "Did anyone see Frannie leave you?"

Jed shrugged, then gazed at him. "I don't know. Unless you or Emmy did."

Will turned to Fielder. "Why aren't there any notes about whether anyone saw Frannie after she left Jed? I thought you questioned her employers about it?" Something vitally important to the case, and the information wasn't there.

Fielder flushed. "I asked around when she disappeared. Asked her employers and her friends. But it's been nearly twenty years, and sometimes things get lost. I don't remember anyone saying they'd seen her at all that day. Only people who saw her that morning were you, Emmy Monday and Jed Louis."

Thorndyke smiled, not a good sign for the sheriff. "Hearsay, Sheriff. Not good enough. Gotta have it on paper to admit it as evidence."

"I'll question her employers again," Will said. He aimed a sharp glance at Fielder before turning back to Jed. "Tell me about this argument." Now came the touchy part. He needed to play this very carefully, or risk Jed losing his temper and only making matters worse for himself.

"You know what it was about." Jed's eyes flashed. With anger or irritation? "I already told you, and besides, you were there. I wanted to go to Juilliard and Frannie wouldn't sign the paper. She thought music was a foolish dream. I didn't.''

"You were angry."

"Hell, yes, I was angry." Jed shook off his lawyer's restraining hand and stood. "But not mad enough to kill her.''

Exactly the answer Will had wanted. No last-minute confessions, but a solid denial of guilt. Now if he could just find someone to attest that Frannie was alive after Jed went out on the lake, Jed would be in the clear. Or at least, a lot better off than he was now.

BY EARLY SATURDAY AFTERNOON, Tessa still hadn't gotten over her frustration with the system in general and Ranger Will McClain in particular. She hadn't heard a peep from the man, and three days had gone by. So much for his assurances of getting right to it. Tired of waiting, she decided to take out her aggressions on the fallow flower beds in the front yard. A couple of hours later, the beds looked great, but her temper still needed improvement.

"Are you doing what I think you're doing?"

Tessa glanced up to see her friend, hands on hips, regarding her with concern. Ellen's brown hair curled madly around her face, flushed from the summer heat. She'd paired screaming pink shorts with a lime tank top, baggy white socks and beat up tennis shoes. Tessa thought she looked about fifteen instead of the early thirties she knew her to be.

Still kneeling, Tessa considered her friend before

answering. Ellen taught anthropology and looked about as far from Tessa's idea of a college professor as was possible. But then, Ellen's nonconformism was one of her charms. Tessa, with the predictability of a Swiss watch, envied her that. She glanced down at her own beige T-shirt, liberally streaked with mud, and an uninspiring pair of baggy denim shorts. Boring, but then who needed to look good when digging in the dirt?

"I'm planting periwinkles. What's wrong with that?"

"You're planting flowers at a rental house," Ellen said, strolling up beside her. "Don't you think that's a little weird?"

Tessa dusted off her hands and stood. "It looks like this is the only digging I'm going to get in anytime soon. Besides, my landlady said to feel free and plant whatever I wanted."

"Of course she did. It's free labor and materials." Ellen glanced at the flowers in question. "They do look good, I'll admit. Maybe she'll give you a break on the rent."

"In my dreams," Tessa said, grinning. "She's tighter than the bark on a bois d'arc tree. Come on in and I'll get us a drink."

"Okay." Ellen followed, chatting about the usual nothing while Tessa washed up. "What happened with your meeting the other day? It must have been important for you to cancel your class."

"It was important," Tessa said grimly, drying her hands on a cup towel. "And totally ineffectual."

"Sheriff Fielder still giving you trouble?" Ellen asked sympathetically.

"No, now I have a new headache." A very large headache in the form of one Will McClain. "I was this close—" she held her thumb and forefinger a scant fraction of an inch apart "—to having Sheriff Fielder's permission to resume the dig."

She jerked open the refrigerator door and grabbed the tea pitcher. After filling a couple of glasses, she slapped Ellen's down in front of her.

Ellen's lips twitched, but she only asked, "What happened this time?"

"Not what. Who." She took a long drink and continued, "The Rangers are involved in the murder case now. An interfering, irritating big lunk of a Texas Ranger vetoed the sheriff's agreement." Tessa ground her teeth, remembering McClain's refusal to listen to her. Listen to her, heck, he had barely acknowledged her existence. That peeved her almost as much as the rest of it. "Five more minutes and I'd have been out of that office and back in business."

"Why did he nix it?"

"Because he's a control freak and he wants to ruin my life, that's why!" Too impatient to sit, she paced the small room. "Will McClain has to be the most arrogant, irritating—"

"Hold it," Ellen interrupted. "Will McClain is the Texas Ranger? Tall? Hazel eyes? Hell-raiser looks?"

Her sharp tone combined with the rapid-fire questions made Tessa stop and eye her curiously. "Yes. Why, do you know him?"

Ellen nodded. "If he's the McClain I'm thinking of, I was a few years behind him in school." She patted her hand on her chest, simulating a fast-beating heart. "Blond, with a smile to die for?"

"He didn't exactly smile a lot." Not a smile she wanted to receive, anyway. "But that's him," she said, thinking about his face, not to mention the rest of him. "He's from around here? From Uncertain?"

"Sort of. He lived here a while." Ellen took a sip of tea, cleared her throat, and added, "With his foster mother and her two other foster children."

Tessa stared at her. Surely not. "His foster mother?" she prompted.

Ellen nodded soberly. "Yeah, his foster mother. Frannie Granger."

"No. I don't believe it. You're telling me...the murdered woman was his foster mother?"

"You got it. If he's the same Will McClain."

Her few remaining hopes crashed abruptly. "I'm sure he is. Too coincidental for him not to be." Besides, she remembered Fielder's reaction. If he'd known McClain as a kid, that explained a lot.

"Oh, isn't this just peachy? He's investigating his foster mother's murder. I'll be lucky if he ever lets me on that land!"

IT TOOK TESSA AWHILE to track McClain down. She'd had to resort to flattering the deputy to convince him to tell her the Ranger's whereabouts. In fact, she'd narrowly escaped a date, and had only been saved by the sheriff calling Kyle to come into his office.

She shouldn't have been surprised to find McClain at the murder site, she thought, squelching her trepidation. In the months that had passed since the discovery of the bones, Tessa had dutifully followed the sheriff's commands and not gone near the land. But enough was enough.

She pulled up beside McClain's monster black truck, thinking that it could squash her ancient Subaru station wagon like a bug. She got out and slammed the door behind her, wincing at the protesting shriek of the hinges. She needed to oil them, but she kept forgetting.

It took her several minutes of hiking to reach the area where she'd found Frannie Granger's remains. She saw McClain first, standing beside what appeared to be a mound of dirt. As she drew closer, her heart plummeted to her toes, bringing her to a dead halt. Mound after mound of dirt piled three to four feet high dotted the landscape. She let out a shriek and ran toward him.

He turned to glare at her. "What the devil are you doing here?"

"Oh, my God, look what they've done!" She moaned, gazing at the unholy mess the sheriff and his men had created. "It's ruined, the entire archaeological site has been destroyed!"

"It hasn't done the murder site much good, either," McClain said.

"What were they thinking?"

"They weren't," McClain said harshly. "Obviously Fielder's experts weren't so expert."

Intent on the disaster surrounding her, she barely heard him. Could anything be salvaged? Anything at all? "They might as well have brought in a backhoe and gone at it!" Her eyes filled with angry tears at the thought of what they'd so carelessly destroyed. "Have they demolished the burial mounds, too?" Her heart stopped, waiting for his answer.

He shrugged. "Haven't looked that far, but it's possible. I haven't been here long." He looked around, muttered something that sounded like a curse. "They were after murder evidence, so this is likely the only area they've massacred. But I wouldn't bet on it."

"I couldn't have done the damage these people did if I'd tried! A nuclear warhead would have been less destructive." Again she looked around, despair growing as she took in the extent of the damage. Then she looked at McClain, tall, unblinking, unemotional. She wanted to slap him. "How can you just stand there, like you don't even care?"

"I care." He turned eyes the color of gunmetal, gray and cold as dawn, to her.

In spite of the heat, she shivered.

"And someone's going to pay, you can count on that. But throwing a tantrum won't solve anything."

Stung by the injustice of the remark, she drew herself up. "I'm not throwing a tantrum."

He lifted one cynical eyebrow. "It looks remarkably like one to me."

"If I'm distraught," she said with dignity, ignoring his snort, "it's because this—" she waved a hand at the piles of dirt "—is criminal. Sheriff Fielder ought to be flogged for letting anyone in his employ do something like this. He's supposed to uphold the law, not use it to wreck things.''

McClain's smile was harsh. She had the odd thought that it promised retribution. He would be a dangerous man to cross. Her heart fluttered a bit. A dangerous man to be involved with at all, she decided.

''Another thing we're in agreement about. Don't worry, I'll take care of Fielder.''

''But what do you intend to do about the site? And what do you intend to do about me?'' She wouldn't cry, not now. Not in front of him. ''I don't even know if I can salvage anything, but—''

''Are you any good?'' he demanded.

''Excuse me?'' What on earth did he mean by that? ''Any good?''

''At your job,'' he said impatiently. ''What are your credentials?''

''My credentials are not in question here,'' she snapped. ''The sheriff's methods are the problem. But I happen to have a master's degree from one of the finest institutions in the country.'' She couldn't bear to think of the Ph.D. slipping through her grasp.

''Could you still work here? Still find evidence, sift through these piles of dirt?''

''I don't—'' Confused, she surveyed the landscape again. ''Yes, I suppose I could. Some of the data would obviously be corrupted, compromised, but—''

He interrupted. ''You could still get information from this area.''

It wasn't that easy, but he seemed to want a simple answer. "Yes. But..."

His gaze locked with hers. He smiled at her, a smile that almost made her forget her name. "Fine. You can start work for me Monday morning."

CHAPTER FOUR

"I BEG YOUR PARDON? Work for you?" Tessa asked, unable to believe her ears. "Are you insane?"

Will's lips quirked. "Not last I checked."

"Why on earth would I want to work for you when the Sheriff's Department is the cause of this—" shuddering, she gestured to encompass the mess "—this debacle."

His mouth straightened into a grim line. "I said work for me, not the sheriff. You'd be dealing with the Rangers."

"Oh, excuse me for not understanding the distinction." Propping her hands on her hips, she glared at him. "Besides, I have a job. I have two jobs. Or I did until Sheriff Fielder and his flunkies destroyed one of them."

His gaze surveyed the land before coming back to meet hers. "Do you want another chance at the archaeological site, or not?"

His way or the highway. He might not have said the words; nevertheless, she heard them clearly. "What other choice do I have?" She shook her head in disgust, admitting defeat. "What is it you want me to do?"

He nodded briskly, as if he'd expected her agreement. "Excavate this area of the site. Where you found the body. If you uncover anything that hasn't been destroyed by whoever tossed this dirt around, I want to know about it. Once you've finished with this area, you can resume work on your Caddo dig. No interference."

She set her jaw. He wasn't running roughshod over her. No sir, not when his lawmen cronies had already destroyed weeks of work, not to mention the integrity of the site. "Not good enough, Ranger McClain. I want part of my team to be allowed to resume work at the Caddo burial mound immediately. I'll need a few people to help me out with what you want me to do, but certainly not everyone."

If work at the archaeological site continued now, she might just finish her thesis after all. That is, if the burial mound had been left alone. Thinking about it, she winced. Probably too optimistic an assumption, given the state of the rest of the land in question.

"Agreed," he said. "But no students at the murder site. Keep them well away from here. Professionals only, and I want you supervising the entire time anyone else is present."

She shrugged an agreement. "Fine by me. The students are interested in the nineteenth century anyway, not the twentieth or twenty-first." Although a number of them probably would be curious about a local murder come to light. "By the way, do you intend to pay us?"

He shot her a surprised glance. "This is an official

investigation. You'll be paid the going rate for a forensic archaeologist.''

"I'm not a forensic archaeologist.''

"Close enough.'' He waved a hand at the wreckage.
"Given the shape this site is in, I doubt it will matter.
You're an archaeologist, aren't you? Which is a hell
of a lot more than these jokers were. At least you
know how to handle what you find and how to run a
dig.''

That she did. Having been involved with uncounted
archaeological sites since the age of twelve had a lot
to do with that knowledge. "And you'll keep the sheriff and his men out of here?''

Will smiled grimly. "No problem there. Don't
worry, the sheriff won't be bothering you.''

"Then I accept. But I won't be able to start Monday
morning. I have classes.''

"Work it out however you can. Just get on it as
soon as possible.'' He put out a hand. "It's a deal,
then.''

"Deal,'' she echoed faintly, slipping her hand into
his much larger one. He shook it but didn't release it.
Their gazes met as she felt the warmth from his palm.
It's just a handshake, she thought. No big deal.

Oh, no? Then why are you tingling, Tessa?

She cleared her throat and he allowed her hand to
drop. Heat crept up her neck and she cursed her fair
complexion, knowing she was blushing. What was the
matter with her? He had simply offered her a job.
Abruptly she turned and began walking to her car.

"I'll go with you," he said, falling into step beside her. "I'm finished here for now."

Dazed, she tried to grasp what had just occurred. She'd agreed to work with the Texas Rangers on a nineteen-year-old murder case. She glanced up at the man beside her. Lord, he was good-looking. And autocratic and demanding, she reminded herself. What would he be like to work with?

"Do you have plans for dinner?"

Well, there's your answer. "If you think I'm starting on this thing now, you really are crazy."

He laughed. "I'm asking you to dinner, Tessa. It has nothing to do with the job."

Shocked, she stared at him. He seemed sincere. Still, even a new haircut couldn't account for a man like Will McClain asking her out. She was hardly his type. Someone like Amanda Jennings, the banker's twice—or was it three times?—divorced daughter, seemed more his style. Blond, busty, beautiful. Or maybe a sultry brunette. Anyway, not a mousy, red-headed archaeologist. Her eyes narrowed as she studied him. She'd already agreed to take on the job. What was he after?

"Why?" she asked after a long pause.

He still looked amused, if a little taken aback. "Why did I ask you to dinner?" They reached her car. He opened her door, gesturing for her to get in.

She nodded and slid into the driver's seat. "I said I'd work for you. You don't have to bribe me."

He laughed and closed the door, placing his hands on the open window. "It's no bribe."

He leaned down, eye level with her. His irises were the oddest color she'd ever seen, like they couldn't make up their minds between green and gray. Right now they glowed spring-grass green. And that smile of his...definite heartbreaker material.

"I'm in the mood for Mexican food and the company of a pretty woman. So, how about it?"

Pretty? Her? Oh, right. She might not be dog ugly, but plain was about the best she could hope for. But she didn't call him on it. Instead, she went at it from another angle. "How do you know I'm not married?"

He glanced at her left hand, which was gripping the steering wheel, then back to her eyes. "No ring." His lips curved upward. "I'm a cop, remember? We notice things like that."

"Maybe I don't wear one. After all, I dig in the dirt for a living."

The smile remained, but for the first time his voice held a hint of exasperation. "Tessa, do you want to go to dinner with me or not?"

She was tempted. Really tempted. In fact, he was the first man she remembered being attracted to in ages. What harm could it do? As long as she remained wary, nothing bad would happen. "All right. I'd like that."

"Are you always this hard on men who ask you out?"

She thought about that for a minute. "Yes." Of course, until very recently she hadn't needed to be hard on anyone.

He smiled and straightened. "I'll pick you up

around seven. Don't dress up. Great food, but it's a dive."

"Don't you want to know where I live?"

"I'm a cop. I'll figure it out."

Tessa watched him walk to his truck, sighing a little over his long-limbed easy stride. She still wasn't sure of his plan, but she decided she didn't care. Dinner with Will McClain wouldn't be a hardship, even if he had a potful of ulterior motives.

STRAINS OF ERIC CLAPTON'S "I Shot The Sheriff" issued from the truck's radio. Appropriate, Will thought, though strangling Fielder with his bare hands might give him more satisfaction. He pulled into the police parking lot behind the jail and jammed the gearshift into park. Unfortunately, as an officer sworn to uphold the law, he could do neither.

His mood dangerous, he stalked inside the building. Thelma Ridell, the evening clerk, sat at her desk, playing solitaire with a deck of greasy cards. Apparently computer usage in the Uncertain Sheriff's Department didn't extend to card games. Deputy Masters was nowhere to be seen. Will assumed he'd taken off for the night. He didn't bother asking for the sheriff. Will had already discovered the widowed Fielder spent most of his time closed up in his office at the station.

"Sheriff said not to disturb him," Thelma called out, laying down another card with military precision.

Ignoring her, Will opened the office door and smiled grimly. He intended to do a lot more than *disturb* the sheriff.

Feet propped on his desk, Fielder looked up when Will entered, his normally taciturn expression turning harsh. His finger marking the spot in the magazine he read, he closed it. ''What the hell do you want now, McClain? Don't you ever go home?''

''Not when I have business to take care of. Like having you booted out of office for incompetence.''

His face turned a mottled red and the magazine fell from his grasp. A fly fishing magazine, Will noticed, surprised. He would have figured the man for a gun enthusiast.

''Incompetence?'' His boots hit the floor with a bang. ''Why you lying—''

Will cut him off. ''I've been out to Beaumarais. To the site. You didn't bring in experts to process that murder scene. The place reeks of amateurs. Who did you use—ditchdiggers?''

Fielder shot to his feet, anger twisting his features. ''Now see here, McClain, we don't have the kind of resources to merit paying some so-called expert a fortune. My boys did their job the best they could. You got no call to interfere.''

''Like hell I don't. Have you even looked at the place since your 'boys' got through with it?'' The expression of chagrin that crossed the sheriff's face was all the answer Will needed. Too bad the man would have to step a lot further over the line before Will could do more than threaten. ''I didn't think so.''

''I've been out there,'' the sheriff blustered. ''And I didn't see a problem.''

''No problem? It looks like a Mixmaster tossed the

site. Your actions and those of your men have compromised this investigation. At least as pertains to the site where the body was found. There's no way of telling, particularly now, whether the murder was committed on site or the body taken there following death.''

''The initial report—''

''I'm aware of the initial report. I've read it. It leaves that conclusion open to further study. Which is now impossible, thanks to you and your wonder boys.''

''What difference does it make where he did it? So what if he did kill her someplace else? Her bones were found there. On Beaumarais.''

Will grimaced and rubbed the bridge of his nose. ''Sheriff, have you investigated a murder before?''

''Of course. They don't happen every day, but we've had several over the years.''

''Then why the hell didn't you use proper procedure on this one?''

He flushed, then glanced away. ''Just because it don't suit you don't mean it's not a perfectly good way to go about it.''

''You know proper police procedure. My God, you've been sheriff here for more than twenty years—you can't help but know. But you didn't bother. You were too damn lazy, or maybe too damn cheap, to do it right, because you're convinced you've already got the perp sewn up.''

Fielder slammed his fist down on his desk. ''I do

have the perp sewn up! Jed Louis is guilty as sin. I know it, you know it. Even if you won't admit it.''

"I *know* you have circumstantial evidence against him. I *know* you have no evidence other than hearsay and gossip linking Jed Louis to the crime. Unless you've kept something from me, or unless some of those missing papers are proof positive, then you don't have enough to charge him."

"Not yet."

Arguing about Jed got them nowhere. Will pushed it aside to deal with later. "The fact remains, you did a crappy job on the investigation because you were complacent. You didn't want to look any further because it was easier to blame it on Jed. I can take this to the city council and you'll be out on your ass faster than you can blink."

His expression thunderous, Fielder glared at him. "I got friends on the council, so I'd watch who and what I threatened, McClain. They know the budget I operate under. Nobody will blame me for trying to save the city money."

"Saving money isn't the issue. Botching a murder investigation is. If you couldn't handle it, you should have called in other resources. Like the Rangers, for instance. Or hell, you had an archaeologist sitting around twiddling her thumbs. Why didn't you make use of her expertise? Instead, it looks like you might have screwed up on purpose."

Fielder took his seat, folding his arms across his chest. Regarding Will for a moment in silence, his bushy gray eyebrows lifted. "Mighty strong words, especially from someone who ain't walking a straight line himself.''

Will's eyes narrowed. "What are you implying?"

He smiled, a smile full of cunning and malice. "I got an idea you didn't tell your captain all the details about this case."

Will didn't speak, waiting for him to go on, though he suspected what came next. Fielder continued, his expression indicating he knew he had the upper hand. "Wonder what your Ranger captain would say if I was to tell him Frannie Granger was your foster mother? And that Jed Louis, the prime suspect, is your foster brother? Sounds like conflict of interest to me."

Returning the smile, Will picked up the phone and handed it to him. "Go ahead. Call him. Captain Roger Sterling."

"You're bluffing." He took the phone, fingers poised over the buttons, eyes on Will.

Will's smile widened. "Try me." He gave him the number and waited.

"Well, I'll be damned." Fielder slammed down the receiver. "You actually told him?"

Will nodded. "The captain's aware of the background. All the background," he added. He knew of no quicker way to get on his captain's bad side than by concealing something pertinent about a case. Besides, not telling Captain Sterling about his past would have laid him wide-open to an attack like the one Fielder had just made.

"He knows and he still assigned you this case?"

"That's right." He didn't mention the captain's

parting injunction. *"You'd better not screw up this case, McClain,"* he'd said. *"Because if you do my ass will be in the sling along with yours."*

Will had no intention of screwing up.

The hostility between the sheriff and him was impeding the case. Murder took precedence over an ancient feud. They would never get anywhere if they kept going at cross-purposes. It was up to him to figure out a way they could work together, because Fielder obviously wouldn't make the first move.

"Look, Sheriff, the way I see it, we both want the same thing here."

"Do we?" he asked, disbelief evident in his voice.

"We both want to solve the murder. I'm going to find Frannie Granger's murderer and bring him in. Whoever killed her will pay for it."

Fielder's gaze met his. "You know, I can almost believe you mean that."

"Believe it."

Fielder pursed his lips and studied him. "And what do you mean to do if Jed Louis is guilty?"

"I intend to bring in Frannie Granger's killer. No matter who it is," Will said.

And pray God it wasn't Jed.

CHAPTER FIVE

"THAT'S A RESTAURANT? It looks more like someone's home," Tessa said as Will pulled into a gravel
lot packed with cars, trucks and SUVs. Across from it
stood a plain whitewashed wooden building with
green trim. Though it had been painted recently, a
home improvement loan still seemed in order. One of
the walls leaned inward and shingles flaked from the
roof. A small sign proclaimed it to be Santiago's.

A smile played over Will's lips. "They live behind
it. Years ago Carlita's mother-in-law fed people from
her kitchen. When the operation grew too big for that,
her husband and sons added a real dining room." He
glanced at her and grinned. "They never claimed to
be in construction."

"It's awfully crowded," she said, noticing the line
of people spilling out the door, down the steps and
winding along the side of the building. "Are you sure
we can get in?"

"Don't worry about it. Best Mexican food in East
Texas," Will promised. He paused before getting out
of his truck. "We can go someplace else if you'd
rather."

His tone was neutral, but she had an idea he really
wanted to stay. And so did she. She heard music in

the background, and laughter, and the aromas drifting from the building teased her senses. Relaxing. Fun, she thought. "No, this is fine. I like Mexican food. Besides, I'm not dressed for anyplace fancy." She'd taken him at his word and wore blue jeans and one of her new purchases—a pale green scoop-necked summer-weight sweater. Luckily, he couldn't know she'd changed seventeen times before settling on the first thing she tried on.

Tessa didn't know how Will did it, but with a touch here, a word there, he slipped past the line and walked right up to the hostess.

Small, dark haired, with deep brown eyes the color of chocolate, she looked both capable and harried. She handed a set of menus to a waitress, then turned to Will, obviously annoyed. Her eyes rounded, she shrieked, "Will!" and launched herself into his arms.

Will caught her and swung her around, laughing as a torrent of Spanish spilled over him. Eventually he set her down and managed to get a word in. *"Hola,* Isabella. *¿Cómo estás?"*

"Muy bien." She flashed her left hand at him, showing off a gold-and-diamond wedding set. "Very well," she repeated with a satisfied smile.

Will answered her in Spanish, something about her breaking his heart and they both laughed. *"¿Dónde esta su mama?"* he asked.

"En la cocina. Come and see her. She'll be so happy!" With a quick word of instruction, she handed the menus to another woman and motioned Will to

follow her. Will grabbed Tessa's hand, pulling her with him.

Towed along in his wake, Tessa listened to the jumble of rapid-fire words coming from the woman who'd greeted him. From what Tessa heard, she conveyed years' worth of information about weddings, babies, jobs and various scandals in a couple of minutes. Tessa hid a smile at the sharp-eyed glance the woman aimed at her before ushering them into the kitchen.

A welter of delicious smells assaulted her, instantly making her mouth water. A slightly older version of Isabella stood at one of the three stoves, snapping out orders, stirring pots of refried beans and sizzling fajita meat, and shouting at half a dozen children who ran in and out of the large room. Will hooked an arm around her waist and gave her a smacking kiss on the cheek. She drew back as if she meant to slap him, but then she squealed, threw her arms around his neck and hugged him, much as her daughter had done.

Tessa couldn't make out her words over the babble of voices, the clanging of pots and pans, running water, and the Latin music blaring in the background, but the woman was plainly thrilled to see him.

She hugged him, kissed him, exclaimed over him in voluble Spanish, and then she hauled off and boxed his ears.

"Ow!" Will rubbed his ears, eyeing her warily. "What was that for?"

"That's for not coming to me when Frannie disappeared." Her expression suddenly serious, she put her hands on his arms and gazed up at him. "We would have made you ours, *hijo.*"

Will touched her cheek and said something in a low voice Tessa couldn't hear. The woman caught his hand and pressed it against her cheek, her eyes bright. After a moment he said, *"Lo siento, Mamacita.* Forgive me?"

Regaining control, she turned her nose in the air and sniffed. *"Es possible,"* she allowed. As if just realizing all activity had stopped with Will's entrance, she shouted at everyone to get back to work. Will took Tessa's hand to pull her forward. "Carlita, this is Tessa Lang. Tessa, this is Carlita Santiago, the best damn cook in all of East Texas. I spent a lot of hours in her kitchen as a kid."

"Corrupting my Rico and flirting with my girls," Carlita added with a smile. "So happy to meet you, Señorita Lang. *Mi casa es su casa.*"

"Gracias, señora. Tessa, por favor. Your restaurant is lovely," Tessa continued in Spanish, adding a comment about the delicious smell of the food. Will's eyebrows lifted in surprise, then he smiled. Carlita beamed, answering her in a flood of the same language.

Carlita escorted them to a small table near the kitchen. The best seat in the house, she informed them, giving Will a wink. "You will have beer," she announced. "And don't worry, *Señor Policía,* my liquor license is up to date."

"Trust Carlita to have already heard the news," Will said, watching her go. "They weren't even surprised to see me. Probably knew I was back before I did.'' He glanced around, his expression thoughtful. ''This place has sure grown since I was here last. The dining room and kitchen used to be all there was to it. They only had a handful of tables, and you had to go through the kitchen to get to the dining room.''

''I like it,'' Tessa said, looking around at the colorful prints and Mexican blankets gracing the walls, the lush potted plants scattered here and there. A three-man mariachi band made the rounds of the tables, belting out traditional fiesta music. ''Great atmosphere.''

''Yeah, looks like it's been discovered.'' He waved a hand at the crowd. ''Good for business, but I miss the way it used to be.''

''Things change. How long has it been since you were last here?'' The minute she asked the question she wished she could retract it. To hear the gossip, he hadn't been back since his foster mother's disappearance.

''A lifetime,'' he said, his eyes turning gray and melancholy.

Not wanting to add to his dark mood, she hastily changed the subject. ''What's good to eat here?'' she asked, studying the menu.

''The special. A little of everything, and then some. Unless that's changed, too.'' Taking her menu, he set it aside with his and motioned the waiter over. ''So, where did you pick up Spanish?'' he asked after giving their order. ''You speak it like a native.''

''So do you. You tell me first.''

He seemed to debate with himself, then shrugged

and answered her. "I grew up speaking it. Where I lived, you heard more Spanish than English. Then when I came here, I fell in with Rico, Carlita's oldest son." One side of his mouth lifted. "He tried to beat the crap out of me when I first moved to town. We spent a lot of time in detention together."

"You made friends with someone who beat you up?" Tessa knew she was a bit sheltered, but sometimes men really were unfathomable.

Will looked surprised. "Sure, why not? If I hadn't, I wouldn't have had any friends. Back then I was always fighting." At her look of complete bafflement, he laughed and added, "Don't worry, I grew out of it." He paused and smiled. "Mostly."

Their beers and chips appeared, served by another of Carlita's daughters. The Santiagos clearly considered Will one of the family. Tessa wondered what it would be like to be welcomed so unreservedly. She didn't remember anyone ever being that happy to see her. Her grandmother, perhaps. But then, her parents were not given to expressing emotion. Her mother in particular considered any show of emotion vulgar.

"I thought you grew up in Uncertain?" Tessa asked after the waitress left.

He shook his head. "Not exactly. I didn't come here until I was thirteen." He chose a chip, loaded it with hot sauce and popped it in his mouth.

Tessa tasted the sauce more cautiously. Even that small taste burned her tongue and had her reaching for water. "I picked up the language in Central America," she said after a moment. "I spent a lot of time there in my teens."

"You didn't grow up there, though. Or Texas, either. That's no Texas twang you have. Your accent's from the South. Makes me think of magnolias."

She smiled at the description. Apparently her youthful accent hadn't totally deserted her. "Good ear," she said. "Georgia. I lived with my grandmother in Atlanta until I was twelve."

"What happened then?"

"My grandmother died and I went to live with my parents." And spent the worst year of her life following her parents around the globe like so much lost luggage.

"I'm sorry."

Simple and sincere. She liked that about him. "Yes, so was I." But she had adapted. The first year had been the hardest. After that she learned to live with the grief, the loneliness, the homesickness for Atlanta and her grandmother's comforting embrace. To hide her true feelings and become the person her parents expected her to be.

"How did you end up in Central America?"

"My parents were both archaeologists. My father died a few years ago, and now my mother is an administrator for archaeological expeditions." Big, prestigious digs, she thought with a grimace. "But back then they were both field archaeologists, and I went with them wherever they happened to go. We lived longest in central Mexico, but I also spent time in Brazil, Chile and Venezuela. Then we went to the

Middle East, but we didn't stay there long.'' Thank God, she thought, repressing a shudder. The conditions on that dig had been the most brutal yet.

He took another chip but kept his attention on her. There was something heady about being the focus of a man's attention, especially when she wasn't delivering a workshop or class, or talking antiquities. She bet he knew it, too. She gave him a sideways glance and barely kept from sighing. *Enjoy it but don't believe it,* she reminded herself. *Everyone has an agenda.*

''So, do you like it? Traveling?''

Did she like it? Funny, she'd never thought of it that way. Her work took her different places. That was her life. She hadn't thought about whether she liked moving around since she was twelve. ''I—I guess so.'' She shrugged. ''Traveling is necessary if you're going to be an archaeologist.''

''Is it? How do the colleges keep teachers, then?''

''Oh, some archaeologists teach. A lot of people retire from the field and teach. But to make a name in archaeology you have to move around a lot.''

His hand curved around his beer bottle. Nice, strong hands, she'd noticed before. And she bet he was good with them, too.

''Is that what you want to do? Make a name for yourself?''

She blinked away her unruly thoughts. ''It's what I'm trained to do.''

He smiled. ''You didn't answer my question. Is that what you want? What you enjoy doing?''

Thankfully, their food arrived. Will let the subject drop, but it continued to bother Tessa. Rather, her own reaction bothered her. Why hadn't she answered him? Why hadn't she simply said of course she wanted to travel? Of course she enjoyed her work?

"Will? Will McClain? Oh, my God, I heard you were back in town." Platinum blond, beautiful and dripping jewelry, Amanda Jennings stood beside their table, her gaze fixed on Will as if he was the ice cream topping her cake. Her tight red knit dress ended well above her knees and fit like she'd put it on with superglue, showcasing opulent breasts. Tessa breathed an envious sigh, wishing she had the guts—and the body—to wear something like that. Amanda spared her a quick glance, then ignored her.

"How could you come to town and not look me up?" Amanda asked, slick red lips moving into a pout.

Though he rose to his feet, Will didn't look particularly interested, Tessa thought, pleased.

"Amanda?"

Another pout. "Well, of course it's me. Now you've hurt my feelings. I can't believe you've forgotten me."

He didn't deny it, he simply smiled. "Amanda, have you met Tessa Lang?"

Glancing impatiently at Tessa, she gestured vaguely. "Yes, I'm sure we've met. Nice to see you." Her tone implied *Get lost*.

"Likewise," Tessa said dryly. Her lips twitched and she caught Will watching her. Their gazes met and they both smiled.

She felt a shiver of pleasure—and surprise—at their silent communication.

Amanda talked for several more minutes before finally saying, "Well, I won't keep you." She put a hand on his tanned forearm, bare beneath his rolled-up shirt sleeve. Her long red nails glinted dangerously as she gazed into his eyes. "Call me, Will. We'll talk about old times." Her voice had dropped on the last two words, holding a husky promise. She trailed her fingers down his arm, smiling provocatively. "I took back my maiden name after my last divorce. I'm in the phone book." She waved a hand sporting a large diamond and walked off, hips swaying seductively.

"Should I call a cab?" Tessa asked sweetly.

Will laughed and took his seat. "Very funny. No, I don't think so."

"That sounded like an open invitation to me. Are you sure you're not...interested?"

"Oh, I'm interested." He picked up her hand and turned it over, his gaze holding hers. "In you."

Her stomach fluttered, her arm tingled all the way to her shoulder. "Um," was the best she could manage.

His mouth lifted at the corners and he released her hand. "Now where were we?"

She could breathe again now that he wasn't touching her. "If the looks Amanda is sending my way are any sign, I'm about to be roasted over a slow fire."

"Forget Amanda."

"She obviously hasn't forgotten you."

"That's just her personality. It doesn't mean anything.'' He smiled cynically. ''We went out a few times in high school.'' His shoulder lifted, then fell. ''Amanda had a thing for the forbidden. Guys her daddy wouldn't let in the front door.''

''And that would be you.'' She could imagine him as a teenager. Those looks of his would have been irresistible. Just like they were now, she thought.

''That would be me,'' he agreed.

''Her father didn't like you?''

His mouth curved upward, into that half smile she found so intriguing. ''Honey, Raymond Jennings hated the air I breathed. He wouldn't have crossed the street to spit on me.''

She sensed a hurt behind the careless words and said the first thing she could think of to soothe him. ''I've met the man. Ray Jennings is a pompous bore.''

He smiled at her, quick and blinding. ''What do you say we move on to another topic?''

Happy to let the subject drop, she nodded agreement. ''Okay. Tell me, do you like being a Texas Ranger?''

''It has its moments. Most of the time I enjoy it.''

''Like when you catch the bad guys,'' she said.

A shadow darkened his eyes. ''Yeah. But that isn't always the way it plays out.''

He told her some stories then, sticking with the more humorous ones and cleaning them up, she suspected, especially when relaying conversations with suspects. They finished eating and he lounged back in his chair, long legs stretched before him. She leaned forward, arms on the table, and never noticed how fast the time slipped away.

A clatter of dishes made her look up. The place was empty of customers but for them. Shocked, she checked her watch. "I had no idea it was so late. I bet they're ready to get rid of us."

"I'll get the check," he said, and motioned a waiter over.

Carlita emerged from the kitchen, highly insulted that Will wanted to pay. After a prolonged argument, which neither seemed to be winning, he stuffed the money into her pocket, grabbed Tessa's hand and walked out.

"You come back soon," Carlita called. "And you, too, Tessa. Next time you don't pay."

"Not likely," Will muttered.

"Why not? If she wants to—"

"They fed me enough times when I was a kid. It's my turn now."

"You always pay your debts, don't you?" she said, struck by his adamance.

He stopped and looked at her. His eyes were dark, edgy, a little frightening. "Yeah. Always."

She had the distinct feeling he wasn't referring to the Santiagos.

They drove home in companionable silence, sated by both the food and the company. She didn't feel the need to fill the silence with useless chatter, and he didn't speak, either. He walked her to her door, waiting while she unlocked it. Suddenly nervous, she turned and held out her hand. "I had a wonderful time. Thank you."

He took her hand and held it in his, smiling down at her. "Is this a hint that you don't want to kiss me good-night?"

Damn it, she was twenty-nine years old. Too old to be flustered at the prospect of a simple good-night kiss. But then, she'd never kissed anyone like Will McClain before. She'd never known a man like him before. "No."

"No, you don't want to kiss me, or no, it's not a hint?"

She frowned and tugged her hand loose from his to put one hand on his shoulder and the other on the back of his neck and pull his head down to hers. Empowered, she caught a glimpse of wickedly smiling eyes before their lips met.

CHAPTER SIX

SHE TASTED SWEET. Sexy. And somehow, innocent, all rolled into one tidy little package. Though he wanted to deepen the kiss, he let her set the pace. And was rewarded when her tongue shyly sought his, slipping into his mouth and withdrawing before coming back to meet his. His hand moved from her waist to stroke her back gently, edging her closer. The throaty little moan she gave notched the heat up even more, as did her arms tightening around his neck.

Regretfully he eased back, knowing if he didn't, she was going to get a real good idea of exactly how much she affected him. And she didn't seem the type to jump into bed with a man she'd known only a few days. Unfortunately.

Her soft sound of distress when he broke the kiss only made him want more. He pressed his lips to the pulse fluttering beneath her jaw and drank in her scent. Magnolias, he thought, like her voice. He raised his head and looked at her.

Her eyes opened slowly, her expression dazed.

Something wound around his ankles, brushing against his leg. It didn't feel like a woman's foot, not any he'd ever felt. He looked down to see a big black-

and-white scarred cat insinuating its rangy body between them.

"Your cat wants your attention," he said, smiling at her still unfocused gaze.

"I don't—" Still dazed, she blinked again. "I don't have a cat."

Will released her and stepped back. The cat ignored him in favor of purring loudly and rubbing up against Tessa's calves and ankles. "Tell that to him."

"Oh, poor thing," she said, bending down to rub between the feline's scroungy ears. "He must be lost."

"Yeah, permanently." Now that Will got a better look at him, he pegged him for a stray. Battle scarred, his coat was dull obsidian and a white stripe ran down his back.

Her fingers stroking the white fur, Tessa frowned. "What's this? It feels hard."

No wonder the stripe looked odd. "Somebody decided to do a Pepe le Pew on him."

"A what?"

"You know, the skunk in the cartoon. Somebody painted a stripe down his back."

"That's—that's horrible!"

Compared to some of the things Will had seen people do to each other, it seemed fairly mild. Still, he hated abuse, whether it be against humans or animals.

Tessa had crouched down and was rur hands over the critter, crooning to him.

"Watch out. If he's hurt, he might sc And something tells me he's not up o

She ignored him, which didn't surprise Will a bit. Given the way she'd ripped into him at the ruined site, he'd already figured out she tended to charge ahead when she felt strongly about something.

Finishing her inspection, she said, "Nothing seems to be broken. He's awfully thin, though."

"Life on the streets is tough." He felt an unwelcome affinity with the animal. "The shelter won't be open until Monday."

"The shelter?" Her expression worried, she glanced up at him, then back to the cat. "I suppose that would be the logical thing to do with him." She stroked his head gently as she spoke. His inner motor revved higher as he arched his back into her hand, begging her to continue her attention.

Will nearly smiled. He didn't think the animal shelter would be getting a new resident come Monday. At least not this mangy feline. "Yeah. Logical." He glanced at the cat, then back to Tessa. His lips twitched. "What are you going to call him?"

Her dimples appeared. "How did you know? Pepe, naturally."

Now he did grin. "You're a sucker."

"I can't help it." Still petting the animal, she glanced up at Will. "Look at him. Who else would adopt him? If I take him to the shelter it's the same as killing him myself."

"No, it's not," Will stated positively. She had a good heart. He liked that about her. In fact, he liked of things about her. Watching her comfort the he felt a tug of envy. What would it be like to have someone care about him, be there for him when he was down? Like family. Will had lost the only family he'd ever had, a long time ago. And the way things were going, it didn't look like they'd be able to put that family back together anytime soon.

Tessa rose. ''I'm keeping him.'' She said it defiantly, as if expecting an attempt to talk her out of it.

He spread his hands. ''No arguments from me. It's your business. What about your landlady?''

''I'll fix it with her. Somehow,'' she muttered. ''I guess I'd better take my new friend inside and see what I can find to feed him.'' She scooped up the cat, glancing at Will again. ''Thank you.''

The cat stared at him from the safety of her arms, his expression gloating. *Eat your heart out, buddy,* he seemed to be saying.

''Spend the day with me tomorrow,'' Will said, not willing to be outdone by this pint-sized Romeo. ''I thought I'd rent a boat and check out the lake. We could swim or just ride around if you'd rather.''

Tilting her head to one side, she considered him. ''You move fast, don't you?''

He smiled disarmingly. ''You might not be in town that long.''

''You might not, either,'' she countered.

He nodded agreement. ''Right. So why waste time?''

She fixed him with a skeptical gaze. ''I'm trying to figure out your angle here, but I can't.''

''Why should I have an angle? I'd like to get to know you better.'' A whole lot better, if he had his way. He asked himself why—what about her appealed to him so strongly? She was pretty, but that wasn't it—or not all of it. Maybe it wasn't so much Tessa as his own state of mind. He was tired of work being the only thing in his life. Not that he expected anything serious with Tessa, but he wouldn't mind the distraction of being with a beautiful woman for however long he'd be in town.

"I intended to go to the site in the morning and plan how to proceed. The sooner I do that the sooner I can get started."

"Good idea. No problem. We'll go boating in the afternoon."

"Does anyone ever tell you no?"

He smiled and stepped closer. "Sure." But women rarely did. "So, how about it? Can I show you the lake?" She took her time, thinking his invitation over. Will wondered why she seemed so wary. Was it him? Or men in general?

"All right." She gave him a reluctant smile. "But I'll pass on the swimming. I'm not a very strong swimmer anyway, and the idea of actually getting in a lake..." She paused and shuddered. "Let's just say that's not an experience I'm anxious to have."

"If you'd rather not go—"

"No, I'd like to. I'm not phobic or anything, I just don't like to swim."

"If you're sure," he said, trying to gauge how much of the truth she was telling him. "Then we'll just ride around."

She nodded. "After lunch, then?"

"Sounds good to me," Will said. "Bubba's dock, around one. You know it?"

"The convenience store on the lake. Yes, I know it."

He stroked a finger down her cheek, lingering at her jawline. "Don't forget the sunscreen." He might have kissed her again, but the cat chose that moment to meow loudly and squirm in her arms, breaking the contact.

"See you tomorrow," she said, and closed the door quickly behind her.

Will left, well satisfied with all but the last few minutes of the evening, when he'd found himself up-staged by a battered feline with shifty green eyes. His investigation might not be going as well as he'd like, but his personal life had definitely taken an upswing.

THE NEXT AFTERNOON, Will met Tessa at the dock while he gassed up the boat. Like him, she'd dressed for the hot, sultry day. She wore shorts and a long-sleeved white shirt, unbuttoned, layered over a pink tank top that should have clashed with her hair but didn't. A wide-brimmed straw hat covered her head, a concession to the brutal Texas sun, he knew. Again he thought of mint juleps on the veranda, rather than fossils in the dirt. She looked cool, beautiful and un-approachable. Until she smiled. Man, she had a dy-namite smile. Warm, inviting…tempting. Especially nice, after the chill he'd gotten from Jed.

He'd run into Jed a little earlier, leaving Bubba's store just as Will had entered. They'd spoken, but neither had made any effort to prolong the encounter. Guiltily Will recalled turning down Emmy's invitation to dinner with Jed and Gwyn, Riley and herself. He'd wanted to go, but with Frannie's investigation like a sword between them, he'd thought it better to keep his distance. It looked like Jed felt the same.

"I brought food," Tessa said, holding out a plastic container. "Sandwiches. I never managed to eat."

"Great. I'll put it in with the water and soft drinks I brought." He stretched out a hand to help her into the boat. "Have you been out on Caddo Lake before?"

"No, never. I've wanted to, but haven't had the opportunity. This is a nice boat," she said as she sat on the vinyl bench seat. "I had visions of one of those army-green, flat-bottomed things with a hand-guided motor."

"I lucked into this," Will said, patting the dashboard. The boat was a beauty, all right. An eighteen-foot Fiberglas, cranberry metal flake bass boat with a two-hundred-horsepower engine. He suspected it would really hum. "I'm staying at the Kit and Caboodle Cottages. I knew the owners when I was a kid, hung out there sometimes trying to score cookies. Mrs. Whitney made great chocolate chip cookies," he added with a reminiscent grin. "Still does. Anyway, when they heard I wanted to rent a boat, they lent me theirs. They're big bass fishermen." Will started the engine.

"I remember when I first saw Caddo Lake," Tessa said as they puttered into the channel. "With all these huge cypress trees and the Spanish moss, I thought I was in Louisiana.''

''Yeah, this part of Texas, particularly the lake, is a lot more like Louisiana than what people tradition-ally think of as Texas. And half the lake is in Loui-siana.'' Will enjoyed watching Tessa. She seemed fas-cinated with the scenery, turning her head from side to side as if afraid she'd miss something.

''What are those flowers?'' she asked, pointing at the lily pads covering the water. ''The ones that look like umbrellas? They're so pretty.''

''The lotus lilies? There's a legend about them.'' He could still hear Murray Rafferty—the local au-thority on Caddo legends—telling Jed and him the story, in a voice hoarse from cigarettes and age. ''They say the wee folk slip out by moonlight and use them for umbrellas. When I was a kid I used to get up in the middle of the night and go down to the lake look-ing for the wee folk.'' He caught her smiling at him and added solemnly, ''I never saw them. Can't tell you how disappointed I was.''

Her lips curved upward and her eyes danced. ''I have an idea you weren't looking for wee folk when you sneaked out at night. But it's a cute story.''

True, he'd generally been looking for trouble and finding it. He grinned. ''Hey, even skeptics don't mess with the wee folks' lotus umbrellas.''

She laughed and returned to watching the scenery. ''It's so beautiful out here,'' she said wistfully. ''And eerie.''

''You ought to see it in the fog. It's even spookier

then.'' He remembered Jed used to tease him about his irrational fear of fog, until Will finally let Jed take him out in the boat early one morning. They'd caught a mess of fish while the fog slowly burned off. He'd never been scared of it again. ''There's nothing like dropping a line in during those early hours when nobody else is out. It's a great feeling. Peaceful.''

''Dropping a line in? I guess that means you're a big fisherman.''

''No.'' He turned the wheel and smiled at her. ''I fished some when I was a kid, but not since then. Jed taught me.'' Jed had taught him to love the lake, as well. Before that Will had never been on a large body of water.

''Jed Louis?'' she asked, sounding surprised. ''That's right, I keep forgetting Mrs. Granger raised you and Jed, and Emmy Gray Wolf, too, didn't she? Jed taught you how to fish?''

''Yeah.'' He laughed, remembering. ''He did a lot of big-brother type stuff. He always did take his responsibilities seriously.'' Will realized Tessa was staring at him looking surprised. ''What, don't you like Jed?''

''I don't mind him,'' she said hesitantly. ''He just hasn't struck me as the...friendly type.''

He raised an eyebrow. ''You and Jed have a run-in?''

''You could say that. Your foster brother doesn't like me much. I had to take him to court to get him to let me dig on his land.'' She shook her head. ''He wasn't a bit happy about having people bothering his land and his horses and anything else of his.''

Will frowned. So Jed had vetoed the archaeological dig. That didn't look good for him, either. Will wondered if Fielder knew that, then realized he was bound to. The sheriff obviously thought Jed hadn't cooperated with Tessa because he didn't want Frannie's remains found. ''You took him to court?''

''I had to. Otherwise he wouldn't have let me set foot on the land. Gwyn was actually the one who recommended I take legal action.''

''Gwyn? You mean Jed's wife told you to do that?''

''They weren't married at the time. I'm sure she wishes she hadn't now.'' She paused a moment. ''After all, I am the one who found Mrs. Granger's remains and everything has been in such turmoil since. I'm not exactly on close terms with either Jed or his wife,'' she said dryly.

''Jed wouldn't hold your finding Frannie against you.'' *Unless he was guilty.* Will pushed the unwelcome thoughts out of his mind. ''At least we know what happened to her now.''

She looked skeptical. ''It would be hard for him not to resent me, especially since he's a suspect in her murder.''

''How do you know he's a suspect?'' Will certainly hadn't told anyone, but Emmy had known. He'd assumed Jed had told her, though. Unlike most investigators, Fielder hadn't minded sharing his suspicions with his primary suspect.

''Sheriff Fielder hasn't been silent about that.

Everyone in town knows Jed Louis is a suspect. It can't be easy for you," she said sympathetically.

"It isn't." Damn it, things just kept looking worse for Jed. "But my job is to find out who killed Frannie. And I intend to do it."

He swung the boat into a familiar channel, surprised at the memories that flooded back as Frannie's dock came into view. It looked old and small compared to Beaumarais's huge dock and boathouse. But someone had kept it up. Jed, he supposed, since he owned the property now, along with his uncle's old place. It didn't look shabby, just comfortable.

He could almost see Frannie out there, Emmy beside her jumping and waving, waiting for him and Jed to pull in on those days they'd been running late. The house looked much as it had all those years before, a small white clapboard, homey and unpretentious. Someone had finished enclosing the porch, a project Frannie had started shortly before she disappeared. The porch she'd intended to make Will's room. He'd been looking forward to a room of his own, something he'd never had before. But Frannie's disappearance shot that hope all to hell. Along with everything else good in his life.

"Will, is something wrong? Is—are you upset because of what I told you about Jed?"

Pulled from his reverie, he looked at her. "Nothing's wrong. I needed to know."

"You looked so sad."

He glanced at the house, letting the boat idle. "Too many memories."

Her gaze followed his. "Was that your foster mother's house?"

"Yeah. I haven't seen it since I've been back." And he hadn't thought it would get to him so much. Hadn't realized that ache he'd felt when he hitched a ride out of town would return so sharply to remind him of what he'd lost.

Impatiently he shook off the unaccustomed melancholy and eased closer to Beaumarais. He wasn't here to indulge in memories; he was here to find a killer.

"I'm beginning to think you had an ulterior motive when you brought me out here," Tessa remarked.

He couldn't help grinning. "You mean other than getting you alone?"

She ignored that comment. "That's Beaumarais you're staring at with such ferocity. You're working, aren't you?"

"No." He laughed at her look of disbelief. "Okay, a little. I didn't think you'd mind. I wanted to see it from the water." To look at it with a cop's eyes, instead of through the eyes of a child. Unfortunately, his cop's vision couldn't tell him whether Frannie had been killed at the site, or brought there after her death. Sure, someone could have docked a boat long enough to dump the body. But why not out in one of the channels? Or in the middle of the lake, for that matter. Weight it down and watch it sink. That would have been the last of it. "Damn Fielder," he muttered, forgetting his audience.

"He and his men certainly made things difficult," Tessa agreed.

He shot her a sharp glance. "Go ahead and say it. They screwed up royally."

"Yes, they did. But I imagine you're as angry about that as I am."

He shrugged. "Nothing I can do about it now." Her face looked flushed, he noticed, conscious of the muggy heat and the sun shining brightly overhead. "Let's find some shade and sit a while."

"Shade sounds wonderful. I'm thirsty, too."

"There's a place just ahead. Why don't you get us a drink while I anchor?"

Anchoring accomplished, Will popped the top to his soft drink and drank thirstily.

"Tell me about her," Tessa said, taking off her hat and fanning her face with it.

"Who?" He finished his drink and tossed the can back into the cooler.

"Your foster mother. Unless it bothers you to talk about her." She moved closer to him, setting her hat on the bench beside her.

Would it? He didn't know. The day stood clear in his memory, though at the time he hadn't realized the sharp-eyed woman who'd marched into the social services office would change the course of his life. She said her name was Frannie Granger, and she wanted to be his foster mother. She told him this time would be different. *Yeah, right,* he'd thought. She took him home with her and explained the rules. She wouldn't tolerate lip, or bad language, or fighting.

He told her to go to hell, and she'd ignored him. So he told her something worse. She said potty language deserved an appropriate job, and made him clean the toilet. She said if he abided by her rules, then he could stay. That she hoped he would, because she wanted him there.

Will didn't believe her for a minute. But Frannie never gave up on him.

"Frannie was something," he said after a long moment. "I remember the first time I saw her. I was thirteen and headed to juvie. She said she wanted me to live with her, but I didn't buy it. I was a foul-mouthed little bastard and I told her what to do with her offer. It didn't faze her a bit."

"She wasn't easily shocked."

"Nope. She was solid. And she'd decided I needed her, and that was that." He smiled, remembering Frannie's passion to help. "She was a tiny little thing. My last foster home—" he hesitated, mentally expunging the worst of it before continuing. "The man was a big sucker, with big fists. I didn't want to do that again. So I figured she was a woman, she was small. I could get around her easier than someone else." He shook his head. "Wrong."

"You loved her."

He glanced at her and smiled. "Yeah, I did. But that came later. At first, I didn't like anybody, and I sure as hell didn't love anyone."

"What about your parents?"

Why was he spilling his guts to her? He didn't hide his background, but he didn't generally talk about it, either. Certainly not to a woman he wanted to sleep with. And he was very, very interested in getting Tessa

Lang into his bed. Still, he found he wanted to tell her, some of it anyway.

So he gave her the basic story. ''Never knew my old man, and I'm not sure my mother did, either. My mother was a junkie who had a different man every month, sometimes every week. Half the time, she didn't know I was there and when she did notice me it was worse. She split for good when I was eight.'' He brushed off the nightmare that had been his life, casually, as if it meant nothing.

Tessa remained quiet for a moment, but her eyes widened then softened in compassion. Seeing that irritated him. He knew better than to tell that story to a woman. He didn't want, or need, her pity. ''Shocked?'' he asked mockingly.

''No, just sad. Is that why you told me? Did you mean to shock me?''

He might not have shocked her, but he had surprised himself. He glanced away from her, stared out at the water. ''I don't know why I told you. I don't, usually.''

She put her hand over his and squeezed. ''I'm sorry it happened. But I'm glad you told me.''

His stomach tightened. Looking into those gorgeous blue eyes dark with emotion, it hit him with fatal force why he'd opened up to Tessa. He wasn't just looking for a good time with her.

He'd fallen for her.

Like a rock slide.

CHAPTER SEVEN

THEIR GAZES HELD. His dropped to her mouth, lingered, raised to her eyes again. She felt as if he'd kissed her, yet only their hands touched.

"That part of my life was over a long time ago," he said after a moment.

"But it still hurts." Tessa knew about old hurts. She remembered those first years with her parents after her grandmother died. How lonely she'd been, trying to carve a place in two people's lives, when they'd taken her out of duty, not love. Realizing she and Will still held hands, she tried to withdraw hers.

He simply smiled and kept hold of her, skimming his thumb over her knuckles. "Okay, no more story of my life. It's your turn. Tell me, what's a beautiful archaeologist from Georgia, who's been all over the world, doing in a podunk town in East Texas?"

"Researching Caddo Indian ruins. And you don't have to do that, you know."

"What?"

"Tell me I'm beautiful. It's a nice thing to say, but I don't like being lied to."

"Tessa." He carried her hand to his mouth, dropped a kiss on it, then continued to hold it while his gaze rested on hers. "Why does it bother you when I tell you you're beautiful?"

Her pulse hammered. She tried to ignore it and failed. "Because I'm not."

"Have you looked in a mirror lately? Never mind," he said when she started to speak. "You obviously don't see what I see when I look at you."

"Men don't— That is, they never used to— Oh, Lord, I wish I'd never started this. Look, I'm just no good at this kind of thing."

"What kind of thing?"

"Flirting." She waved her other hand. "Men. Whatever you want to call it. I don't have a lot of experience with men. Not like that, anyway."

"A lot, or any?"

Stung, she raised her chin. "I had a relationship in college." And she didn't intend to tell him what a disaster that had been. "But since then I've been a lot more interested in my work than in men." Safer that way, she thought. Much safer.

Still gazing into her eyes, he ran his thumb over the pulse at her wrist. It beat fast and even more erratically than a moment earlier, to her irritation.

"Was it serious?" he asked.

"I was serious. He wasn't." That summed it up perfectly, though the whole story was sordid and humiliating to her even years later. "Oh, God, I can't believe I'm telling you all this. Is this how you get suspects to talk to you?"

"By asking?" he said with a grin, leaning closer.

"By listening." She stared at him, her eyes widening when she realized his intention. "Will—"

He cupped her face in his hands and looked deep into her eyes. "Tessa," he murmured, and kissed her.

The man knew how to kiss, she gave him that. His lips were firm, yet soft and warm. He took his time, gently rubbing his lips over hers before dipping his tongue into her mouth, sweeping it leisurely, tantalizing her with promise. She sighed and gave into the urge to put herself in the hands of a master. It was only a kiss. She couldn't get into trouble with a kiss.

Could she?

Oh, yes, she could.

Why not just enjoy it? she thought. Quit analyzing things to death and for once go with her feelings. So she wrapped her arms around his neck and kissed him back, meeting his tongue with hers and melting even closer to him. She wasn't prepared for the instant torrent of heat exploding between them. His lips cruised down her neck and she moaned, her breath coming in gasps. He said something, maybe her name, then covered her mouth again. Her fingers curled into the soft silky hair at the back of his neck as she poured herself into the kiss. She tingled, vibrated, every nerve ending alert and ready for his touch.

He cupped her breast and rubbed her nipple with his palm. She flattened her own palm against his chest, felt the warmth beneath his T-shirt and wanted desperately to run her hands over his bare chest. She arched into his hand, wanting more, silently asking for it. He hesitated and, afraid he'd stop, she pulled her mouth from his and whispered, ''Yes.''

His hand slid under her shirt, slipped inside her bra. Her nipple tightened almost painfully. She gave a strangled groan and kissed him, their tongues tangling, their breathing labored.

Moments later he was half reclining on the bench seat, while she, barely conscious of their cramped position, lay stretched out on top of him. Their gazes locked, his legs tightened on either side of hers and his hands pressed her inexorably closer. She could barely breathe, but she could feel, every rock-solid inch of him hard and fully aroused against her.

Her head descended to kiss that delicious mouth of his when the harsh sound of a horn split the air. Startled, she looked up to see a boat passing by, its passengers laughing and waving at them.

Oh, my God, what was she doing? Her face flaming, she scrambled up, trying to get away. ''I don't— I can't— Oh, I can't believe—''

Releasing her, he smiled. A wicked, charming smile that made her insides flutter. ''Relax. I'd like nothing better than to make love to you right now, but this isn't exactly the place I had in mind.''

She put a hand to her forehead, aghast at her reaction. ''I don't do this. I don't have sex with men I barely know.'' And she'd never, ever burst into flame when a man touched her before. It wasn't possible. Maybe she had a fever.

A corner of his mouth lifted. ''We didn't have sex.''

But she would have. It blew her mind to realize

she'd have let him make love to her right there in the boat in the middle of the lake where any passerby could have seen what was going on. Let him, hell! She'd practically ripped his clothes off! She'd only known him a matter of days. How could she respond to him so strongly?

"Tessa," he said, sounding amused. "Don't get so bent out of shape. It was only a kiss."

Maybe for him. It had been a hell of a lot more than that to her. She struggled for breath. "I'm not like this."

"Like what?" He straightened in his seat, that gorgeous mouth of his smiling provocatively. "Passionate? Beautiful? Sexy?"

She gave a strangled laugh. "Hardly. I'm dull and boring and—"

He grasped her shoulders and kissed her, quick and hard. "I don't know who did such a number on you, but you need to let it go. You're a beautiful, intelligent woman. I'm attracted to you. And you're attracted to me. Sooner or later, we'll end up in bed. Why is that a problem?"

"It's too fast. For heaven's sake, we've only known each other a few days!"

"Things like this don't work on a timetable, Tessa. I wanted you the first time I saw you."

Her eyes narrowed and she folded her arms across her chest. "No, you didn't. You didn't even notice me. You were focused on Sheriff Fielder."

He smiled and flicked a careless finger over her cheek. "The second time I saw you, then. When you chewed me out in front of my truck.'' He released her and flipped the key in the ignition. The motor caught, revved. ''Why don't we just take it one day at a time and see what happens?''

She sucked in a deep breath and watched his profile as he steered the boat into the channel. His blond hair fell over his forehead, and she itched to smooth it back. Her gaze traveled down, over his chest, to his arms, looking tan and powerful in a short-sleeved T-shirt. Pretty, sleek muscles, not bulky. She closed her eyes and swore to herself.

If she didn't cool it, she was going to fall into bed, no, make that jump into bed, with a man she'd known a matter of days.

Bad idea, she thought. But tempting. Extremely tempting.

BY WEDNESDAY, Tessa had seen Will a couple more times, briefly, at the murder site. Attempting to curb her disappointment that he hadn't called, she told herself it was for the best. True, he'd said he'd been following leads and was out of touch, but she hadn't been sure whether he was trying to let her down easy or really meant it. Given her track record with men, she figured he'd already dumped her, even before they'd gotten started. Still, he had looked discouraged when she'd gotten a glimpse of him, so maybe he'd been telling the truth.

The phone rang as she headed out the door. Hoping it was Will, she snatched it up, but the well-modulated voice she heard was feminine. ''Hello, Mother.'' Tessa closed her eyes and bowed her head. *Great, the last person in the world she wanted to talk to right now.*

"Theresa," Olivia Lang said, "I've been trying to reach you for days. Where have you been?"

Tessa always wondered how Olivia—God forbid anyone call her Liv or Libby—managed to convey disgust, anger and irritation without ever raising her voice. "Sorry. I've been working. Why didn't you leave a message and let me get back to you?"

Her mother sailed right past that with a disdainful sniff. "You know I don't talk to machines. When will you be able to leave for Peru? They're making up the team as we speak."

"Peru?" For a moment Tessa couldn't figure out what her mother was talking about. "Oh, the Donovan expedition. I don't think I can make it." Fingers tightening on the receiver, Tessa tensed and waited for the explosion. A very calm, controlled, and hideously uncomfortable explosion for those on the receiving end, she knew from experience.

"That is not acceptable, Theresa." Ice coated Olivia's voice. Tessa could imagine her eyes, blue and cold as a permafrost, flashing with anger. "What is the delay?"

"I told you I'd been denied access to the Caddo dig because of the murder." Had told her several times, in fact, but her mother had chosen to forget that. "I can't possibly leave the country until my thesis is complete. But there has been progress. The police—the Rangers, actually—have now asked me to excavate the murder site and—"

"Really, Theresa." Her mother's tone progressed to frigid and disapproving. "The police? Now you're involved with the police? How utterly *common*."

Tessa ground her teeth but remained silent. There was never any point in trying to explain something her mother didn't want to hear. She considered anything Tessa told her about her current situation to be merely an excuse. Olivia Lang did not tolerate excuses.

"It doesn't matter," Olivia stated dismissively. "You must, simply must, find a way to be part of that expedition. The prestige of being on the team, well—" she laughed indulgently "—you'd be made for life."

I don't want to be "made for life," Tessa thought rebelliously, then wondered where that had come from. After all, she'd spent the past two years, and several before that, buried in her career. She should want to be "made for life." But the fact remained, she didn't. She set those troubling thoughts aside to consider later, when she didn't have to deal with her mother on top of everything else.

"I'm sorry, I don't have time to chat now. I have a class I don't want to be late for."

"What do you mean, you have a class?" Olivia asked sharply. "You've been working at that Caddo burial site. Not that I ever understood why you chose Caddo Indians for your thesis, but we won't get into that again."

Damn, damn, damn, now she'd done it. She hadn't meant to tell her mother about her teaching job. Too late, though, she'd have to come clean. Twisting the phone cord around her finger, she drew in a breath. "I accepted a teaching position here. At Caddo Lake College.''

''Caddo Lake College?'' her mother echoed, making it sound as if she had named another planet. ''I've never heard of it.''

''You wouldn't have. It's quite small.''

''What on earth possessed you to take a teaching position at a place like that? What could it possibly offer you?''

''Oh, I don't know, Mother,'' she snapped, unable to hold her tongue. ''I'm kind of fond of food.''

There was a stunned silence before her mother's arctic tones filled the air. ''I don't appreciate your sarcasm. If I'd known you wanted to teach—'' She hesitated and Tessa knew the wheels were turning. ''Caddo Lake College. No, that won't do at all,'' she stated briskly. ''I have some contacts, or possibly I could call in a favor or two. Harvard, or perhaps—''

''It's temporary. Don't worry about it.''

''How can I not worry? When my only child has forgotten all sense of responsibility, has involved herself with the police, and if that isn't enough—''

''Gotta go,'' Tessa interrupted, knowing she'd pay for it later. ''Pepe just spit up a hair ball and I'm late for class.''

''A hair ball? What in the—''

Tessa quietly replaced the receiver, breathing a huge sigh of relief. A slow smile spread over her face. She didn't often get the last word in an argument with her mother. She'd have thought by her age that she'd have learned to deal with Olivia better, but she never had.

Things hadn't been so bad when Tessa's grandmother was alive, but a few years ago, when her father died, her mother had entered into the administrative area of archaeology. Her interest in Tessa's career had quadrupled. That was a mixed blessing, because although Olivia had undoubtedly helped Tessa's career along, she also wanted to manage it, just as she had her husband's and her own. Tessa didn't intend to let her.

At least she'd shown some backbone this time. Her step unconsciously lightening, Tessa left for class.

A FEW HOURS LATER, Tessa slid into the pea-green vinyl seat of a booth at the Caddo Kitchen, the café where she planned to meet Ellen for lunch. Her goal, a quick bite and then on to the site. Her progress hadn't been as rapid as she'd have liked, but at least she had started, and her crew was proceeding with the burial mound itself.

She waved when Ellen arrived, though in a place the size of a postage stamp, the woman could hardly miss her. Today her friend looked practically subdued, in a striped sundress the colors of a package of Starburst candy.

"Tessa!" she almost shrieked as she took her seat. "You're not going to believe who asked me out!"

Cassie, the waitress, appeared and after the obligatory chat, they gave their orders. "Guess," Ellen commanded as Cassie left.

"Robert Morrison," Tessa said, referring to the dean of the Business College. It was widely held that Morrison had never cracked a smile, so the thought of him going out with the exuberant Ellen was a funny one.

"How did you know?" She seemed a little crestfallen that Tessa had guessed. "Aren't you even shocked? I thought the man loathed me. Actually, I think he asked me out against his better judgment." She primmed her mouth, then laughed.

"He watches you at faculty meetings. I've noticed it several times."

"No way!" Ellen said, her eyes rounding. "Really?"

Tessa nodded. "Discreetly, of course. I think he's nice. Are you going?"

"Absolutely." She snatched up a cracker packet and ripped it open. "I can't afford to turn down a free meal."

"That's not the only reason you're going," Tessa said shrewdly. "Admit it. You like him, too."

"Where is that Cassie with our drinks?" Ellen said, fanning herself with a paper napkin. "I'm parched."

"And I'm right," Tessa said with satisfaction.

"Speaking of liking, what's up with you and the very hot Ranger McClain?" She waggled her eyebrows. "Hmm?"

The very hot Ranger McClain had walked up just in time to hear Ellen's comment. He couldn't possibly have missed it, and considering his smile, Tessa would bet he hadn't. "Nothing. A big, fat nothing," she said, looking at him.

Ellen turned her head and her mouth dropped open comically. "Oops. Hi, Will."

"Hi, Ellen. Tessa." He nodded, a lazy smile curving his perfect mouth. No man should have a mouth that luscious, she thought. It simply wasn't fair.

"Mind if I sit with you ladies? I hate to eat alone."

"Have a seat," Ellen said before Tessa could answer. Her lips quivered and she added, "Funny thing, we were just talking about you."

"Is that a fact?" Will slid into the booth beside Tessa. Lord, he was big, she thought. And so...close in the tiny booth. Even though she'd scooted over against the wall, their thighs rubbed against each other. *Take a deep breath,* she told herself, trying her best to ignore the tingling.

He signaled Cassie, who came instantly to his side. After giving his order he clasped his hands together on the marbled Formica table and looked at Ellen. "Tessa's mistaken. There's definitely something going on between us."

Tessa choked in midsip. "Or there will be if I have anything to say about it," Will continued easily, turning to Tessa. "Would you like to go to dinner with me tonight? There's a restaurant in Jefferson you might enjoy. Not far from the river."

Ellen watched them with fascination. Recovering, Tessa said, "What I'd *like* is to kick you."

He gave her a reassuring grin. "Okay, as long as you'll go to dinner with me." He covered her hand with his, prompting her to look up at him. "Tessa, I haven't stopped thinking about you since I met you. I'd really like to be with you tonight. Say yes."

Her heart took a slow tumble as she gazed into his

eyes. If he wasn't sincere, he sure gave a good impression of it.

"If you don't, I will," Ellen interjected. "Robert wasn't anywhere near that smooth."

"Yes," Tessa said, capitulating recklessly.

The rest of the meal passed uneventfully, though Tessa discovered that Will had spent the past two days buried in work. Strain showed around his eyes and she wondered if part of that was due to worrying about his foster brother.

Ellen said she had an appointment, leaving Tessa waiting outside for Will, who had insisted on paying the bill. A pitiful yelp from several yards away snagged her attention. Two young boys and a large dog, she thought, smiling at the picture. But as she looked more closely, her smile faded. They were dragging the animal to the end of a dock by a rope, with something—a brick—tied to it. Incredulous, she started toward them, then saw one of them kick the dog as the other tugged harder on the rope.

"Stop! Stop it! Don't you dare throw that poor animal in the lake." Panting, she reached the group a second after the boys had succeeded in shoving the dog off the end of the dock. Flailing desperately, the animal managed to stay afloat, but she knew it was only a matter of time before he'd be pulled under by the weight of the brick.

Dimly aware of the boys scattering, Tessa kept her eye trained on the spot. She gave a brief, panicked thought to what jumping in that brackish water would feel like. But it didn't matter, she couldn't stand by and watch the poor thing drown.

Drawing a breath, she said a quick prayer and jumped in, as close to the animal as she could get. The water closed around her, dark and frightening, as vegetation and other nameless things brushed against her skin.

The dog disappeared beneath the surface just as she reached him. She grabbed for the rope around his neck, but missed. Cursing silently, she held her breath and went under. Opening her eyes, she saw the dark shape through the murky water. She wrapped her arms around him and kicked for the surface.

He squirmed, fought. She broke water, gulped in air before the struggling dog pulled her back under. Again she battled for breath, the dog clasped against her chest. The dock—so close, but it might as well have been a million miles. Strength ebbing, she closed her eyes in despair.

Let go, she thought. *You'll drown if you don't.* She sucked in more water, choked. *No choice.* With a last desperate surge, she fought her way to the surface. She heard a splash and opened her eyes just as Will's strong arms closed around her.

"What the hell are you doing?" he asked, pushing her toward the dock.

"Help—the dog—" she gasped, her arms weakening, her mouth filling with foul water.

Though he cursed, he took the dog from her arms and pushed him up on the dock. The water closed over her head, but Will grabbed her and dragged her over to the dilapidated pier. Seconds later, he climbed out and hauled her onto the dock beside the hapless dog. Racked with coughs, she collapsed against him.

"Are you all right?" he demanded, his fingers digging into her shoulders. He looked angry, and something else she couldn't quite define.

She nodded, still coughing. She tried not to think of what had been in the water or how much she'd swallowed. Neither spoke again for several minutes while Tessa regained her breath. Will pulled the brick up from the lake and placed it beside the now shivering animal.

"What the hell were you thinking, jumping in like that?" He finally asked, his voice harsh and angry. "You could have drowned!"

"I was thinking about saving the dog," she retorted, placing a hand on the cowering animal's back. His tail thumped. He seemed to realize she wanted to help him. "I didn't have a choice. Some horrible boys threw him in." She tried ineffectually to untie the rope, hampered by both the wet knot and the dog's attempts to lick her face. "See, they tied this brick around his neck." Though she'd stopped coughing, she still tasted the nasty water.

"Tessa, you can't swim enough to save yourself, much less this mutt. It was crazy for you to jump in."

"I can swim." Just not very well. And if Will hadn't come in after them... "Thank you for helping me." He'd saved the dog's life, and possibly hers.

"That's not the point. You had no business going in after that dog. Why didn't you call for help or—"

It occurred to her what she saw in his eyes. Fear. For her. "Will, I'm all right."

He glared at her. "I thought you were drowning. It scared the hell out of me." He sighed and rubbed a hand over his face, pushing his wet hair back. He looked at her a moment before a reluctant smile lifted his lips. "I guess it's too much to expect you to pass up any creature in need."

Or for him, either, she thought. She raised a hand to his cheek. "Thank you," she repeated softly.

Shrugging it off, he rose, worked a hand into his pocket with difficulty and withdrew it, holding a pocketknife. "We can cut the brick off, but I'm going to leave the rope on him to use as a lead."

"They were trying to drown him," she said, rising, her voice hitching as she watched him deal summarily with the rope. "How could they?"

"People do," Will said, handing her the cut end of the rope. "It sucks, but it happens. I don't know about you, but I could stand a shower. Let's go to my place. I'll find you something to wear."

At her blank look, he pointed to the Kit and Caboodle Cottages, across the road. "It's right over there."

She stared down at the dog, now sitting on his rump and happily panting. "Cruelty to animals is illegal, isn't it? I want you to arrest them."

He spared her a frustrated glance. "If I had a hope in hell of finding them, I could do that. Did you know them?" She shook her head. "Get a good look at them?"

"Sort of. I might recognize them if I saw them again."

"Asking around about who's been drowning dogs lately isn't likely to gain me any answers. You're probably going to have to settle for saving the mangy mutt's life."

At least she'd been dressed for the field, she thought gloomily as she sloshed across the road after Will. He'd been dressed in his usual jeans and button-down shirt, which now lay plastered against that powerful body. Oh, well, everything would wash, she thought philosophically. But her shorts would never be the same, with the muck and slime from the lake soaked into them. And her best running shoes, the ones she worked in, were a total loss. The dog didn't help matters by jumping up and planting his enormous muddy paws squarely on what had once been a white T-shirt. Apparently unaware of his close call, he was winding the rope happily around her legs, trying to trip her.

"You really can't arrest them?"

"Not if I can't find them. Give me a description and I'll ask Fielder. He might know who they are." He stopped at the door and smiled at her. "But if you ever do see them, just let me know. I can sure as hell haul them in and scare the bejesus out of them. Okay?"

"You're a nice man," she told him.

"Don't believe it." He grinned. "How do you know this isn't a ploy of mine to get you naked?"

"I'm sure I'm incredibly appealing right now," she

said, conscious of mud trickling down her face and back.

"More than you know." He didn't give her a chance to respond but said, "Tie him up out here for a minute. I'll go get you some clothes and then I'll hose him down while you're in the shower."

"Absolutely not. You shower first. It's only fair since you're the one who saved him."

He looked unconvinced, but she finally persuaded him.

"He'll have to stay out here until he dries off," Will said as he started to go inside. "Mrs. Whitney would have a stroke if I let a wet dog in the place."

Cleaning up the mutt took longer than she'd expected. The hose scared him and he kept shying away and shaking water all over her, but finally she had him about as clean as she could hope for.

He looked like a cross between a shepherd and she didn't know what. Maybe a Great Dane, but whatever it was, he hadn't exactly gotten the best of both breeds. His medium-length fur was an uninspiring dingy brown and beige, and a black circle ringed one eye. Added to that, his paws were about four sizes bigger than the rest of him, indicating he had some growing to do. No American beauty, this dog.

"You are a goofus," she told the dog severely as she tied the dry rope Will had brought her securely around a post on the porch. Unchastened, he gave a woof and wagged his tail, whacking it against the wood column. Startled, he turned around, as if wondering what could have made the noise. Goofy, she thought, naming him. It fit him to a tee.

She entered through the kitchen and saw Will on the phone, buttoning his shirt as he talked. Spying her, he gestured toward the hallway. The bathroom opened off the hall. Small and tidy, it made her wonder if Will was that neat or if there was a daily maid service at the cottages.

Noticing he'd laid out a pair of wind shorts and a shirt for her, she turned on the taps and stepped into the shower gratefully. She lathered her hair lavishly, rinsed it and sighed with pleasure as the warm water flowed over her. Rubbing a bar of soap slowly over her body, she thought about what Will had said at lunch. *He hadn't stopped thinking of her. He wanted to be with her.* How was she supposed to hold out against that? Especially when it was spoken in that deep, seductive voice, as though the two of them had been the only people in the universe.

And really, she asked herself, why was she fighting him so hard? A gorgeous, sexy man wanted to take her to bed. She understood as well as he did that theirs wouldn't be a lasting affair. But why not enjoy it while she could? Enjoy him while she could?

Why not be the new Tessa Lang that Ellen insisted she could be, instead of the insecure and, yes, boring, woman who rarely dated and would never have imagined in a zillion years going out with someone like Will McClain. She shivered, even underneath the warm water. A man who knew what a woman wanted and had no problem giving it to her.

She still hadn't talked herself into it by the time she finished showering. But she was awfully close to crumbling. The shirt he'd loaned her was a button-down powder-blue like the one he'd been wearing the first time she saw him. She tried on the wind shorts, but couldn't keep them up. If he had a safety pin, or some kind of belt, they might stay up.

Tessa wandered into the living room, leaving her wet clothes in the tub until she figured out what to do with them. "Will? Do you have a sack for those clothes? Or a clothes dryer? And I need a safety pin."

He stood with his back to her. "The washer and dryer are in the hall, but I don't have a—" He turned around and broke off in mid-sentence, staring at her. His gaze stroked her from the tips of her very bare toes to the top of her wet slicked-back hair. "Sorry. What did you say?"

She held up the shorts he'd given her. "I need a safety pin. The shorts are too big and I don't think I'd better drive home like this."

"No, I don't think you'd better." His eyes lit with an appreciative glow. "You'd cause a riot if you had to get out of the car."

She laughed. "I doubt it. I must look like I'm twelve."

"No." Not taking his eyes off her, he shook his head. "Trust me on this. You don't look twelve. If you did, I'd have to throw myself in jail for thinking what I'm thinking."

"What are you thinking, Will?" she asked, hardly

daring to breathe. She crossed the room, halting a few inches in front of him.

"Can I ask you a question?"

She nodded silently.

"Are you wearing anything underneath that shirt?"

CHAPTER EIGHT

"NOT A THING," Tessa said, and smiled. Her heart pounded until she could hardly breathe. She took another step forward, wondering where this sudden courage had come from.

Will closed his eyes. "Damn, I was afraid of that."

"Is that a problem?"

"No." He opened his eyes and his gaze swept over her body in a long, hot journey. "It's a dream come true. The problem is I have to leave."

Which is probably a good thing, she told herself. *You're not sure you want to do this.* Then she looked at him, felt the heat of his gaze and amended that thought. Oh, yes, she wanted him. She just wasn't sure having him was wise. But instead of saying something sensible, she asked, "Right this minute?"

His jaw tightened. "Soon. Too soon to be able to do what I really want to do with you."

Something about wearing a man's shirt with absolutely nothing on beneath it, and having that same man stare at her as if he wanted to start at her toes and devour her whole, gave her courage. She tossed the shorts onto the couch and laid her hand on his chest, palm flat against his heart. It beat fast, erratic, keeping time with hers. "We could be quick." She could hardly believe she'd said that, but when she opened her mouth that's what had come out.

His mouth lifted in a devastating smile, eyes a hypnotic green. He shook his head slowly. "No, we couldn't. Not the first time. We're going to need a long time. All night."

Her stomach fluttered, her skin tingled. She stayed silent, certain she'd stutter if she tried to speak.

He gathered her to him, chest to chest, staring down at her intently. There wasn't a speck of gray in his eyes; they were forest-green, kindling with what even she recognized as desire. "Kiss me goodbye." His voice was deep, dark and quiet, sending shivers of anticipation up and down her spine. "It's probably a mistake, but to hell with it. I'm not leaving without tasting you again."

He crushed his mouth to hers in a kiss that had all the blood draining from her head and every nerve in her body aching for more. His arms tightened around her, his tongue slid inside her mouth, slow, wicked, knowing. She clung to his shoulders, certain his arms were the only solid thing that could anchor her suddenly shifting world.

When her heart pounded like a pneumatic drill, and every coherent thought had fled her mind, he released her. "Tonight," he said, and walked out.

RESIGNED TO OWNING yet another stray, Tessa decided to drop Goofy off at the vet on her way to Beaumarais. Her house had a fenced yard, but Mrs. Brindle, her landlady, hadn't been thrilled about a cat. Tessa would have to do some fast talking to get her to consent to a dog.

She glanced at him, stretched out in the back seat of her little car, covering the area from port to starboard. Did he have to be so big? Oh well, she thought, if she was lucky Mrs. Brindle would never set eyes on him.

Forty-five minutes later, alone at the dig site, she set to work quickly, aware she'd wasted a good deal of time. Though she could hardly call what had happened between her and Will a waste of time. Whenever she thought about that parting kiss she became hot and shaky all over again. It shot her concentration to hell and back.

In the distance, she heard the sounds of her crew, working at the Caddo burial mound. Although they were too far away to see exactly what they were doing, she did see signs of activity. Surprisingly, it hadn't bothered her as much as she'd imagined to be forced to turn that dig over to someone else while she worked at the murder site. She was involved in this murder, by virtue of finding the victim's remains. That tied her to it in a way she couldn't deny.

She'd decided to work alone at the murder site, at least at first. Since she had told Will she wouldn't use students, it left her a bit shorthanded, because she felt she needed the more experienced people at the Caddo mound. If she ran into trouble, though, she could always pull someone from the other site to help her.

Tessa had decided to begin with the actual place she'd found the remains rather than the mound of dirt tossed up beside it. On her knees on the ground, she brushed dirt onto the tray, then sifted through it to see if anything of interest showed up. When nothing did, she placed the screened dirt in a large bucket, to be dumped into a wheelbarrow later. Then she repeated the process, one tray at a time. Monotonous work, but a find would make it all worthwhile.

She thought about teaching her classes, and realized that she hadn't found her job monotonous at all. Not even grading papers. And her students were a joy, or most of them were. Bright, eager to learn, some of them hung on her words as if she were giving them the keys to the universe. It was an exhilarating experience after being virtually ignored at some of the bigger digs she'd taken part in. Before she took the job with the college, she'd never have imagined that she'd enjoy her time in the classroom so much.

Bending to gather dirt for the seventh tray, she saw something glinting in the sunlight. A small object lay half-buried, in almost the exact spot where she'd found Frannie Granger's remains weeks before. Cautiously she swept the soil away with her brush. Careful not to add her fingerprints to any that might be on the object, she scooped it up with her diamond-shaped trowel and inspected it.

A ring. Taking tongs to it, she turned it to catch the light and peered more closely. Bright gold, with a garnet stone gleaming bloodred in the center. An Uncertain High School ring, she thought, her heart beginning to beat unsteadily. She shifted the ring to look inside and saw that the initials had been inscribed. J.L.

J.L. She closed her eyes, sucked in a deep breath. Jed Louis. Will's foster brother.

Oh, God, she thought, her stomach plunging as she opened her eyes and stared once more at the damning evidence. Evidence she would have to turn over to the police. *What would Will do?*

WILL HAD AN OFFICE of sorts now. A small room at the Sheriff's Department with a desk, a hard wooden chair with a gimpy leg and a phone. No window and barely enough room to turn around, but he didn't much care. He'd worked in worse.

Phone receiver against his ear, he tapped his pen impatiently on the desk. On hold for the Marshall, Texas, Police Department, he'd spent the past twenty minutes listening to canned announcements, interspersed with something he supposed was music. He should have gone over there himself, but he'd hoped for once he could accomplish something over the phone instead of having to drive halfway to hell and back.

Finally his contact came back on the line. ''I found the records you requested, Ranger McClain. Sorry it took so long. I had a little trouble locating them. A Hank Belmonte, I believe you said?''

''That's right. Belmonte.'' He spelled it out and the clerk reconfirmed. This was Will's only lead, other than Jed. The only remotely suspicious person he'd found who'd been in Uncertain at the time of Frannie's disappearance. Hank Belmonte was a drifter who'd taken handyman jobs in the area. Frannie had hired him to convert her porch into a bedroom for Will shortly before she disappeared. And then the man had vanished—the same day as Frannie. Will hadn't found any evidence that Belmonte had ever returned, either.

A few days before, Will had interviewed Joleen Berber, Frannie's good friend. She'd told him Frannie had been ready to fire the man for drinking on the job. So Will had traced Belmonte's whereabouts, which was why he'd called the Marshall police. Reports indicated the man was last seen in a bar in Marshall, the evening before Frannie disappeared.

"Yes," the officer said. "Hank Belmonte was in custody from 2:17 a.m. the morning of May 4, 1982 until late the following afternoon."

Will managed not to curse in her ear. Scratch one promising suspect. The jerk had been in the drunk tank the entire time in question. Talk about a great alibi. Will thanked the officer and hung up.

Dead ends, damn it. He rubbed his temples and wished for an aspirin. Nothing but stinking dead ends. He intended to check with Frannie's employers again, though Fielder maintained it was a waste of time, pointing to his notes from years before. None of her employers had shed any light on her disappearance. In fact, if Will read the reports correctly, Ray Jennings, the banker Frannie had worked for, had been mad as hell he'd even been questioned. Will smiled, thinking he'd enjoy questioning Mr. High-and-Mighty Jennings again. It ought to really tick him off to have the riffraff who'd once dated his daughter on the sly question him about a murder.

Will had tried investigating Fielder, as well, without tipping him off. It hadn't been easy, and so far he'd had zero luck in either verifying the sheriff's whereabouts at the time in question or assigning him a motive for killing Frannie.

Disgusted, Will began to pace the tiny office. Yeah, that was the kicker. Why would Fielder have killed Frannie? Other than the fact that he was so determined to pin the crime on Jed, Will wouldn't have given a thought to suspecting him. Still, in Will's professional judgment, Fielder seemed just a little too obsessed with charging Jed Louis with the crime, especially given the circumstantial nature of the evidence.

He sat again, bending over the desk to study the copies of Fielder's files, leafing through them slowly until he came to Amanda Jennings's statement. The morning after Frannie's disappearance, Will, Jed and Emmy had gone to school as usual. Amanda had overheard Jed and Will discussing the previous day's argument. That dovetailed nicely with the information Fielder had managed to drag from Emmy and Will. Will remembered that interview well, because directly after it, he'd left town. One good thing—Amanda wasn't likely to mind discussing the situation with Will all over again. Though Will doubted her memory of the events would be particularly good, it was worth a shot.

The call came in as he was headed out the door for Amanda's house. "McClain."

"Will, it's Tessa."

Checking his pocket for his Ranger identification,

he stopped. Her voice sounded odd. Tight and upset. "What's wrong?"

"I'm—I'm at the site. I found something, Will."

"Hot damn. Finally, a break."

There was a strained silence before she said, "I don't think it's the break you wanted."

Shit. He didn't ask what she'd found. He'd know soon enough. "On my way. I'll be there in ten minutes."

THE MINUTE HE HEARD her voice on the phone, he knew it was bad. One look at her face told him it was worse. She waited for him, standing beside one of those huge mounds of dirt the sheriff's men had so carelessly made.

"I called you as soon as I found it," Tessa said, handing him a clear plastic bag with a small object inside. "Luckily, I had a cell phone with me so I didn't have to leave the site."

He looked at the bag, turned it over to get a better view. It held a ring. A high school ring with some kind of dark red stone. He smoothed his hand over the plastic. A garnet. He read the lettering around the stone with a sense of unreality. Uncertain High School, 1982. Jed's senior year. The year Frannie died. "Did you touch it?"

"No. I used tongs. I found it where Frannie's remains were. Almost exactly at the spot." She gestured toward the ground beside them. "In the original excavation I made a grid showing where that is. I don't know how the sheriff's men missed it, or how it managed to escape being thrown out with the rest of the dirt. It's small, so I guess it slipped through their tools.''

His stomach twisting, Will stared at the evidence, then looked at Tessa. ''Any distinguishing marks?''

She nodded, her gaze solemn on his. ''It's engraved. With—'' She hesitated, glanced away, then met his eyes. ''Will, the initials inscribed inside the band are J.L.''

He'd known it, of course. The minute he'd recognized it as an Uncertain High School Senior ring, he'd known. Still he said, ''That doesn't necessarily mean—'' Breaking off, he looked at the engraving for himself. Pulled the plastic tight so he could see inside the thick gold band. A squared off *J,* a serif on the *L.* The letters looked like mirror images of each other. The same image Jed used on his letterhead.

There could be an innocent reason why the ring had been there. They couldn't even guarantee it had been left there at the same time as Frannie's body. But with this evidence, Fielder would be on the phone to the D.A. quicker than a paid informant shot off his mouth. And Jed would be charged and arrested for Frannie's murder.

''I need to take this with me,'' he told Tessa after a long moment. ''You may be—no, I'm sure you'll be called in to testify about exactly where you found it. We'll need to see the original grid you drew up, as well.''

''All right. Just let me know. Will, I wish...'' Her

voice trailed away. She laid her hand on his arm and squeezed sympathetically.

He couldn't stand her compassion right then, couldn't deal with it, or with what was happening. "You'll call if you find anything else," he said, cutting off whatever else she might have added.

"Of course, although I'm not sure how much longer I'll be here today. Will—" her fingers tightened on his arm "—I'm so sorry. I know how this must hurt you."

He met her gaze, seeing her blue eyes dark with pity, concern. "I'm not hurt. I don't know what I am." Numb, that's how he felt. Not hurt, or shocked, just numb. He needed to think. Alone. He brushed her hand off and looked away. "I can't talk about this." His throat closed up. He wanted to put his fist through something, but nothing was going to help clean up this mess.

"I know. But if you need to talk...if I can help, you know where to find me."

"I have to go," was all he could manage.

A SHORT WHILE LATER, Will stalked into Fielder's office. Fielder had just returned from a call and was hanging his hat on the rack as Will entered. His face must have given him away, because the sheriff said sharply, "What have you got?"

He tossed the bag containing the ring down on his desk. "New evidence."

Fielder took his seat, picked up the bag and looked at it a moment, before reaching into his chest pocket for his glasses. Slipping them on, he brought the bag closer and studied it silently. "It's a high school senior ring." His gaze lifted to Will's. "From Uncertain High."

"That's right." He would keep his voice calm, level, no matter what it cost him. He was a professional, and he had a job to do.

"Where did you find it?"

"Tessa Lang found it at the murder site. Almost exactly where she found Frannie's remains, she said." He didn't add that Fielder's men had missed it. What was the point?

An expression of chagrin crossed his face, but he only said, "Fingerprints?"

"It needs to go to the lab, but fingerprints aren't likely after this amount of time and given the composition of the object. Tessa didn't touch it, except with tongs."

Studying the ring, still encased in clear plastic, Fielder said, "Looks like writing inside the band. I can't quite make it out... J—" He broke off and laid it down, then fixed Will with a hard stare. "My eyes aren't as good as they used to be, but those initials sure look like a *J* and an *L* to me."

"They are," Will confirmed, his voice hard, void of emotion. "And it's not standard engraving."

"Well, well," Fielder said musingly, leaning back in his chair. "Anything else you want to tell me?"

Nothing he *wanted* to talk about, but he knew he had to. Besides, Fielder would find out easily enough. "It's a squared-off *J* and the *L* has a serif on top, so

they look like mirror images of each other.'' He
paused and added deliberately, ''Just like the initials
on Jed Louis's stationery.''

Fielder simply nodded, clasped his hands together
across his belly. ''Do you want to call the D.A. or
should I?''

''What, no discussion?'' Will paced a few steps,
attempting to control his temper. ''No I-told-you-so?''

''What's to discuss? And why should I tell you
something you know as well as I do? You're not stupid,'' he said, gesturing at the plastic bag. ''You know
what this means.''

Fielder looked pleased, but then why wouldn't he
be? The ring went a long way toward proving his theory. ''There could be an innocent explanation for why
that ring was found in the same place Frannie's remains were. With the mess the site was in, we can't
even be sure when it was put there. It could have been
dropped—hell, even planted—at a later date.''

''Could have been, but you don't believe that,''
Fielder said shrewdly. ''That's a mighty far reach,
McClain. Are you trying to say you don't believe we
have enough evidence to charge Louis now? That
this—'' he held up the evidence bag ''—this ring isn't
a solid piece of evidence to present to the D.A.?''

How could he answer that, except with the truth?
''No, I'm not arguing that,'' he said harshly. ''Call the
D.A.''

Fielder's bushy gray eyebrows lifted as he stared at
him. ''I have to say, McClain, you've surprised me.''

Will shrugged that off. ''This evidence isn't rock

solid, you realize. His lawyer will likely shoot all sorts of holes in our case.'' And with good reason, he thought. But would it be enough to get Jed off?

"Maybe not rock solid,'' Fielder said, ''but pretty damn strong.''

Will slapped his palms down on the desk, standing nearly nose to nose with Fielder. ''That ring is compelling evidence, and has to be taken into account. But if you think any evidence, other than a full confession from Jed himself, is going to make me believe he deliberately murdered Frannie Granger, then think again.'' He straightened and stalked away, hanging on to his temper by his fingertips.

"Understood and noted,'' Fielder said. ''I don't impress easy, McClain, but you've impressed me. I figured you'd do whatever it took to protect Louis, feeling as you do.''

"I'm here to find Frannie's killer, *whoever it is*. If that's Jed, and I don't believe it is, then he'll pay for his crime.''

Fielder pursed his lips, nodded. ''Do you want me to bring him in?''

"No. I have to do it.'' Bad as it would be, Jed would do better if Will brought him in rather than Fielder.

Staring at Will, the sheriff shook his head. ''You're not the punk I always thought you were. And you got a respect for the law, and your job. You might not realize it, but I got a respect for that law myself.''

He didn't give a damn about Fielder's respect, he wanted to prove Jed innocent. ''I haven't given up on finding the real killer. And I won't, until I'm satisfied we have him in custody.''

Fielder nodded again, placed the call to the D.A. A short time later, he hung up. ''The D.A. agrees we should be able to prosecute with the new evidence. Judge Rimmer will issue a warrant for the arrest of Jed Louis in the murder of Frannie Granger. Are you willing to make the collar?''

''Yes,'' Will said, wondering how the hell he'd managed to get into the position of having to arrest his foster brother for the murder of their foster mother.

Better him than Fielder, he told himself. It was the least he could do for Jed, even though he'd rather get caught in cross fire during a drug raid. Jed wasn't going to be happy to see him this time.

And no matter how it turned out, even if Will cleared Jed by bringing in the real killer, he knew Jed might never forgive him for what he was bound to see as betrayal. Hell, Will couldn't blame him. He wasn't sure he could forgive himself. *Assuming Jed was innocent.*

He had no choice. He'd taken an oath, sworn to uphold the law. He had a duty, and a promise to the woman who had saved his life. Those two things took precedence over anything else. Even a brother.

CHAPTER NINE

WILL REACHED BEAUMARAIS about six-thirty that evening. Still full daylight, it was hotter than Hades, and would stay that way until long after the sun went down. As always, June, Jed's housekeeper, answered the door. For a change, she looked pleased to see him. Jed had told him last time he was there that she'd decided Will wasn't so bad after all.

She'd change that opinion quick enough when he arrested her employer.

''I'll wait in the parlor,'' Will said. Why arrest him in the library and ruin Jed's favorite room for him?

June seemed surprised but left him there and went to get her employers. A few minutes later Jed entered, with Gwyn following. Gwyn smiled at him warmly. She wore a pale blue summer dress that emphasized the blue of her eyes. A pretty, classy lady, he thought, who seemed to suit Jed very well. Not for the first time since having met Gwyn, he wondered what it would be like to have a woman so solidly behind him. To have a woman believe in him like that.

''How are you, Will?'' Jed asked. ''And what are you doing in the parlor? I can't imagine why June put you in here.'' They shook hands, and Will was struck by how happy he looked. Jed had Beaumarais, a career he excelled at, a beautiful wife who obviously loved him and who he just as plainly loved. And now Will was about to bring it all crashing down around him.

"Never mind," Jed continued. "Gwyn, why don't you tell June to set another place for dinner before she goes home?"

"Of course," Gwyn said, but she looked sharply at Will. "Can you stay for dinner, Will?"

"No." The word shot out, abrupt and stark. "This isn't a social call." No sense dragging it out. In the long run that would only make it harder.

Jed's eyes searched his face. "I see," he said slowly. "What's this about?"

"I have to take you in. To the station."

"For questioning, you mean," Jed said. His expression changed. Became shuttered. "No. Been there, done that, and I don't intend to do it again. I've already answered all the questions I'm going to. As I told Fielder, check the notes."

"Not just for questioning. I'm sorry, Jed." He drew in a breath and said it, quickly, to get it over with. "A warrant has been issued for your arrest in the murder of Frances Granger."

Jed's eyes went blank with shock. Then he gathered himself together and spoke. "You're sorry? You're arresting me, booking me for murder, and all you can say is you're *sorry?*" His blue eyes had darkened with fury, carefully controlled.

"I don't have a choice." Will glanced at Gwyn, who'd gone sheet-white and clung tightly to Jed's hand. "It was me or Fielder. I thought it would be

easier for you if I did it.'' Jed didn't speak, he just
stared at Will in a way that made him feel lower than
a snake's belly. ''Goddamn it, Jed, do you think I'm
enjoying this? Do you think I'd be here if there was
any way out of it?''

''I don't have a clue, Will. I thought I knew you,
but obviously I was wrong.''

''What brought this about?'' Gwyn asked, speaking
for the first time since Will had dropped his bombshell. ''Why are you arresting him now? What's happened?''

''New evidence. That's all I can tell you. Call his
lawyer,'' he said, his gaze meeting Gwyn's. ''Tell him
to meet us at the station.''

He saw the moment the reality hit her. With a
choked sound, she turned into Jed, burying her face in
his shoulder. His arm came around her protectively,
and he looked down at her. For a moment tenderness
softened his face, displacing the anger.

''Don't worry,'' Jed murmured. ''We'll get through
this, Gwyn.''

''I know,'' she whispered, her hand coming up to
clutch his shirt. ''I know we will.''

Gwyn was one tough lady, Will thought, watching
her straighten and turn her head to fix him with a cold-
eyed stare. Good, he had a feeling she'd need to be.

''I hope you can live with yourself after this,'' she
said. ''I'm going to call our lawyer. I'd appreciate it
if you didn't take my husband away before I return.''

Will nodded, saying nothing. But Jed's angry voice
exploded into the silence. ''I have one question for

you," he said. "If you have the guts to answer it honestly."

"Ask it. But you shouldn't talk to me, or to Fielder without your lawyer present." And thank God, he had a good one.

Jed brushed the warning aside. "I'm fully aware of that. I still want an answer. Do you really believe I killed Frannie? Is that why you're here, arresting me in my own home?"

"What I believe doesn't matter. The evidence matters."

"Answer me, Will. Do you believe I killed Frannie? That I killed her and buried her on Beaumarais, then did nothing while social services took Emmy and you skipped town for good? Do you think I'm capable of killing her, *my foster mother,* and hiding the fact for nearly twenty years? Of just going about my business, as if nothing had ever happened?"

Gwyn returned and went swiftly to Jed's side. They stood together now, facing him as if he were the worst piece of pond scum they'd ever seen. And that's exactly what he felt like.

"Nothing would make me believe you killed Frannie deliberately," he said, echoing his earlier words to Fielder.

"Not deliberately," Jed repeated, emphasizing the last word. "Well, there's my answer." His voice turned cold as ice, and his gaze was hard enough to slice a man to the bone. "So how did I do it? In a fit of anger? Did I choke her? Hit her with a rock? Shoot her? Stab her? Beat her? Tell me, Will, how did I do it?''

"Goddamn it, I didn't say you killed her."

"No?" Jed laughed, a harsh, bitter sound. "Yet you're arresting me for murder. I'd say that gives a damn clear view of your opinion, Ranger McClain."

Will read him his rights. And died inside with every word.

THE DIGITAL CLOCK on Tessa's bedside table glowed pale green in the darkness. 1:17 a.m. Three minutes later than the last time she'd checked it. Two hours of tossing and turning and she was no closer to sleep than she had been to begin with. *Face it,* she told herself, sitting up and flicking on the light, *you're not going to sleep until you hear from Will.* She rose and grabbed her pale yellow cotton robe from the end of the bed. Why she was so certain he'd call her, she didn't know. But she was.

She didn't know enough about the law to know if he would have arrested Jed. Was the ring enough evidence to charge him with the murder? She didn't have a clue. But if Will had arrested Jed…that's where her imagination broke down. She'd heard the affection in his voice when he'd spoken of his foster brother that day on the lake. He obviously cared about the man.

In search of a sleeping aid, Tessa walked through the living room to the kitchen. Pepe, the cat, blinked at her as she passed, and lashed his tail, but didn't offer to get up. He had appropriated the easy chair in the living room for his bed and looked too comfortable to move. After a struggle that she hadn't been too sure she'd win, Tessa had convinced Goofy to sleep on a pallet in the kitchen. She could hear him in there now, woofing in his sleep.

The animals had been a little wary of each other at first, and then Goofy had tried to make friends. Pepe had put the dog in his place with a swipe across his nose that drew blood. Even though he outweighed the cat by a factor of ten, Goofy knew when he'd met his match. Since then Goofy had kept his distance from the cat and lavished his attention on his new mistress. Regardless of his name, Goofy was pretty bright about who to bother and who to leave alone.

And thank goodness her landlady hadn't laid eyes on the dog yet.

Just about to put some water on for tea, Tessa heard a knock on her front door. Her heart leaped and she hurried to open it, not even questioning who it was. Will. She felt it, with an awareness that sizzled through her bloodstream.

He stood in her doorway wearing jeans and a white button-down shirt, one hand propped against the door-jamb. He didn't speak. Didn't have to. She looked into his eyes and saw the despair that raged inside him. Wordlessly she opened her arms and he stepped inside, pulling her into his embrace and kicking the door shut behind him. For a long moment, for an aeon, they simply stood there, holding each other. Tension, anger, utter sadness—he radiated all those emotions and more.

''I'm so sorry,'' she said, her arms tight around him,

knowing it was inadequate but not knowing what else to say. "It's going to be all right."

He pulled back and stared down at her, grasping her upper arms. "No." He shook his head slowly. "No, it's not. I arrested my foster brother tonight. I can't change that, or fix it, either."

Reaching up, she pushed his hair back from his forehead, then pressed her palm against his cheek. She wanted to lay his head against her breast and soothe him, comfort him. Wanted, so much, to ease his pain. She'd never felt that way before, and didn't know what to do with the rush of emotion bombarding her. "Do you want to talk about it?"

His arms encircled her, pulling her tightly against him. She felt his cheek come to rest against her hair. His breath sighed over her head, ruffling her hair. "No. I want to forget it. For a little while, I just want to forget."

Ordinarily she'd never have been so bold. But this wasn't an ordinary situation, and he wasn't an ordinary man.

And she wanted him. Why deny it when she wanted to be with him more than anything? So she stepped back and took his hand. Led him to her bedroom. Sat him on the bed and stood in front of him. She started to reach over to flick off the light on the bedside table, but he caught her hand and carried it to his lips.

"Leave it," he murmured against her palm.

Slowly, a little hesitantly, she untied the sash of her robe, slipped it from her shoulders to pool at her feet. She wore a white cotton floor-length gown with a tiny row of buttons marching down the bodice. No femme fatale, she thought, wishing she had worn something at least a little bit sexy. But this was the real Tessa, and it seemed important that he know that.

He didn't say anything more, beyond the murmured injunction to leave the light on. Didn't reach for her, though he kept hold of her hand. He just sat on the side of her bed and stared at her, his expression impossible to read. Finally he touched her cheek, rubbed a thumb over her mouth. ''Are you sure you want to do this?''

''I'm sure.'' Sudden doubts swept her and she added, ''If you're sure you...want me.''

He smiled, the smile that never failed to set her insides to jumping. ''I want you, Tessa. That's never been in question.''

Funny how liberating those simple words were. She smiled and stepped forward, between his legs, shivering with anticipation as her legs brushed against the denim covering them. His hands reached up and he began undoing the row of tiny buttons, not stopping until he released the last one. Holding her gaze, he spread the bodice and slipped his hands inside. He stroked, caressed, palmed her nipples, which had already hardened and strained against those deliciously rough palms.

''Tell me something,'' he said, his voice low, seductive. A midnight tide in the still of the night.

Anything, she thought, her eyes closing, as long as he didn't stop touching her. ''What?''

''Are you a virgin?'' Her eyes snapped open and

she stared at him. His hands never stopped their motion, but his intense gaze settled on her face.

"I'm twenty-nine years old. What do you think?"

"That's not an answer," he said, and moved one hand to her waist to pull her forward. He kissed her, a long, slow, drugging kiss that implied he had all the time in the world and intended to savor every moment. He murmured against her mouth, "Are you?"

"No," she managed, feeling dizzy.

"Good." His lips journeyed down her neck, leisurely sampling her skin. "I don't want to hurt you." He took her mouth again, his tongue dipping inside in a lazy, taunting motion. She melted closer, twined her arms around his neck and kissed him back, her tongue meeting his, retreating, drawing his inside.

He raised her gown, sliding it slowly up her legs. She thought about her small breasts, the slight pooch of her tummy, her hips that seemed to attract fat like honey catches flies. She was certain he'd seen worse, but she was equally certain he'd seen and touched a whole lot better.

"The light," she managed to say. "I could turn it out."

He stopped with the gown around her thighs and looked at her. "Then I couldn't see you."

"That's the point." Flushing, she turned her head away.

"I want to see you. Is that a problem?" He kept raising the gown, then paused when he had it to her waist, waiting for a response.

Aware she was overreacting, she shook her head.

But it had been a long time since a man had seen her naked, and she'd never been entirely comfortable with it. Will finished drawing the gown over her head and tossed it aside. She repressed the urge to cross her arms over her chest and was rewarded when he said, "Beautiful" and cupped his hands around her breasts before his mouth settled on one painfully tight nipple. He licked it, suckled it, making her throb. His lips traced across her chest to her other nipple, which he subjected to the same thrilling torment. "Sweet. You taste sweet."

His hands slid to her hips, covered only by white bikini panties, and pulled her against him. She wanted to touch him, touch his bare skin, and her fingers scrambled at the buttons to his shirt. Soon, it was on the floor beside her gown, and she stroked her hands across his chest, while he did the same to her. Then he lay back on the bed with her on top of him. Even though he'd left his jeans on, his arousal was obvious. She stared down at him and swallowed.

"Don't look so scared," he said, amusement in his voice. "It'll be fun." He gave her a wicked grin along with a roll of his hips. "I promise."

"I'm not scared," she lied. Fun? Maybe, but her previous experiences with sex made her wonder about that. She'd only had one lover, and her few times with him had been uncomfortable and over quickly. But Will wasn't Kirk. Thank God.

"Kiss me," he said, his eyes glinting. "And prove it."

So she kissed him, while she pressed her hips against him.

He rolled over, taking her with him. He toyed with her mouth, sliding his tongue in, beckoning her to flirt with him. Moments later, he left her long enough to stand, pull some foil packets from his pocket and toss them onto the bedside table. Then he removed the rest of his clothes.

She stared at him, a little awed by the sight of him naked. He truly had a beautiful body. All masculine planes and angles. Sleek, rippling muscles. When he lay down beside her again, he pulled her panties down her legs and tossed them aside. She gasped, her hands clutching his shoulders. His skin was warm, smooth, and felt lovely beneath her palms.

His mouth crushed hers, he thrust his tongue in her mouth and his finger inside her in the same compelling rhythm. She wanted to scream, but couldn't breathe well enough to do it. Her back arched, her hips rose, keeping time with the tantalizing rhythm he set. He groaned again, breaking the kiss and said, "I want you, Tessa. So much."

He reached for a condom and ripped it open. Her eyes widened while she watched him cover himself. She couldn't have moved if the bed was on fire. He entered her slowly, inch by glorious inch. When he was deep inside, he smiled at her. His head lowered and he kissed her mouth.

Her heart raced madly, her hips thrust against him, meeting him as he plunged in and withdrew, a faster and faster rhythm. Tension built, bright like the sun—

until she exploded in a burst of light. He said her name, drove inside her with a final, deep thrust as his release shuddered through him.

After a time, he rolled aside and snuggled her against his chest, leaning down to kiss her, slow and gentle. Tessa didn't know what to say, so she simply kissed him back and hoped that she hadn't made a huge mistake making love with him.

Their relationship had *temporary* stamped all over it. The last thing she needed was to fall madly in love with Will McClain. And she had a feeling it would be fatally easy to do just that.

CHAPTER TEN

JUST BEFORE DAWN, Will sat on the side of the bed, leaned over and kissed Tessa. Still asleep, she smiled and flung her arm across his leg. He hated to wake her, but didn't want to leave without telling her goodbye. That would make their night together seem too much like a one-night stand. If Will had anything to say about it, last night was only the first of many he intended to spend with Tessa.

They had made love again in the predawn hours, and then Tessa had fallen into an exhausted sleep. Will hadn't slept much, and what little he managed had been marred with nightmarish images of arresting Jed, questioning him, booking him. It was the first time in his life he regretted having gone into law enforcement.

''Will? Are you leaving?''

At the softly voiced question, he looked down. Tousled red hair streamed to her shoulders as she sat up on one elbow, clutching the sheet to her chest. Her mouth was full and pouty, her eyes slumberous, with the faint circles beneath them accenting the blue. He wondered if she had any idea how tempting she looked just then. Probably not. Tessa didn't seem to have a vain bone in her body. The opposite, in fact. He wondered again who had done such a number on her.

In spite of the day ahead of him, he smiled. "Yeah. Jed's bail hearing is set for eight this morning. I need to go by my place and clean up first." She shifted and the sheet fell, exposing one pale, perfect breast. Noticing the direction of his gaze, she started to cover herself. "No, don't do that," he said, catching her wrist and holding it lightly. "I like looking at you."

She smiled and made no move to pull up the sheet.

He released her wrist to trace a finger over the slope of her breast. "Whisker burns," he murmured. "I should have shaved again. Next time I will." She had a true redhead's skin—pale, fragile, soft as magnolia blossoms. His hand itched to touch more, but he knew if he did, he wouldn't leave. And he had a job, and a duty to fulfill.

She didn't speak but he saw relief flare in her eyes. "Did you think last night would be enough?"

"I—didn't know. I wasn't really thinking," she said, blushing.

"It wasn't enough for me. I want to see you again, Tessa. Be with you again." He leaned down and kissed her, taking his time, slipping his tongue in to tease hers. "And I've got to tell you, I'm going to be real disappointed if you tell me it was enough for you."

Her lips curved upward and she shook her head. "It wasn't," she said huskily.

"Good." He kissed her one last time, allowed himself to hold her for a moment, before he regretfully released her. "I'll see you tonight."

THE BAIL HEARING was every bit as tough as Will had expected. At least the judge dismissed the D.A.'s attempt to deny bail, and he set a reasonable one, as well. Judge Rimmer had been around for a long time, and he told the crestfallen D.A. he didn't think a man who'd lived in the area nearly his entire life, and who owned property and had a wife who was also anchored to the community was any threat to skip town.

While Jed wouldn't look in Will's direction at all, Gwyn's killer glare didn't do much for his mood. But hell, what did he expect? To top it off, Emmy and Riley attended as well, and Will could tell simply by looking at Emmy's angry expression he was going to catch an earful later.

The hearing was mercifully short. When it ended, Jed walked out of the courtroom without a word, though he did level a long, unsmiling look at Will. After that, Will's day got worse. Emmy marched up to him, obviously loaded for bear.

"I want to talk to you, Will," she said, her expression unnaturally solemn.

Will glanced at Riley, standing solidly behind her. Riley had always been hard to read, even when they were kids, but impassive as his expression was, Will had an idea of what the other man was thinking.

He owed it to Emmy to talk to her. He shrugged, and led her and Riley into the city commissioner's office, which appeared to be empty. He definitely didn't want to discuss Jed's case where anyone could overhear them.

"I know what you're going to say," he told her

wearily before she could begin. "You don't understand, Emmy." He turned to Riley. "You're a lawyer. Talk to her. Explain my position so that she can understand it."

Riley shook his head and spoke for the first time. "I know you're between a rock and a hard place, but I have to agree with Emmy." He folded his arms across his chest and fell silent, waiting for his wife to continue. Which she did.

Hands on hips, Emmy stared at him. "You're right, I don't understand. How could you arrest Jed? What were you thinking, Will?"

"I had no choice."

"Of course you did. You chose to arrest Jed. What's the matter with you?"

He shoved a hand through his hair, wishing he wasn't having this discussion. Not with Emmy, who had always looked up to him. She didn't look up to him now. "Should I have let Fielder do it? Because that's what would have happened if I hadn't arrested him."

"But why? Why arrest him at all?"

"You know why. The new evidence doesn't look good for Jed."

She threw up her hands in disgust. "This is ridiculous. Why haven't you put a stop to it?"

"How do you expect me to do that? I can't ignore the evidence, and even if I could or would, Fielder sure as hell wouldn't."

"Oh, Fielder," she said, waving a hand in dismissal. "I thought you were in charge of the case. I thought the Rangers were a big deal."

"Do you expect me to just ignore the facts? I swore an oath to uphold the law, and that's what I'm going to do."

"At Jed's expense."

"I'm a Texas Ranger. I can't disregard the law, no matter what my feelings are. No matter what I think, I've sworn to uphold the law to the best of my abilities. And Frannie, of all people, deserves nothing less."

She stepped closer, gazing at him earnestly. "Will, you know as well as I do that this arrest business is a crock. Jed is innocent."

If only he were as certain of that as Emmy and, apparently, Riley were. "How do you know?" Will asked softly. "Why are you so sure of that?"

Her eyes rounded in surprise. "Because I know him. And so should you. Jed would no more have hurt Frannie than—"

"Accidents happen."

She stared at him. "No. He wouldn't have, he couldn't have..."

"It's a possibility that I can't ignore," Will said grimly. "Especially given the evidence, and that damned fight. You may be able to blow that off, Emmy, but I can't. And neither will the sheriff."

"I'm not blowing it off! If Jed had killed Frannie, even accidentally, he'd have owned up to it." Chest heaving, eyes sparkling with moisture, she faced him.

"Would he? He was young. Angry. He'd have been

frightened, scared witless, in all likelihood, if an accident like that had happened. Think about it, Emmy. Think before you answer.''

''I don't have to think about it. And I can't believe that you do.'' She put her hand on his arm and locked gazes with him. ''Who are you? You're not the Will I knew.''

He shook her off, turned away. ''No, I'm not. I'm a Ranger, and I have to do my job.''

''No matter who it hurts.''

He spun away, walked a few steps and turned back to her. ''Damn it, it's hurting me, too! How do you think I felt, arresting Jed? Do you think I wanted to do it?''

She shook her head, her eyes filling with tears. ''I don't know what you want anymore. I don't understand you at all.''

''It's not so hard to understand. I owe it to Frannie.''

''You owe it to Frannie to betray Jed?''

How to get through to her? How to make her understand? Will finally asked, ''What do you want me to do, Emmy? Hide the evidence?''

She shook her head slowly. ''No, but the problem isn't the evidence. The problem is that deep down, you think Jed might be guilty. You actually believe he could have done it.''

He said nothing. How could he, when she only spoke the truth?

''I feel sorry for you, Will. Sorrier for you even than for Jed. Because Jed at least has a heart. You seem to have lost yours somewhere along the way.'' She looked at her husband. "Come on, Riley. It's obvious—'' her voice cracked but she continued "—we aren't doing any good here.'' She turned her back and rushed out the door.

Riley looked at him a moment, then said, "You did your job, Will. But you're going to regret the hell out of this.''

"I already do," Will said. "Believe me, Riley, I already do.''

Riley left without another word.

Will had a heart all right, he just couldn't allow it to matter.

PACING THE COURTHOUSE hallway, Tessa saw Emmy Gray Wolf and her husband Riley leave the city commissioner's office. Her nerves tightened as she waited for Will to come out. It had been a stupid idea to come down here, she thought. What if he thought her interfering? Why did she think her presence might help him? After all, it wasn't as if they had a long-term relationship. They'd spent one night together. Big deal.

It was a big deal to her, though.

And she wanted to help, so she'd come. Unsure if it was proper for her to be present at the hearing, she had waited outside. Occupied with his foster sister and her husband, Will hadn't seen her when he emerged from the courtroom. Tessa had watched them disappear into the commissioner's office and settled down to wait for Will.

The door opened a moment later and Will halted in midstride. "Tessa?" His gaze homed in on her like a laser. "What are you doing here?"

Her stomach jumping, she said, "I—I thought a friendly face might help."

He smiled, an unguarded, happy smile, and her stomach relaxed a fraction. "It does help. Especially when it's your face." He held open the door for her to enter.

But she was still nervous. Maybe he was simply being polite. He was a nice man. He wouldn't be rude, no matter how he felt. "I hope you don't mind. I wasn't sure what you'd— If you want me to go—"

He shut the door, backed her up against it and kissed her slowly, thoroughly. Like he meant it. When she started to speak, he kissed her again. "You're babbling," he said, amusement in his voice.

"I know. I can't help it. I babble when I'm nervous." Oh, that wicked, lazy smile of his got to her every time.

"I'm glad you came. You're the first person today who hasn't looked at me like I'm a cross between Attila the Hun and Darth Vader."

"I'm sorry. I was afraid it would be bad."

He shrugged, as if it didn't matter, when she knew it did. He stroked her cheek, smiling at her again. "Much as I'd like to, I can't stay. I have some interviews to conduct."

"That's all right. I didn't mean to bother—"

He interrupted her by laying his fingers on her lips. "Don't apologize. You did a nice thing." His lips claimed hers again, briefly. "It might be really late tonight before I'm finished."

"I don't care," she said recklessly. "I'll be up late." As late as she needed to be.

"Good. I'll see you tonight, then."

Her heart still pounding, Tessa watched him go.

WILL'S FIRST STOP after the hearing was the Cypress Bank and Trust, Uncertain's only bank. Raymond and Catherine Jennings, the bank president and his wife, had been one of Frannie's longtime employers. Their original interview with Fielder, along with several others, was unaccountably missing. Will walked into Raymond Jennings's office and gave the secretary his name, showed her his badge, and waited while she buzzed her boss over the intercom.

"He wants to know what this is concerning," the secretary said, gazing at him over half glasses.

"Murder," Will said pleasantly, enjoying himself for a change. Questioning the man who'd once threatened to castrate him if he came sniffing around Amanda again appealed to his sense of humor. No, he didn't think Mr. Jennings would like what was going down one bit.

She relayed the message, then said, "Go right in, Mr. McClain."

"Thanks. And it's Ranger McClain."

Raymond Jennings's office oozed cool, rich elegance. Burgundy leather chairs flanked an imposing dark mahogany desk. Against one wall stood an antique telephone table, on top of which sat a silver tray with fine crystal water glasses and a decanter. Several golf knickknacks of silver and gold adorned the bookshelves behind the desk. The desktop didn't lack for expensive doodads, either, Will noticed, from a set of gold engraved cuff links to a silver glasses case with finely etched carvings on the lid.

Will figured the man's wife must have decorated the room. That or a professional, because he didn't think Ray had an elegant bone in his body. He'd married money, tons of money, and thought that gave him class. Will thought Jennings had a lot of class, all of it low.

"State your business and then get out," the bank president said, rising. "We don't want your kind in our bank."

Jennings wasn't as big as Will remembered, but then, he'd only been a kid when he left town. The banker's hair was a lot grayer, too. And he'd grown a pencil-thin mustache. But he still had the same snotty attitude he'd always had, at least toward Will. "You have something against the Rangers, Mr. Jennings?"

"Not the Rangers. Just you. I remember you, McClain. I know your type. No badge is going to change that. Your type never changes."

His type. A street kid. To this man, and others like him, no matter what Will became, what profession he practiced, he'd always be trash. So it gave him a great deal of pleasure to say, "If you prefer, Mr. Jennings, I can take you down to the station, book you and arrange for questioning, oh, say some time tomorrow. Maybe a night in jail will change your attitude." Jennings hissed in a breath and glared at him. "Or we can do it here and now," Will continued. "Your choice."

"Ask your questions," Jennings snapped, and sat down. "And you'd better be damned quick about it."

Will took his time, dragging up a nearby chair and arranging himself in it comfortably. He sensed Jennings growing angrier with each passing moment. Good. Anger often led people to say things they shouldn't. He pulled out a notepad and pen, in case Jennings actually told him something useful. "As you know, I'm here about the murder of Frances Granger. Specifically, I'm looking into her actions the morning she disappeared, May 4, 1982."

"I don't know anything about the woman's actions. Not that morning or any other."

"You didn't see Frances Granger that morning."

"No. And I probably wouldn't remember if I had." A sneer marked his expression. "I don't make a habit of keeping up with the domestic help."

"Are you saying you never saw her? She cleaned your home for four or five years, didn't she? Isn't that a little far-fetched?"

He gritted his teeth. "Of course I saw her. Shuffling through with her cleaning buckets and mops and whatnot, usually at the most inconvenient times, too. I don't remember if I saw her that specific morning, however. The help was and is my wife Catherine's responsibility, not mine."

"Did you ever talk to Mrs. Granger? You were Jed

Louis's trustee. Did you ever discuss him with Frannie?''

''I really don't remember. I doubt it. As a rule, I don't chitchat with the hired help.''

He looked a little uneasy, Will thought, and wondered why. ''You can't think of anything that might shed light on Mrs. Granger's disappearance?''

''No, I've told you that.''

Just then a strident female voice echoed in the outer office. ''Ranger McClain and I are old friends. I'm sure he won't mind if I pop in.''

As the door to the office opened, Jennings looked, if possible, even more irritated than before. ''Amanda, what do you think you're—''

''Don't mind me, Dad.'' She gave him an airy wave. ''I just came in to see Will.''

''I'm having a business meeting here, Amanda. How many times have I told you not to interrupt me?''

''Business? Oh, you must mean about poor Mrs. Granger's murder. I remember the day like it was yesterday. I'm sure I could help, Will.''

''As a matter of fact, I would like to talk to you, Amanda. But—'' he glanced at Jennings, who seemed ready to bust a gut ''—I don't think your father wants us using his office for another interview. Why don't you come to the station with me? We can talk there.''

A shudder shook her. ''The station? Oh, I couldn't possibly. I have far too much to do right now.'' She reached out to stroke his arm. ''But you can come to the house. I'm at my parents' place for the time being.

In the guest house, actually. Say, eight o'clock tonight?''

He didn't particularly want to put it off, and he didn't have any interest in her angle in asking him over. But then again, he didn't mind jerking Jennings's chain. And Amanda was likely to be a lot more talkative in a relaxed atmosphere. After a couple of drinks, who knew what she might spill.

''All right. Eight it is.'' He turned to the banker and said, ''Thanks for your help, Mr. Jennings. I'll be in touch if there's anything else.''

He managed not to smile at the snarl Jennings couldn't restrain.

CHAPTER ELEVEN

BY THE TIME Will made it to Tessa's that night, his mood was in the toilet. Then she opened the door to him, and her welcoming smile hit him square in the heart Emmy had accused him of not having. He walked in, took her in his arms and kissed her soundly. "Thanks for coming to the courthouse."

"I was afraid you'd think—you'd think I was interfering. Or clinging."

Clinging? He'd had women cling before. That was the last word he'd use in connection with Tessa. He had to smile again. "I thought you were sweet. Thanks." He kissed her again, then released her.

"I kind of gathered the bail hearing didn't go well." She took his hand, leading him to the couch, stepping over a snoozing Goofy as she did.

"Not much of a watchdog, is he?" Will said, seeing the dog twitch in his sleep.

She smiled wryly. "No, that doesn't seem to be his forte. Once he's asleep I don't think a cannon blast would wake him. So tell me what happened."

"The best thing I can say about the bail hearing is that the judge didn't deny bail. Other than that, it was a bust." He rubbed his fingers over his temple. "The rest of the day didn't get any better. I interviewed every one of Frannie's employers, those who haven't died or moved away, and came up with zip. No one saw anything, no one heard anything. We'll start on the ones who moved away tomorrow. If we can trace them," he added grimly.

Amanda hadn't been any help, either. They had talked about Amanda overhearing Jed and him discussing the argument between Jed and Frannie, but Will remembered it better than she did. She'd spent most of the evening making it clear she wouldn't mind time between the sheets with him. When he'd told her he was involved with someone else, she'd stared at him blankly for a moment before asking, "And that's a problem?"

"No leads at all?" Tessa asked.

"*Nada.* I even tried Frannie's best friend, Joleen Berber, and that was as unproductive as the rest of the interviews. Not to mention, weird."

He thought back. Joleen had sure acted strangely when he questioned her. Though she'd answered his questions about whether she'd seen Frannie on the fateful morning, or if she knew anything about her plans, she'd been jumpy as a barefoot kid on hot asphalt. If Will didn't know better he'd think she was hiding something. But what? He didn't believe she'd killed Frannie, because he couldn't see a motive. Maybe being around the law made her nervous. It affected a lot of people that way, though he wouldn't have thought someone who'd known him since he was a teenager would have felt that way, lawman or not.

"Jed's upset with you," Tessa said.

"Jed and Gwyn hate my guts," he said flatly. "Riley seems to be withholding judgment but thinks I'm misguided. Emmy is upset with me, and asked me if I'm the same person she used to know. I don't think she hates me. Yet."

"I wish I could help."

"You do." He caught her hand and squeezed it gently. "You're the only person around here who's actually objective about the case." The only person he could talk to and not have to defend his every move. The only one who couldn't possibly have killed Frannie, and more, the only person who didn't have a stake in who had done it. "But that's enough about my lousy day. Let's talk about yours."

"I didn't get out to the site. I was tied up with classes all day. But I did have something exciting happen."

"What?" He smiled as her eyes brightened.

"I had my first convert." He must have looked confused because she went on to explain. "One of my students told me today he'd decided to change his major to archaeology. Because he liked my class so much."

"Yeah? You must have gotten a kick out of that."

She nodded excitedly. "I didn't know teaching could be like this. I'd never taught a class, not for any length of time. Not a college course." Her eyes clouded, and a wistful look crept into them. "For the first time I felt that I mattered. That I made a difference."

Before he could speak, the phone rang. Tessa excused herself and reached for it. Pepe came over and lashed his tail, sitting down to lick his paws and stare at Will. He looked a lot better, with nearly all the paint gone and his black hair almost shiny. Tessa must brush his fur daily, Will thought. The cat would never be a beauty though. Will decided if the looks the critter aimed at him were any sign, he'd make a better watch-dog than Goofy. "I met her first," he told the cat. Pepe seemed to smirk, then licked his other paw.

Although he didn't try to eavesdrop, he couldn't help overhearing Tessa's part of the conversation. Every drop of animation had drained out of her voice. She spoke in monosyllables and twisted the phone cord around her finger as she talked.

"Yes. No. I don't know." Her fingers tightened on the receiver, whitening noticeably. "No, Mother, I've already told you that's impossible."

Mother? Will tried to remember what Tessa had said about her parents, but beyond the fact that they had both been archaeologists, and that her father was dead, he couldn't think of much.

"I'll call you when I know," Tessa said. "Yes, as soon as I know."

"Family problems?" he asked as she hung up.

"Not exactly." She smiled, but it lacked warmth. "Just my mother trying to get her way." He didn't speak, but lifted an eyebrow in question. Tessa sighed and added, "She wants me to go to Peru. It doesn't matter how much I tell her about my obligations here, she just won't listen."

"Peru? What for?"

"An archaeological expedition. She's determined to get me in on it."

"Why? Is it such a big deal?"

"Yes. Not as big as she's making it out to be, but it's big. But that's beside the point. I can't leave here to go on a dig for six months or more."

Six months? He hadn't realized a dig took so long. But then, he didn't know much about archaeology. "Did you explain your work here?"

"Only a million times. She's totally ignoring the work for the police, and she doesn't consider a temporary job at a small college to be a deciding factor."

"Do you?"

"I honor my obligations. I said I'd teach until fall, at least. Until they find a replacement."

"And then you're gone."

She met his gaze, hers solemn. "It's what I had planned on doing. Assuming I'm through with my thesis work."

"What about teaching? I thought you liked it."

"I do. But it's a temporary thing. They knew that from the start."

Temporary. He wondered if she considered their relationship temporary as well. Why did it bother him so much that she probably did? After all, he'd acknowledged the same thing when they first met.

"What if you changed your mind?" He stretched his arm across the couch and toyed with the ends of her hair. "Decided to stay?"

"Changed my mind? You mean, take a permanent

position at the college?'' She looked totally shocked, as if the thought had never occurred to her.

''Yeah. You like teaching. Why not?''

''Because I can't just give up my career. I've been working for years to get to this point. To get my Ph.D.''

His hand slid around to the back of her neck, urging her closer. ''You wouldn't be giving it up, just changing the focus.'' His lips cruising her jawline, he murmured, ''You'd still get your Ph.D, wouldn't you? That's what the burial mound is all about.''

''Um, yes.'' She sighed. ''But that's not the— What are you doing?''

''Getting you out of your clothes,'' he said, unfastening her last shirt button. ''Any objections?''

His hands closed over her breasts and her eyes turned smoky blue. ''I've forgotten what we were talking about,'' she said huskily. He popped her bra clasp and they both groaned as he filled his hands with her bare breasts. ''The bedroom—''

''Too far,'' he said, lying back and pulling her down on top of him. She rubbed her naked breasts against his chest, and even through the fabric of his shirt he could feel her nipples stiffening. No way was he going to last until the bedroom. ''What's wrong with right here?'' His hands slid to her rear, pressed her into him. ''Right now.''

''Not a thing,'' she said, and kissed him.

TESSA ARRIVED at the Catfish Corner the next day a few minutes early for her lunch meeting with Ellen.

She didn't mind waiting. The past couple of days, she hadn't been much good for anything beyond daydreaming. Still, nights like the ones she'd spent with Will certainly deserved a little dreaming.

It's not going to last, she reminded herself, and felt a pang of longing. But she intended to have fun while it did. She sighed, knowing she must have a goofy look on her face, but she couldn't help it. For the first time since she was twelve, she felt young and carefree. As if anything was possible. Almost anything.

She looked around, noticing that Amanda Jennings and a woman she didn't know sat at the table next to her booth. Amanda's voice carried clearly, and Tessa heard every word. But she didn't pay much attention until she heard the other woman say, "Will? You mean you and Will McClain? Tearing up the sheets?"

"Not just the sheets." Amanda laughed. Her gaze flicked over Tessa without recognition. She leaned forward, closer to her friend, and lowered her voice, but Tessa heard every word, sounding a death knell in her heart. "I have to tell you, Tracy, it was unbelievable. I've been married three times and thought nothing could surprise me, but Will—" She sighed and laid a hand over her heart. "He's amazing."

Tessa's stomach plummeted. Not again, she thought. I can't go through this again. Not with Will.

"Tessa? Are you all right?"

Stunned, she looked up. Ellen was beside the table, her round face creased with concern, eyes dark with worry. Solid, dependable, *loyal* Ellen.

"No, I'm not. I have to leave." She stood on shaky

legs, throwing down a couple of dollars for the tea. "I'm sorry, I can't stay for lunch."

"Wait, I'm coming with you," Ellen said, charging after her. "You look like you're about to throw up," she said as they reached Tessa's car.

"I am." Tessa propped her hands against the car door and hung her head, sucking in air desperately. She needed to calm down. To think about this logically. Forget that, she needed to kill Will McClain.

"Are you sick?"

Dizziness subsiding, she shook her head. "No, I'm stupid. Terminally stupid."

"I don't get it. Did I miss something?"

Tessa straightened and looked at her friend. "Just Amanda Jennings talking about what a great lover Will McClain is."

Ellen winced. "Oh, crap." After a long pause she said, "You're sleeping with him."

"You got it. And apparently, so is Amanda."

"You're sure you didn't misinterpret what she said?"

"Please, it was crystal clear. Her friend asked if they'd been tearing up the sheets and Amanda said, 'Not just the sheets.'" She closed her eyes, remembering the rest of what she'd heard. *"It was unbelievable,"* she mimicked.

"Oh...crap," Ellen said again.

Tessa gazed at Ellen fiercely. "Will was with me last night, too. After Amanda. Oh, I can't believe I've been this dumb again!" She pounded a fist on her car door, not even noticing the pain. "I swore after college

I'd never let another man make a fool of me, and look what I've done!''

"I could point out you're jumping to conclusions here.''

"Logical conclusions. Wouldn't you?''

Ellen frowned, tapped a finger to her cheek. "I don't know. Do you and Amanda know each other?''

"We've met. Not that she'd recognize me,'' Tessa said bitterly, leaning back against her car door. "She was too busy drooling over Will to remember me.''

"Did she know you could hear her?''

Tessa thought about that. "Yes. She looked right at me when she talked to her friend.''

"Convenient.''

Tessa's eyes narrowed. "What are you saying?''

"Isn't it obvious? What if she's making it up?''

"Oh, come on, Ellen. Why would she?''

"Because she wants you to dump him. To leave him free for her to go after.''

Too good to be true, Tessa thought. "Do you really believe that?''

"Why not? Amanda has always been a liar. Even though I was a few years behind her in high school, I heard the talk. That woman couldn't tell the truth if somebody offered her a million bucks. Lying about Will would be perfectly in character for her.''

But what if Amanda was telling the truth? Tessa and Will hadn't made any promises of exclusivity. A mistake on her part. She should have made her feelings about that clear at the outset. "I want her to be lying,'' she said, voice low.

Ellen patted her arm. "Talk to Will. He's a good guy, Tessa. He'll tell you the truth."

Would he? Somehow, she thought he would. But would the truth be something she could live with?

ON HIS WAY OUT for a quick bite of lunch, Will jerked open his office door. He didn't know who was more surprised, him or the man standing there, his hand raised to knock. Silently they stared at each other. "It's about damn time you showed up," Will said finally, then broke into a smile. "How the hell are you, Rico?"

Rico Santiago flashed a grin, teeth white against his olive skin, and lowered his hand to extend it in greeting. Will gripped it, feeling another one of those odd rushes of emotion similar to what he'd experienced the first time he saw Jed and Emmy again. Damn, he was getting sappy in his old age. He stepped back and let Rico in, closing the door after him.

"*Muy bien. ¿Como estás,* Will?" Slapping him on the back, Rico added, "But I think it's the other way around. It's about time you showed up here. Why did you run off like that? You know Mamá and Papá would have taken you."

"The last thing your parents needed was another kid to feed. Besides, your mother's already lectured me about that." Remembering, he rubbed his ear.

Rico laughed. "She told me. I'd have come to see you sooner, but I just got back in town. Been on vacation with my wife and kid."

Rico Santiago with a wife and kid. Will shook his

head, thinking back on some of their wilder adventures, and Rico's reputation with women. "How many kids?"

"One." He smiled proudly. "A beautiful little girl."

"Isabella said you married Layla St. Cloud. How'd you manage that? I know you always had the hots for her, but when I left, you couldn't even get her to go out with you."

"There was this storm. The rest is history," he added with a wicked grin.

"Someday I want to hear that story."

"Oh, I don't think so," Rico said, and they both laughed.

"I thought your mother was going to bust when she told me you'd become a doctor. You did good, Rico."

"I had a lot of help, and it was still hard. I can't imagine what it was like for you. It must have been tough."

"It wasn't much fun," Will said, then shrugged away the memories. "But I survived."

"And became a Ranger. I was surprised at first, but when I thought about it, it made sense. I could see you as a Ranger. It's hard to imagine you working with Fielder, though."

Will smiled briefly. "He's not real thrilled about it."

"Why don't you come to the restaurant with me?" Rico said. "I've got something to talk to you about and I don't want to do it here." He frowned at his surroundings.

"About the case?"

Rico didn't look happy. He nodded. "And you're not going to like it."

WILL WAITED until after they'd finished lunch before broaching the subject that occupied both their minds. "Okay, give. If you've got something about Frannie's case, why not tell me at the station?"

Rico leaned back in his chair, but he didn't look comfortable. "I didn't want Fielder in on it. It's about Jed. I heard you arrested him."

"Yeah." He frowned, a picture of Jed as he'd looked that evening flashing into his mind. "Not one of the days I want to relive."

"No, I don't imagine you would. It must have been...hard." Will nodded, saying nothing. "I also heard you were looking for anyone who saw Mrs. Granger the morning she disappeared."

Will brightened. "Why, did you see her?"

Rico leaned forward, propped his arms on the table. "No. But I saw Jed."

Again Will didn't speak, just waited for his friend to go on.

"I hooked school that day and went down to Bubba's dock. I decided to con Rob Boulder out of some night crawlers so I could fish. Around eight-thirty, maybe a little later, I saw Jed pull up in his boat. He didn't see me."

"What are you saving, Rico? Just tell me."

His friend's bleak gaze met his. "There was blood

on his shirt, Will. A lot of blood. More than just a cut finger would account for.''

"Shit.'' He thought a moment. "He could have hurt himself fishing. It's easy to do.''

"Except he probably hadn't been fishing yet.''

Given the timing Will was forced to agree. "You're absolutely sure he was bloody before he gassed up his boat?''

Rico nodded. "I'm sorry, Will. I never told anyone because we didn't know Mrs. Granger had died. It didn't seem important at the time. Then when they found her bones, well, I thought about it, but I just couldn't see going to Fielder. You know how he is with the Hispanic community.'' He made a crude gesture that signified what he thought of the sheriff. "Besides, I didn't want to implicate Jed if that's all there was to go on. But when I heard you'd taken over the case, I knew I had to tell you.''

"Damn it!'' Will pounded his fist on the table. "Damn it, why did it have to be Jed?'' After a moment he said, "You did the right thing, telling me. I just wish to hell you hadn't seen anything.''

"Me, too, *amigo*. Me, too.'' They were both silent, then Rico added, "Look, Will, I'm no cop, but I see a lot of people in my practice. See them hurt, upset, grieving, angry. And I don't think Jed did it. He looked angry and upset, but he didn't look or act like he'd just killed someone. He was too—'' he shrugged "—too normal.''

Small consolation. The D.A. would steamroll right over that comment. "It doesn't make sense. I can't see him burying Frannie under a bush and going off fishing. I just don't see it.''

"No, I don't, either. Do you have to tell Fielder?''

He heard no censure in Rico's voice, but that didn't stop him from feeling like hell. He nodded slowly. "Fielder and the D.A. I can't conceal evidence pertinent to the investigation.'' No matter how damning for Jed.

One more nail in Jed's coffin.

AFTER MAKING PLANS to get together later in the week, Will had Rico drop him back at the station. He immediately called Thorndyke, Jed's lawyer, arranging to question Jed about the new development later that day. He sure as hell hoped Jed had a good explanation for the blood, but he had a sinking feeling he wouldn't.

Deciding he'd better bring Fielder up to speed before the questioning, he sought him out, finding him in his office. "I've got something new on the case,'' he said without preamble.

"About Louis?''

"That's right.'' Will told him the story, with Fielder giving the expected response. The sheriff brushed aside Rico's comments about how Jed had looked, focusing instead on his bloodstained clothes.

"She died of a blow to the head,'' Fielder said. "There'd have been a good bit of blood. Especially when he dragged her around to bury her.'' He shook his head, all but rubbing his hands together in pleasure. "It sure don't look good for Louis.''

Standing by the window, Will frowned at him. "We

haven't questioned Jed yet. Maybe there's a reasonable explanation for the blood.''

The older man snorted scornfully. ''You betcha. It's called murder.''

''You're so convinced of Jed's guilt, you can't see that this isn't logical.'' He crossed the room to stand over the sheriff's desk. ''Be reasonable. You've got an eighteen-year-old kid who kills his foster mother, the woman who raised him since he was six. You think he's going to bash her head in, bury her under a bush, and go off fishing like nothing had happened?'' he asked scornfully. ''And not even look upset?''

Fielder leaned back in his chair, lacing his fingers together over his stomach. ''I'm not saying he meant to do it. Maybe he just wanted to scare her and things got out of hand. You gotta admit, the blood don't look good.''

Of course, the blood didn't look good. Not a damn thing looked good for Jed. ''Okay, so he tries to scare her to get his way and ends up killing her. You think he'd have been that cool about it? He probably wouldn't have realized she was dead. Don't you think he'd have gone for help?''

Fielder nodded. ''Yep, his lawyer'll say that all right. But I don't buy it.''

Will smacked a fist down on the desk in frustration. ''And I don't buy that Jed Louis killed his foster mother and then went fishing like not a goddamn thing had happened. We've got an eyewitness who'll swear Jed didn't look like he'd just murdered someone.''

''Could be he don't remember.''

"If he remembers the blood, then he'd remember what Jed acted like, what he looked like. And Rico Santiago is a doctor now. His word, his professional opinion will carry some weight."

"It's up to the D.A.," Fielder said stolidly, "what we do with this new development."

Someone knocked on the door. Glaring at each other, they both ignored it.

"I plan to talk to the D.A., too," Will said. "I intend to make sure he pays full attention to Rico's statement. All of it, not just the part that screws Jed."

"Sheriff?" Deputy Masters called through the door. "Is McClain in there with you? Tessa Lang is out here and she says she needs to see him. Says it's important."

"Tell her I'll be right there." He looked at Fielder grimly. "Think about it, Sheriff."

He found Tessa in the waiting room, bag in hand. As he led her to his office, he was almost afraid to ask what was in it. He couldn't decipher her expression. "Bad news?"

"I don't know." She stared pointedly at the bag, not at him. "I think, though I'm not certain, that it's a glasses case."

He looked at it through the clear plastic. "A glasses case? What kind?"

"It's badly tarnished and corroded, but I believe it's silver."

He turned it over in his hands, but really couldn't tell much about it, so he took Tessa's guess as to what it was. Glasses. Jed didn't wear glasses. And if he did, he sure as hell wouldn't have had a silver case for them. Neither would Frannie. For the first time, a little hope stirred in his chest. "Found in the same location?"

She nodded. "Very near where I found the ring."

"How the hell did the sheriff's men miss something this size? The ring I can understand, but this thing should have stood out like a beacon."

"They might have found it and thought it was trash," she offered. "It's hard to tell unless you've been trained."

But they should have kept anything from the site, trash or not. Staring at it, Will frowned. Something about the object was ringing a bell. He'd seen something like it, but he couldn't place where or when. He looked up at Tessa and smiled. "This is the first break Jed's had. If I can date this case, find its origin, it might cast suspicion on somebody else." For a change. Finally, something good to report.

He glanced at Tessa and noticed she was looking at him oddly. "Is something wrong?"

"No, nothing." She bit her lip, then said, "No, that's not true. I—I need to talk to you."

He stepped forward and put a hand under her chin. Beneath the slight sunburn, she looked pale, fragile. "The heat's getting to you." His fault, since his job had kept her out in the sun.

She jerked back, away from him. "It's not the heat," she snapped. "I'm an archaeologist, I'm accustomed to being in the sun."

"What is it, then?"

"I don't think this is the place to talk. It's personal." Her hands twisted together nervously.

Personal. He cocked his head and studied her. He wasn't sure he liked the sound of that, especially considering she looked anything but happy. What could be so bad? "Okay. I have to get this to the lab, but I can come by after work."

"I'd rather come to your place."

"All right. I'll call you."

She nodded, then started for the door. Will caught her arm. "Tessa, wait. Don't go back to the dig. It will keep until morning."

Her gaze met his. Once again, he couldn't read her expression. "I'm not sick, Will."

Maybe not, but something was sure as hell wrong. "Trust me. You don't need to go back there today." An odd look flickered in her eyes. He bent to kiss her, but she turned her head and his lips landed on her cheek. "I'll see you later," he murmured, releasing her.

Tessa tore out of his office like she was running from a wildfire.

Women are really weird, he thought, and then, since he couldn't do anything about Tessa, he got down to business. The business of finding something to clear Jed.

CHAPTER TWELVE

THAT EVENING, Tessa arrived at Will's with her course of action planned. Giving herself a pep talk, she raised her hand to knock. She intended to be calm. Dignified. She would simply ask him for the truth. And if he admitted he had been with Amanda? What then?

Simple. She'd kill him.

Will opened the door and pulled her inside. Before she could speak, he covered her mouth with his. He kissed her as if it had been days, not mere hours, since he'd last touched her. In spite of herself, her muscles began to go lax, her body throbbed.

Had he kissed Amanda like this?

A swift pain stabbed her heart. Tessa put her hands on his chest and shoved him, at the same time, turning her head. "Stop. We have to talk."

Clearly baffled, he released her. "All right. Do you want to sit down?"

She shook her head, choosing instead to walk to the window and stare sightlessly out of it. Asking about Amanda was even harder than she'd imagined.

"What's on your mind, Tessa?"

She took a deep breath and let it out. "I realize we haven't— That is, we never talked about our— I don't know what your feelings are about it, but I can't—"

"Tessa." He put a hand on her shoulder and turned her to face him. Instead of their usual green, his eyes were gray and filled with concern. "Just tell me."

Could he look at her like that, so sweet, so sincere, and all the while be sleeping with another woman? Other men have done it, she thought bleakly. "I realize neither of us is looking for anything permanent, but I— You may think I'm old-fashioned, but I—" Furious with herself that she couldn't even get the words out, she broke off. Totally mystified, Will stared at her.

She blurted out, "I can't be with a man who's sleeping with another woman." Her throat closed. To her horror, she sniffed. "I know I should have said something in the beginning, but I didn't think—" Composure cracking, she halted again.

"That's what you're upset about? You think I'm sleeping with someone else?"

She nodded miserably. "Are you?"

"Of course not. I'm involved with you."

He said it so easily. So quickly. As if it shocked him that she'd even imagine such a thing. "That doesn't matter to—to everyone," she said, thinking of Kirk. He had thought nothing of chasing everything in a skirt, all the while telling her he loved her.

"It matters to me." He put his hand under her chin and forced it up, holding her gaze. "I don't want to be with anyone else, Tessa. Don't you know I'm crazy about you?"

Startled, she blinked. "No. I mean, I knew you liked me but—"

"Then you haven't been paying attention." He took her in his arms and kissed her mouth gently. "Because I'm seriously—" he pulled her closer and kissed her again, harder this time "—seriously crazy about you."

He smiled at her and her heart gave the funny little lurch it always did when he looked at her that way. As if…as if he really cared about her. He didn't look guilty, or worried that she might not believe him. Will expected people to believe him, she realized, because he didn't lie. With Will, what you saw was very much what you got. A man trying to do the right thing, no matter how much it hurt him. A man of his word.

How could she have believed him capable of anything else? He was nothing like Kirk.

Sighing, she leaned into him, her forehead against his chest, content to feel his arms around her. "I'm sorry. You must think I'm an idiot."

He rubbed her back. "No, I think you've been burned. And if you want to talk about it, I'll listen." He led her to the couch and sat, pulling her down beside him. Taking both her hands in his, he kissed them. "But first tell me where this idea came from. What happened?"

Glancing away, she bit her lip. "You know what they say about eavesdroppers never hearing anything good. At the Catfish Corner, I heard Amanda Jennings talking to a friend. She implied you and she were lovers." Drawing a breath, she looked at him. "More than implied, she flat out said it."

He sighed and rubbed the bridge of his nose.

"Damn, I knew better than to tell her about you. I should have known she'd take that as a challenge."

"What do you mean?"

Dropping her hands, he leaned back and wrapped an arm around her shoulders, settling her against his side. "Last night, before I went to your place, I stopped by Amanda's to question her about Frannie's case." He smiled wryly. "Amanda had other things in mind. So I told her I was involved with someone. I guess she figured out it was you. Seeing us together at Santiago's would have been her first clue."

So Ellen was right. Amanda had been making sure Tessa heard her. "She's a beautiful woman. I'm sure she's wondering what you see in me."

"Don't do that," he said, frowning. "Don't run yourself down."

"It's not running myself down to recognize that I'll never look like Amanda."

"So? You look like Tessa. That's better. I'm partial to redheads, myself. Redheads named Tessa." He leaned over and planted a soft kiss on her lips. "Forget Amanda. Tell me about him."

"Who?"

"The guy who did the number on you." He held her hand, rubbing his thumb gently back and forth over her pulse.

She'd never told anyone. Who had there been to tell? Until Ellen, she hadn't had any close girlfriends. Her mother wouldn't have understood—or even cared. But Will cared. So she told him.

"His name was Kirk. I dated him in college. Our

senior year. He was great looking. The kind of guy girls were always falling over.'' Like you, she thought, but she didn't say it. ''I thought I was so lucky to have him. I thought—oh, I was young and stupid. He told me he loved me and I believed him.'' She gave a short, humorless laugh. ''Seems he loved a lot of other women, too. While he was seeing me.''

''Jerk,'' Will said.

''You can say that again. And that's not all. I found him with another girl right before finals. One of many, I discovered later. He said he wasn't sorry I'd found out, but he wished I'd waited until after finals.'' She forced herself to meet Will's gaze when she finished the story. ''That was when he planned to dump me. He said he only dated me for my brains, that it sure as hell wasn't because of my looks. It's…humiliating to realize you've been used as a study aide rather than a girlfriend.''

Will surprised her by smiling. ''And you bought that? Honey, he handed you a line. He was just trying to save his ego by making you feel bad.''

''It worked. I believed him for a long time.''

''I think you still do sometimes,'' Will said shrewdly. ''I wish I could go back and punch him. Right in his lying mouth.''

She laughed. ''He wasn't much of a fighter. Too afraid to mess up his perfect face.''

''His face wouldn't have been perfect when I got through with it.'' She needed reassurance, Will thought, and he wanted to provide it. ''Forget the twerp. I can think of much better things to do with our time.''

She smiled, but he sensed a certain reserve. He thought she believed him, but maybe she still harbored doubts. After that story, no wonder. Damn Amanda for putting that hurt look in Tessa's eyes! He hated that he'd been the cause, even inadvertently.

Distraction, that's what she needed. He drew his finger down her nose. ''Your nose is a little sunburned. Did I ever tell you that turns me on?''

She shot him a look of disbelief. ''Oh, right. I'm sure it's amazingly sexy.''

''On you it is.'' He kissed the tip of her nose, trailed his lips over her cheek. ''And these little freckles, I like them, too.'' Gazing deep into her eyes, he unfastened her blouse and spread it open. ''But I like that you cover up this part,'' he said, stroking a finger over her chest. ''Your skin here is so pale, it gleams in the moonlight. Did you know?''

She choked out a whispered ''No.''

''Smooth. Creamy.'' Dropping his head, he strung kisses across her collarbone, then her chest, smiling against her skin when her breath hitched. ''You taste like cream.'' Above her bra, he tested the curve of her breast. ''Sweet cream.''

''Are you—'' She moaned when his mouth latched onto her nipple through the fabric of her bra. ''Are you trying to seduce me?''

''Honey, I am seducing you.'' He stripped her slowly, stopping to thoroughly kiss each portion of skin he uncovered. To stroke her, to watch his hands caress that fine, pale, magnolia-petal skin.

"You're still dressed," she said, her voice husky. "I want to touch you."

"You will. Later. Right now—" his lips lowered to kiss her stomach, to trail farther down "—I'm touching you." And touch her, he did. With his hands, with his mouth. Again and again, until she hovered a step away from the edge and he knew it wouldn't take much to push her over. "Tessa, open your eyes."

Those gorgeous blue eyes, hazy with passion, blinked open. He pressed his hand between her legs and slid a finger inside. Withdrew and did it again. And again, until she convulsed around him, crying out his name. Watching her climax shot whatever self-control he had.

He picked her up, carried her into his bedroom and placed her in the middle of his bed. In no time flat, he got rid of his clothes, wasted precious seconds fumbling with a condom, and then was beside her.

"Hurry, Will." Her warm hands slipped over his chest, then went lower to caress him, to drive him even wilder with need.

She spread her legs and he entered her. He wanted to make it last, and knew there wasn't a hope in hell he could. She locked her legs around his hips and he thrust harder, deeper, over and over, until he exploded inside her with a scalding release.

It was a long time before he moved. When he would have, she held on and murmured, "Don't go yet. I like it."

"You like not being able to breathe?" But instead of leaving, he raised up to rest his weight on his arms on either side of her.

"I like having you inside me." She rubbed her cheek against his arm.

"I like being here." He kissed her mouth, slowly, lingeringly. "Tessa?" When she looked at him, he had the satisfaction of knowing he'd wiped any sign of doubt from those beautiful eyes. "There's another reason why I wouldn't have been with her. With anyone else."

Smiling, she raised her hand to his cheek. "What's that?"

"I'm in love with you."

Her eyes widened, but she didn't speak. She simply stared at him, then her mouth curved into a smile and she pulled his head down to hers. He made love to her again and neither spoke for a very long time.

WILL FELT GOOD. Better than good. More like fantastic. Lying in bed with Tessa gave him a contentment he'd been missing in his life. And it wasn't just the sex, though that had been incredible. He'd finally fallen in love. He hadn't expected it, hadn't even known he'd missed it. But now he knew why every other one of his relationships had ended. He hadn't loved any of those women. He'd liked them, enjoyed them, but he hadn't loved them. Until Tessa.

Why had it happened now? he wondered. Was he just ripe for falling in love, being back in the only place he'd ever called home? Seeing Jed and Emmy again had brought home to him how much he missed the family they'd been. A family he probably would never have again…unless he had one with Tessa.

And what did Tessa feel? She still hadn't said a word about his confession, when he said he loved her. He knew she cared for him, because she'd never have gone to bed with him otherwise. But did she love him? If she did, she wasn't saying.

Her fingers traced his chest, halting at one of his scars. "What's this from?"

He glanced down to see which one she was talking about. "Gunshot wound. Courtesy of a drug dealer with bad aim." He didn't think she'd get off on his scars, the way some women did. He figured she was just curious.

"Do you get shot at often?"

He couldn't help smiling at her look of horror. "Sometimes. Not so much now that I'm not busting drug dealers all the time." Which was nice, actually. He'd gotten used to not being shot at.

She kissed his scar, which made him smile again, and resumed trailing her fingers over him. "And this?" she asked, tracing a long, thin line that ran down his side. "Did a drug dealer do this?"

It would be easier to let her think that, but he found he didn't want to look into those deep blue eyes and lie. "No. That's not a line-of-duty scar." He sighed, thinking how best to tell her. "After I left Uncertain I lived on the street for a while. A couple of guys decided I looked like fair game, and when I didn't persuade easy, they pulled a knife. Lucky for me, the

cops showed up on another call and scared them off.''
Just not before they left him with a permanent reminder of that night.

The cops had taken him to the hospital, of course,
and he'd cut out as soon as they stitched him up and
pumped him full of antibiotics. Even so, he knew now
he'd been damn lucky not to get an infection. But he'd
known where he would have ended up if he'd stayed.
At seventeen, and given his background, he wouldn't
have been high on the list for another foster home. No,
he'd have landed in the nearest juvenile hall. Or worse,
a real jail.

Her eyes widened with distress. "You mean they—
they were trying to force you to— Oh, God, Will, I'm
sorry. I'm sorry I asked about the scar.''

"Don't be. It's over and I was lucky. But it's an
ugly world out there. Or it can be.''

"Is that why you became a cop?''

"Partly. They were…they were the good guys, and
they were decent to me.'' He hooked his hand behind
his head and leaned back against the headboard. "But
mostly I did it because of Frannie.''

"Did she want you to be a policeman?''

"Not especially. She wanted me to make something
of myself. And I owed her.''

"For taking you in.''

He shook his head, his gaze holding hers. "For saving my life.''

"Tell me,'' she said softly.

He wanted to tell her, he realized. Wanted her to

know him like few other people did. "I told you some
of it, that day on the lake."

"I remember. But there's more, isn't there?"

"Yeah, there's more. I was thirteen. Frannie was
my last shot at foster care. If I'd gone back to the
street then, or to juvie, I'd be dead. Or an addict and
better off dead."

She made a sound of denial.

"But thanks to Frannie, I didn't. I had a smart
mouth and the guy at the last foster home didn't much
care for it. When I came to Frannie she noticed I was
hurting. Made me take my shirt off and called Joleen,
her friend who was a nurse, to come over. Turns out
I had a busted rib."

"They just let him get away with that? With abus-
ing the children in his care?"

Will shrugged. "I think they're a lot tougher nowadays. Anyway, I'm sure he got his. Frannie lodged a
complaint and they pulled his license."

"She sounds like a wonderful woman."

"Frannie was great. She swore no one would ever
hurt me like that again." All these years later, he could
still see her, hear her promising him he was safe. "I
didn't believe her." He smiled wryly. "I didn't have
much reason to trust the system. It had never been very
good to me."

"But Frannie was different."

"Yeah, she was. She loved us. If she could have
afforded it, she'd have adopted all three of us."

"Did your foster brother and sister love her as much
as you did?"

"Yeah." He pulled his arm from behind his head to skim his hand over Tessa's hair. "Emmy was with her almost from birth, and Jed came to her when he was about six." He didn't doubt that they had loved Frannie. Which was one more reason his suspicion about Jed hurt so badly.

"Then why—" She broke off abruptly.

He looked down at her and finished her sentence. "Why did I arrest Jed?"

"Well, yes. If he loved her, why would he have killed her?"

"I don't think he would have. Purposely."

She stared at him a moment. "But you're afraid he did it accidentally."

He hesitated, nodded. "What I think doesn't matter, anyway. I have to uphold the law. The new evidence gave Fielder enough to ask for an arrest warrant." Jed's insistence that he had lost the ring days before that, so couldn't have been wearing it, hadn't mattered, either. It was still his ring, found at the murder site. "And everything since, every item of evidence except that glasses case, has only made things worse for Jed."

Thank God for that glasses case, Will thought, remembering the session earlier that day with Jed and his lawyer. Just as he'd been afraid of, Jed's account of why he'd had so much blood on him left a lot of room for doubt. After a hard time remembering initially, he'd admitted he recalled washing blood out of his T-shirt that night. But he swore he'd cut his arm on a nail while loading the boat. Which was just about impossible to prove nineteen years after the fact.

"But now you have a new lead," Tessa said. "You can look for the owner of that case."

"Assuming I can date it. But yeah, I can tell you one thing. Neither Frannie nor Jed would have owned something like that." He frowned, wishing he could remember why that thing had seemed so familiar.

"Why aren't you happier about it? If this might prove Jed innocent, you ought to be ecstatic."

Wearily he scrubbed a hand over his face. "I don't know if it's enough. Or if it was put there later or during the same time period as Frannie's murder. The evidence—damn it, the evidence is stacking up against Jed." And Will was very much afraid it would continue to do so, no matter what he did.

He had a shot at proving Jed innocent, though, and he sure as hell intended to try.

CHAPTER THIRTEEN

TESSA WOKE in her own bed, surrounded by Will. Still asleep, he had taken over her entire bed, sprawled out in blissful comfort. Which, she supposed, was why she had slept practically on top of him. Self-defense.

She needed some time to think, time alone after a night spent with him. Careful not to wake him, she eased out of bed and padded to the closet, grabbing her robe before going to the bathroom to take care of necessities. Late the evening before, they'd returned to her place to care for the animals. Will had stayed over, as he had every night since the first time they made love. It surprised her how quickly she'd become accustomed to his presence. She hadn't lived with anyone else since college.

She wasn't living with him, though. He stayed over because it was easier that way. Just as it was easier for him to keep a toothbrush and change of clothes at her place. But none of that meant he was actually living with her.

Her morning routine seemed mindless by now, even though established only a few months before. In urgent need of caffeine, she went into the kitchen. Goofy stood whimpering at the back door, so she let him out into the yard first. Then she turned on the coffeemaker and, while she waited, set out a bowl of kibble for Pepe, scratching him behind the ears when he came sauntering in.

Midway through the cycle, she siphoned off a cup of coffee and took it out to the front porch with her, content to sit on the swing and slowly awaken. Across the way was the lake, in all its eerie early-morning glory. A fine mist hung over the stands of tall cypress, trailing fingers of fog down to the water and sprinkling fairy dust across the gray Spanish moss that dripped over the trees. She smiled at her whimsical thoughts, for until she came to Caddo Lake she'd never known she had that streak in her.

The water was still, breaking into ripples only when an occasional water bird or a johnboat slipped quietly by. The air swelled with the tang of pine and warm dew, overlaid by the scent of wild dill and sweet honeysuckle.

Sipping coffee, she thought about the night before. As unlikely as it seemed, Will claimed to be in love with her. Even stranger, she believed him, or at least, believed he *thought* he loved her. But what did she feel about him? Unconsciously, she rubbed a hand over her heart.

Dazzled. No other word described it half as well. He simply dazzled her. His looks—hell-raiser looks as Ellen called them—were a part of that, but only a small part. She liked how he made her feel. Wanted. Needed. And even pretty. She liked how he made her laugh, then turned around and shared painful moments as well. And she admired how he did his job, regardless of the personal cost, because he believed in it, believed in what being a lawman meant.

He was a nice man, an admirable man. But she'd known nice, admirable men before and had never been in danger of losing her heart to any of them. She'd thought herself immune, thought she'd be too afraid to ever allow a man that close again. Yet somehow Will had battered down those walls without her even being aware of it.

Oh, Lord, maybe she was already in love with him.

She hadn't intended to fall in love. What she and Will shared had never been destined to be permanent. They had no future together. Soon her work would be finished, and she would leave. And her next stop would likely be several thousand miles away. Will's life, his career, was here in Texas. And hers...wasn't.

It could be. Unbidden, the traitorous voice whispered in her mind.

She glanced at the doorway and saw Will, leaning against the door frame sipping from a steaming mug, wearing a pair of jeans and nothing else. Her mouth went dry as her gaze wandered over the broad expanse of bare chest, tanned, golden skin, past the faded denim covering powerful thighs, to his bare feet. Stubble shaded his jaw, making it look even stronger than normal. It appeared as if he'd raked his fingers through his blond hair, pushing it back from his face, though a shock of it rebelled and fell over his forehead. He looked dangerous, a little disreputable, and utterly tempting. And then he smiled and her heart tumbled.

"You seem awfully serious for so early on a Sunday morning," he said. "Deep thoughts?"

Unsure if she wanted to talk about those thoughts, she returned the smile and shook her head. "No, not really. I'm still half-asleep." She tucked her feet up beneath her and Will crossed the porch to sit beside her. The swing creaked with his weight, moving forward a little before settling.

"This used to be Jed's favorite time of day," he said, cupping his hands around the mug and lifting it to his mouth. "Frannie liked it, too. Sometimes I'd wake up and they'd be sitting on the porch swing, just like we are now, doing nothing in the early-morning light." He smiled. "Emmy never could understand how they could sit there and not say a word."

"I've met Emmy, but we've never talked much. What's she like?"

"Loyal. True blue." His gaze met hers and he sighed ruefully. "She doesn't understand why I can't believe in Jed's innocence as wholeheartedly as she does."

"Why can't you?"

He stared at her a minute, as if struck by a thought.

When he didn't speak, Tessa continued. "You obviously care about him. You don't want to believe he's guilty, yet a part of you does. I know there's evidence, but what does your heart tell you?"

"My heart?" He scoffed. "I can't afford a heart. Not when I'm on a case. I'm a Ranger. I look at the facts, not my feelings."

But he had a heart, nonetheless, she thought, and it was hurting. "Isn't the evidence circumstantial?"

"Yeah. Pretty damning circumstantial evidence. And that's not all. I can't find a motive for anyone except Jed. Frannie had no enemies. Not that I can discover. She was honest, hardworking, dependable. No one hated her, no one had it in for her. As far as I can tell, she wasn't a threat to anyone."

Startled, she asked, "Jed had a motive to kill her?"

Will scrubbed a hand over his face. "Possibly. They argued, the morning of her death. Emmy and I witnessed it. It's common knowledge, thanks to Amanda overhearing Jed and me talking about it."

"Do you really think he was angry enough to kill her?"

"Like I said before, not purposely. But accidents happen. More often than you might think."

"Could it have been a random act of violence? Obviously, it's too late to tell whether—" She stopped, unwilling to voice her thoughts.

"Whether she was sexually assaulted," he finished. "It's possible. But with Jed sitting there with motive, means and opportunity, not to mention a boatload of circumstantial evidence, it's going to be damned hard to convince anyone of that."

She set her coffee mug down, put her hand over his and squeezed. "I'm sorry."

He laced his fingers through hers and brought her hand to his lips. "Me, too. And I can't move forward with the investigation until I get the report back on that glasses case you found."

''When do you think you'll get it?''

''Hard to tell.'' He shrugged. ''Not for a few days, anyway. Which leaves me free today. What about you?''

''I don't have anything special planned.''

''Good. Let me take you to Jefferson. I never did manage to, and I think you'll like it.'' He set his mug on the porch beside the swing. ''How does a riverboat ride sound to you? We can go this afternoon, see the sights, then eat dinner at a place I know. The Black Swan. Cajun and Creole food. Sometimes they have entertainment, too. A jazz piano player, or even a Cajun band.''

''It sounds like you're romancing me,'' she said, charmed.

His mouth lifted in a wicked grin. ''I am, honey. That's exactly what I'm doing.'' He took her face between his hands and planted a lingering kiss on her lips.

She was so caught up in him, in the kiss, she didn't even hear the car drive up. The first hint that they had company came when she heard a disgusted voice say, ''Theresa, really. You're making a spectacle of yourself.''

Her eyes flew open. Lips still on hers, Will chuckled before his hands dropped and he released her. She turned her head and stared at the woman who had halted a few feet away. Red hair, perfectly styled in a short, straight pageboy. A classic linen suit in shades of ivory. An aristocratic face with frigid blue eyes gazing at her disdainfully.

"Mother? What in the world are you doing here?"

"Obviously, I'm here to see you." She turned her attention to Will, studying him with a scholarly detachment. "And this is?"

Tessa flushed and stood, Will rising with her. "Sorry. Mother, this is Will McClain. He's the Texas Ranger who hired me to work at the murder site. Will, my mother, Dr. Olivia Lang."

Will stepped forward, offering a hand. "Nice to meet you, Dr. Lang." Though he wasn't smiling, Tessa could see his lips twitching. She wanted to smack him. No, she wanted to smack her mother. Why in the world had she chosen to show up on Tessa's doorstep before eight o'clock on a Sunday morning? Tessa hadn't seen her in months and hadn't expected to see her for several more.

Olivia took the proffered hand and shook it briskly, inclining her head regally. "Mr. McClain."

"Ranger McClain," he corrected, "but call me Will." He turned to Tessa, flashing a smile. "I'll leave you two alone. I've got some errands to run, anyway."

"Don't go," she said, a little desperately. She really didn't want to be alone with her mother. Not given her ominous expression.

"You sure?" When she nodded, he said, "I'll go catch a shower, then."

Tessa resisted the impulse to tell him not to do that, either. Might as well get it over with. She was a grown woman, not a twelve-year-old child. Her mother shouldn't be able to inspire dread in her anymore.

Except she did.

"Come inside, Mother," she said as Will left them. "Can I offer you a cup of coffee?"

Olivia glanced at her watch and frowned. "No, thank you."

"How have you been?"

"Quite well, thank you. I don't have time for idle chitchat, Theresa, so I'll get right to the point."

Her mother swept into the room, a look of revulsion crossing her face when she saw Pepe lying on the couch. Tessa stifled a giggle when she thought of what Olivia's reaction to Goofy would be. A good thing the exuberant dog was out in the yard, she thought, eyeing her mother's immaculate suit. It occurred to Tessa that she'd never seen her mother mussed. Even after a day in the field, she appeared neat and tidy. How she managed it, Tessa couldn't imagine.

Choosing Goofy's favorite chair beside the couch, Olivia waited to speak until Tessa also sat. "I have come, at great trouble to myself, I might add, to see what could possibly be so important that you felt you needed to jeopardize your future career for it. And what do I find when I arrive?"

Assuming it was a rhetorical question, Tessa remained silent, merely reaching out to rub Pepe's head. Somehow the contact steadied her.

"A man." Olivia's expression, if possible, grew colder. "I couldn't believe my eyes."

A quick spurt of temper had Tessa asking, "What exactly couldn't you believe, Mother? That I might have taken a lover? Or that any man might be interested in me?"

Olivia sailed past that question. "This is why you refused to go on the Peru dig. So you could indulge in a tawdry affair. Where are your priorities? Have you lost your senses?"

Don't get mad, Tessa reminded herself. *It never helps.* She drew in a breath and fought for calm. "First of all, Will is not the reason I said I couldn't go. I've explained several times why I refused, you simply haven't listened. Second of all, I'm not having a tawdry affair."

"What?" Olivia's well-modulated voice rose and she sat forward in her chair. "I saw you with my own eyes, sitting in your robe on your front porch with a half-naked man. That was no innocent kiss."

"I didn't say he wasn't my lover. I said I wasn't having a tawdry affair." She raised her chin and locked gazes with her mother. "There's nothing tawdry about it."

Olivia's jaw tightened, her eyes snapping with glacial fury. She seemed about to say something, but apparently thought better of it. "I can see it's futile to talk to you about this—this affair. So we'll say no more about it." Nodding decisively, she swept on. "I didn't come here to discuss your love life, but something much more important. Your career."

Her personal life had never been important to Olivia. Why should Tessa think that had changed? "Please, if you're going to harp on about Peru again—"

"Not Peru. Another opportunity." Her eyes sparked

with purpose. "An even better one. I must say, I can't believe your good fortune."

Tessa's head ached, tension tightening her neck muscles. "Mother, I can't do anything right now. I have commitments here in Uncertain."

"This expedition won't begin until fall. You'll have the summer, at least, to finish up your Ph.D. and whatever else—" her gaze cut to the open hallway and back "—you think you need to remain here for."

Whatever else, Tessa thought. Meaning Will.

"Aren't you even going to ask where it is?"

"All right. Where?"

"China. The Lost Emperor's tomb," she said, referring to a famous, and supposedly mythical Chinese emperor. "Imagine, Chang Su Lin's tomb. And I can tell you right now, the word is this find will make Tut pale in comparison."

"China? How did you manage to get a position for me on a dig like that?" The Chinese weren't much on Westerners invading their territory. Her mother was right. This was a one-of-a-kind opportunity, if it worked out.

Olivia waved a hand. "I happen to be one of the administrators for the American contingent. But that doesn't matter. What matters is that you can't pass on this opportunity. Not if you have any intention of developing a brilliant career." She sent her a scathing look. "Or have you abandoned that goal in favor of having affairs with men you hardly know?"

"I haven't abandoned my career or my goals. None of this has anything to do with my relationship with

Will. And not that it matters, but I do know him."
Better than she knew the woman sitting across from
her. Olivia might have been a stranger for all the care
she showed her daughter. But then, Tessa had always
been a disappointment to her mother. Why else would
Olivia have foisted Tessa on her grandmother?

"You're infatuated. These things pass, Theresa.
Your career is more important than a temporary sexual
fling. However exciting that might seem now."

"What if I said it was serious?" Will had said he
loved her. That sounded serious, even if it wasn't permanent.

She gave a smile of disbelief. "Is it?" When Tessa
didn't respond, she said, "I thought not."

"Why is it beyond the realm of possibility that I
might have a serious relationship? Am I so unworthy
that I don't deserve—" *Someone to love me,* she
thought, breaking off. Her hands curled into fists of
helpless anger.

"You're overreacting, and I find it very unbecom-
ing. We were discussing your career. The one you're
busily throwing away."

A brilliant career. What she'd always believed she
wanted. "I'll have to think about it. I can't just decide
on the spot like this. I need more information."

"Of course. But if you let this go, Theresa, all because you're caught up in a tangle of hormones, then
you're a fool."

"Thank you, Mother. It's reassuring to know some
things never change. Such as your opinion of me."

"My dear." She stretched out a hand, let it fall.

"I'm concerned about you. I'm not blind, you know. He's very...attractive. It's no wonder you're infatuated. But really—" she laughed indulgently "—what could a man like him see in you? Have you asked yourself that question?"

"Your daughter's a beautiful woman," Will said, walking into the room. "Haven't you noticed?" He came to stand beside Tessa and smiled down at her.

Tessa felt slightly nauseated, as she always did when her mother berated her. It didn't matter that she was a grown woman—when she heard that voice, those tones, she felt like a grieving, vulnerable child again, trying desperately to live up to her mother's expectations. But Will's response steadied her, and so did the reassuring squeeze he gave her hand when she slipped it into his.

"Sweet words for any woman to hear, Ranger McClain."

"But true," he said. "And it's Will."

Olivia examined Tessa as she might have an archaeological find, her gaze sharp, assessing. Finally she said, "You've done something different to your hair."

Tessa nearly laughed. "Yes, I did. But we can leave this discussion until another time. How long will you be staying, Mother?"

"Not long. I'm flying out of Shreveport early this afternoon. In fact—" she glanced at her watch again "—I really must be going."

"I could show you the Caddo dig...if you stayed until tomorrow." Though Tessa made the offer reluctantly, somewhere deep down she wanted to share her work with her mother. Hoping for an approval she would never gain.

"I couldn't possibly. I'm sure it's quite interesting," she said in a lofty tone that meant she believed no such thing. "However, I only scheduled an hour with you. I wanted to tell you about the China expedition personally."

"Thank you," she said, because it was expected. But she didn't feel thankful, just confused. And hurt.

"It was no easy task to make this happen for you, Theresa," her mother said sharply. "I have your best interests at heart. Surely you can see that."

How many times had she heard her mother say that very thing? Her best interests. Her career. "I'll be in touch about it."

"See that you are. And don't wait too long to decide. It's not as though they won't have others who can recognize their good fortune at being offered such a coup." She stood and gave a terse nod. "Fascinating to meet you, Will."

"Likewise," he said, with a wealth of meaning to the single word.

Tessa walked her to the door. "I'll expect to hear from you," Olivia said. "Very soon."

Tessa closed the door behind her. Shell-shocked, she turned to look at Will.

"Man," he said, and whistled, lifting an eyebrow. "Is she always like that?"

She couldn't help smiling, and wanted to hug him

for making her feel better. "Yes. Especially when she isn't getting what she wants."

His mouth quirked as he met her gaze. "I don't think your mother likes me."

"That's okay," she told him. "She doesn't like me, either. She never has."

CHAPTER FOURTEEN

"Never?" Will asked. He had started to say something soothing, but one look at Tessa's face and he couldn't do it. The truth hurt, but lies crippled.

She smiled and crossed the room to him. "You have no idea how refreshing it is that you didn't tell me I must be wrong. That she cares about me, and it's simply her personality."

Tilting his head, he studied her. "Maybe it is. And maybe she does like you, but from what I saw, she sure as hell didn't act like it." He didn't believe Olivia Lang gave one good damn about her daughter's feelings, but he wouldn't be that blunt. Besides, Tessa obviously knew it. "She didn't exactly treat you like her best friend."

Tessa gave a humorless laugh and stuffed her hands into the pockets of her robe. "No, we're not friends. Never had a chance to be, and she never showed any interest. Until I was twelve and my grandmother died, I only saw my parents a few times a year. I didn't know them, and they didn't know me." Catching his gaze, she asked, "Do you know what it's like to be taken care of only out of duty, not love?"

"No. My mother was never big on either one." She

hadn't had a responsible bone in her body, nor, as far as he knew, any love.

Regret flashed in her eyes. "I'm sorry. I—I forgot. Here I am whining about my childhood when yours—"

He interrupted before she could beat herself up any more. "Tessa, you have a right to your feelings. Just because I had a lousy childhood doesn't mean yours wasn't bad."

"It wasn't like yours. At least I had my grandmother." Her expression softened. "She was a wonderful woman. She loved me, and I always knew it. That carried me through, even after she was gone."

"I had Frannie," Will said, thinking about the unconditional love she'd given him. Given all of them. "For a while, at least."

"Will—"

"But we were talking about your mother." They'd talked of Frannie and about Will's past, but never much about Tessa's. And he had a feeling she needed to talk about it. "Why doesn't she like you? Do you know?"

After a long, assessing look, she accepted the return to the original subject. "I'm not sure. My mother is a very driven person. Her career—and my father's while he was alive—have always been the most important things in her life." Her laugh was strained. "Certainly more than me. I've always been an inconvenience and an annoyance to her. And I'm certain I wasn't planned." She closed her eyes, then opened them to gaze at him. "If she'd wanted me, why would she have given me to her mother to raise? Why wouldn't she have made an effort to see me more than twice a year?''

Good point, he thought. ''Some people aren't cut out to be parents.'' His mother hadn't been. Funny he and Tessa should have that in common.

''What about your father?''

''Father?'' She looked surprised. ''Father was... oblivious. Sometimes I wonder if he even remembered he had a daughter, he was so immersed in his work.'' She shrugged. ''He didn't dislike me, he just...was never really there. When he died—'' she smiled wryly and continued ''—my mother had more time to spend on a new project. Me.''

''Sounds uncomfortable.'' He knew he wouldn't like to be seen as anyone's project. A telling choice of words there.

''It can be,'' she said. ''Especially if we don't agree on what my best course is.''

''Why did she come?'' he asked. ''I thought you said she wanted you to go to Peru, but I heard her mention China as she left.''

''The first job was in Peru. Since that didn't work to get me out of here, she looked for something else. Now she's found me a position in an expedition going to China.''

China? It just kept getting farther away. His tone carefully neutral, he asked, ''Is that what you want? To go to China?''

She sighed and rubbed the back of her neck. ''I don't know. It sounds like...something I should do. If it doesn't fall through it would be an unprecedented opportunity.''

''How long would you be gone?''

''A year or two. Maybe three, depending on the size of the find.''

Two or three years? His stomach bottomed out. ''So it's a big deal.''

''Yes, a very big deal. But I don't know all the details. I can't make up my mind until I do.'' Her hand stopped massaging her neck and she looked at him and smiled. ''Don't worry, it's not until this fall. I wouldn't leave you high and dry. I'm almost through with the site work, anyway.''

For once he wasn't worried about the damn site. He was just beginning to understand how much he wanted Tessa to stay. With him. In Uncertain, the only place he'd ever felt he could really call home. But she obviously wasn't ready to hear that. Not now, coming on top of the scene with her mother. So instead, he changed the subject.

''You know what you need?''

''Besides a mother who doesn't come on like Catherine the Great? Or maybe I'm thinking of Bloody Mary.''

He laughed. ''Can't help you there. But I can take you to Jefferson. Get dressed and let's have some fun.''

She put her arms around his waist and hugged him, laying her cheek against his chest. ''Thank you.''

''For what?'' He rubbed his hand over the soft, silky material of her robe, wishing he could make the hurt go away. Wishing he knew the right words to make her want to stay. The prospect of not seeing Tessa for two or three years wasn't one he wanted to think about.

"For letting me talk. For being here. For not leaving. My mother can be a bit...overwhelming. Most men would have been out of here in seconds flat."

Most men weren't in love with her, Will thought, but he didn't say it. After the first time, he hadn't told her he loved her again, but he didn't believe she'd forgotten. He tugged her hair so she'd look at him. When she did, she grinned. "I'm a Ranger, honey. We eat trouble for breakfast."

Her face came alive with laughter. "And take your lines from Arnold Schwarzenegger movies."

Still holding her, he laughed, too. As he stared into her eyes, the laughter faded. "Your mother was wrong. I see a whole lot in you to interest me." He lowered his head, captured her mouth slowly, his tongue tracing her lips, urging them open. Her tongue answered his, and his body tightened with desire. "Maybe Jefferson should wait a while," he murmured.

"Good idea," Tessa said, and they walked hand in hand to her bedroom.

THREE DAYS PASSED before Will received the report on the metallic object Tessa had found at the murder site. Definitely a silver glasses case, manufactured by a firm that had gone out of business fifteen years earlier. And not available anywhere in Uncertain nineteen or more years ago. So Will's search to find a store that might have carried it would take him to Marshall, Longview, Shreveport, Louisiana, and possibly even Dallas. Even so, finding who sold it was a long shot. For all he knew, it could have come from anywhere in the country. Still, he had to try.

He'd be better served to discover who might have owned a case like the one in question. And where he'd seen something similar. Something nagged at him, just beyond reach. He pinched the bridge of his nose and thought about it for the fiftieth time, at least. Nothing. It just wouldn't come clear. Knowing Fielder had been sheriff in Uncertain for nearly twenty years, he decided to go to him. Maybe he could shed some light on the object.

As for who might have owned the thing—anyone with money. There were a few wealthy families in the area. Raymond and Catherine Jennings probably had the most money of any of the permanent residents. The Osgoods, who had owned the local grocery, had been well-off, but not wealthy. The Barkers, he remembered after some thought, had been nearly as wealthy as the Jennings. The local doctor had been doing okay, as well as the attorney whose practice Riley had taken over. Will picked up the file of Frannie's employers, noting which ones he knew had had money years before. Fielder would know about the rest.

During the summers there had been, and still was, an influx of people staying at their summer homes. Frannie had cleaned several of those vacation homes. Could she have found something damaging at one of them? Something damaging enough to prompt a murder? And how was he going to find out, after so many years had passed? Especially given the fact that the summer people changed every few years. The rental agencies would have records, but he doubted they would go back nineteen years. They'd probably only kept them for the required seven years.

As usual, he found Fielder in his office. Sometimes Will felt a surprising flash of sympathy for the man. The sheriff had no family and, apparently, few friends. Other than an occasional fishing trip, Will didn't think he even took a vacation. Much as Will loved his work, he didn't want to end up like Fielder, alone and married to his job.

"Got a minute, Sheriff?"

Fielder looked up from the paperwork spread over his desk. He was surprisingly conscientious about keeping up with it, Will thought. At least, he was now. Someone had sure screwed up in the past, though, losing some of Frannie's case files. No telling what else was missing.

"Something new?" He took off his glasses and laid them on the desk.

"Yeah. The report came back on that object Tessa found. It's a silver glasses case, manufactured about twenty-five years ago. No prints or anything, and no identifying mark from a particular store."

"I don't envy you that search," Fielder said, shaking his head. "You sure as hell won't find a store around here that would've carried it. Maybe in Marshall or Longview, but I doubt it."

Thinking he might be there a while, Will took a seat. "No, I'll probably have to go to Shreveport or Dallas, and that could take forever. We did have one break, though. That particular item was only manufactured for a limited time. From 1975 to 1985. So it's possible to place it at the site at the time of the murder."

Fielder merely grunted in response. Will propped his boot on his knee and drummed his fingers on the leather. "Who would have had the kind of money to use a silver glasses case?" Or the kind of personality, he wondered. Carrying around a silver case on a daily basis sounded pretentious in Will's book, at least in a town the size of Uncertain.

"You don't know if it was dropped there at the time of the murder."

"We don't know that it wasn't," Will countered. "Come on, Sheriff, help me out here. It won't hurt you to consider another option besides Jed Louis. Who had money back then?"

Fielder snorted, muttering something like "wild-goose chase," before he huffed out a deep breath and spoke. "Ray Jennings and his wife, for one. And the Farrs," he added after a moment, naming a longtime resident architect and his wife, even wealthier than Catherine Jennings's family was purported to be. "Maybe the Hartfields, but that's about it, unless we're talking some of the summer folk."

"Are the Hartfields still around?"

"The old lady is. Old man Hartfield passed on a few years back."

Will handed him the police artist's sketch of the restored glasses case. "Ever run across anything similar to that around here?"

Fielder picked up his reading glasses and slid them on. After studying the drawing for a long moment, he looked up, over the lenses. "As a matter of fact, I have. But I don't think it's gonna help you much."

"Where?"

Pursing his lips, he tapped a finger on the sketch. "Seems to me Ray Jennings carries something along those lines. Not exactly, but close enough."

Will sat up straight, both boots landing on the floor. "I knew I'd seen something like this, but I couldn't place it. He had a case like that on his desk at the bank. If he has one now, it's possible he had one back then."

"Possible," Fielder said, nodding agreement as he laid his glasses down again. "But so what?" He leaned back and eyed Will skeptically. "You still got no motive, even if you can prove it was his and that he lost it at the time of the murder. Which you aren't likely to be able to do."

"It's a start, though. And Frannie worked for the Jennings. Maybe she discovered something one of them wasn't too happy about her finding." Considering that, he added, "Or maybe she overheard an argument or something."

Fielder snorted. "Simplest thing would be if she found proof that ol' Ray had an eye for the ladies."

"Did he?"

Fielder shrugged. "Rumor had it he was one for

tomcattin' around.'' He cracked his knuckles and added, ''Still is, according to the talk. He's just a lot more careful nowadays. Anyway, years ago his wife caught on to one of his shenanigans and laid down the law to him. Said her daddy wasn't gonna be happy about it.''

''Meaning she threatened to cut off his funds. She's the money in that family.''

''Yep. But before you go getting all excited about this, I gotta tell you, Jennings came down here breathing fire the first time I questioned Jed Louis. Wanted me to look into that drifter who was hanging around at the time of Frannie Granger's death. Kept saying he likely did it and why didn't we leave Louis be.''

''Hank Belmonte.'' Will reviewed what he'd learned. ''Yeah, well, his alibi is rock solid. He was in jail in Marshall during the time in question.''

''Drunk tank?''

''You got it.'' And it was too damn bad.

''But if Jennings was guilty, then why would he care if I arrested Louis? Seems like he'd have been happy someone else was already suspect.''

''Anyone but Jed, possibly. He was Jed's trustee, years ago. And I think he helped him out some, too. Maybe he felt guilty, because of Frannie, and that's why he helped Jed out.''

Fielder shook his head. ''I don't buy it. Besides the fact I still think Louis did it, I just don't see how knowin' Ray Jennings fooled around on his wife does you any good.'' Leaning back in his chair, his expression skeptical, he continued. "So what if he did? And so what if Frannie Granger found out? Lots of men have done the same and never murdered anyone on account of it."

"Lots of men don't owe all their wealth and position to their wife's family," Will said, standing. "Lots of men wouldn't be totally ruined if their wife divorced them."

Skepticism turned to pity. "You're wasting your time, McClain. Louis is guilty as sin, and you just can't admit it. Don't forget the ring. And the blood."

"We'll see, Sheriff. Thanks for the information."

Regardless of Fielder's doubts, Will was more hopeful than he'd been yet. Who knew what he might turn up in another interview with the banker—and his wife?

"EARTH TO TESSA. Yoo-hoo, anyone home?"

The voice sounded distant at first, then grew closer. Tessa glanced at the open door to her office to see her friend Ellen regarding her with a quizzical eye. "Hi, Ellen."

"Hi, Ellen, she says." She propped her hands on her hips. "I've been standing here calling your name for five minutes. What's with you?"

"Shock, I guess. Sorry."

"Is something wrong?" Ellen walked in quickly, coming to stand by her desk.

"No, nothing." Tessa shook her head to clear it. "It's—just a surprise, that's all. The chairman of the sciences department just called and offered me a full-time professorship, with all the perks." Not to mention a chance for advancement once she successfully defended her Ph.D. thesis.

"Hey, that's great!" Ellen leaned a hip against the desk and peered at her more closely. "Isn't it?"

If only it were that cut-and-dried, Tessa thought. "Yes. At least, I suppose it is, but I don't know what to do. I don't think I told you about the position my mother found for me."

"Sure you did. Going to Peru."

"No, a different one. To be part of an expedition to China. To the Lost Emperor's tomb."

"No, you hadn't mentioned that one. China, huh? So, do you want to go?"

Want to? Why did everyone keep going on about whether she wanted to or not? Didn't they understand, careers weren't about what one *wanted*. Careers were about duty. Opportunity. Advancement. Not about wanting at all. "I'd be crazy not to go. It would be a huge step forward in my career."

Ellen cocked her head, studying her. "What about Will?" she asked after a moment.

"Will has nothing to do with this."

Ellen made a rude sound and boosted herself to sit on Tessa's desk. "Except for the fact that you're madly in love with the man and living with him." She glanced down at her nails. "Nah, I guess he doesn't have a thing to do with your decision."

"I'm not living with him. Exactly."

Her eyebrows arched in disbelief. "I suppose you're

not in love with him, either. And he's not in love with you.'' She rolled her eyes. ''Yeah, right.''

''He—he said he loved me. Once.'' Flushing, she remembered just exactly when he'd told her. After making love. When he was still inside her. ''It might have been the, er, heat of the moment.'' But she didn't really believe that. He hadn't sounded carried away. He'd sounded very sure of himself.

''Horsefeathers,'' Ellen said succinctly. ''He wouldn't have said it if he didn't mean it. He's not the type. Believe me, I know all about the type who tells you what they think you want to hear, whether it's true or not.''

''Yes, so do I,'' Tessa said. ''And no, I don't think Will is like that. But I'm also not sure…'' She threw her hands up in frustration. ''Oh, I'm not sure of anything. This is my career we're talking about. My entire future.''

''And what is Will? Where does he fit in?''

''I don't know.'' Tessa put her head in her hands and rubbed her temples. Glancing up at her friend, she said, ''I thought it—the two of us—would be just a temporary thing. A summer fling.'' She smiled ruefully. ''It isn't.''

''Tessa.'' Ellen laid a hand over hers. ''What do you want to do with your career?''

''My mother thinks this—''

''No.'' She shook her head. ''Don't tell me what your mother wants or thinks. Tell me what you want. What you think is the best thing for you to do.''

Reluctantly Tessa said, ''The best thing for my career would be to go to China.'' What she'd always wanted. Wasn't it? A chance to shine. The opportunity to make her mother take notice. To make her proud.

''Well, that depends on the kind of career you want. Personally, I'd rather slit my throat than deal with the kind of pressure that comes with a high-profile career like that. Which is why I teach at a small college in East Texas. Where I'm appreciated. Where I know I'm doing some good.''

''But this is what I've always wanted, what I've always planned. I'm interested in field archaeology, not teaching.'' No, teaching wasn't for her. Not until she'd made a name for herself in the field.

''Then you shouldn't have a problem,'' Ellen said cheerfully, hopping off the desk. ''It's simple. Turn down the teaching position and kiss Will goodbye.'' She grinned and added, ''I'm sure there'll be plenty of women anxious to console him after you're gone.''

''Thanks,'' Tessa said shortly. Amanda would be first in line. ''I really needed to hear that.''

''Hey, face facts,'' she said in the same perky tone. ''And the fact is, a man like Will won't be alone for long. If you're willing to leave him to go halfway around the world, you have to expect the inevitable.'' She glanced at her watch. ''Oops, I'm going to be late for class. Let's have lunch tomorrow, okay? Give me a call.''

Ellen left with a wave. Tessa felt a surge of irritation at her friend's cavalier attitude. Not to mention her crude comment about Will finding solace with other women. The fact that Ellen had only spoken the truth didn't make it any more palatable. She could see Amanda licking those fire-engine-red lips at the chance for another shot at Will.

The chairman of the department had asked Tessa to give her decision within two weeks. Two weeks wasn't much time to decide the rest of her life.

CHAPTER FIFTEEN

WILL DIDN'T MANAGE to make it to Tessa's place until late in the evening. His day hadn't been anywhere near as productive as he'd hoped, either. Nothing new turned up during his interview with the Jennings, even though he did confirm that the couple's tastes ran to a lot of gold and silver. But beyond that, the day yielded zip.

Tessa wasn't there, but she'd left him a note saying she'd gone to the pier across the street from her house. Once upon a time, the old dock had had lights and the locals had fished there at night, but no more. Besides, after eleven, no one would be out. Uncertain still shut down early, just as it had when Will was a kid.

Will took the time to change into shorts and a short-sleeved T-shirt before searching Tessa out. Smiling, he realized most of his belongings had migrated to Tessa's. With the animals to care for, it made more sense to stay at her place. He wasn't sure why he kept his cottage at the Kit and Caboodle. Maybe because he and Tessa had never discussed living together, it had just happened naturally.

Sure enough, he found her on the pier, bare feet dangling off the edge. The night was clear and moonlight spilled over the dark water, painting it with pale streaks of muted color. A slight breeze swept through the trees and muffled notes from someone's stereo carried across the lake. A frog croaked, was silent and croaked again.

Peaceful, he thought, taking in a deep breath. The night breeze was cool for a change, with the damp smell of the lake and hints of honeysuckle underlying it. A perfect summer night waiting to be shared. And there was no one he'd rather share it with than Tessa.

Not wanting to frighten her, he called her name before walking up behind her. She turned around and smiled, beckoning him to her side. Kicking off his shoes, he eased down beside her, pulling her to him for a long, steamy kiss. Though she returned it, he sensed a hesitation in her response and wondered why.

"What are you doing out here so late?" he asked, lifting his mouth from hers. His cop's mind worried about her, even though Uncertain had a low crime rate. "Have you been here long?"

"A while. I had some…thinking to do."

He wrapped an arm around her shoulder, caressing the bare skin of her arm. So soft. So smooth. "You're cold," he said. "It's cooler tonight than it's been. And not muggy. Must be the breeze." She leaned her head against his shoulder and sighed. "What is it? You seem kind of down or something."

She shook her head but didn't address his question. "I've finished with the murder site. It's yielded everything it's going to. Everything I could find, anyway. I'm sorry I couldn't come up with more."

His hand stopped its caressing motion. Murder

seemed to have no place here, yet it was his reason for returning. And why he'd met Tessa. "You found the only piece of evidence that indicates Jed didn't do it. You won't hear me complain."

"Still, I wish I'd come across something to clear him."

"You might have. Maybe the glasses case will tell us something." If he could discover where it had come from…but his investigations into its origins hadn't been successful yet.

"I hope so."

"Yeah, me, too." They fell silent a moment. "I guess this means you'll start working on the Caddo burial mound again. On your thesis."

"Yes. Tomorrow I'll be back with my crew."

"Is something else going on?" He let go of her and put a hand under her chin, studying her. The moonlight was bright enough for him to see her troubled expression. "You look upset." His thumb brushed over her mouth. She looked solemn, thoughtful. Like she had something serious on her mind.

Drawing back from him, she shook her head. "Not upset, but I had a job offer today." Her gaze met his. "For a full professorship at Caddo Lake College."

He didn't speak for a moment. To him, it sounded like something that suited her right down to the ground. Her love for teaching had been clear from the first time he'd talked to her. Judging by her expression, though, she didn't feel that way. "Are you going to take it?"

"I—they gave me two weeks to decide." She rose

and paced the dock, the worn planks creaking as she passed over them. "I should have told them right away, but I was surprised by the offer and I didn't."

"Told them what?" he asked, but he had a sinking feeling he knew.

She halted a few steps away. "About the China expedition. I should have turned down the job when they offered it, instead of letting them think I might take it."

He moved to stand beside her. This wasn't what he wanted to hear. "You're not even going to consider the job offer?"

"How can I? I decided a long time ago I would do field archaeology. Everyone thinks—everyone feels it's what I'm best suited for. If I stay here, I can't do that."

"What about the Caddo ruins? Isn't that field archaeology?"

"Yes, but it's not..." Her voice trailed off. She turned to look out at the water.

He put a hand on her shoulder, keeping it there until she finally faced him. "It's not important enough, is that it? Not some big deal like the China thing."

Raising her chin, she met his gaze. "It's important. But it's not a—a once-in-a-lifetime opportunity. I wish it were, but it isn't."

An owl hooted while they stared at each other. Water lapped at the pier, the wind rustled the leaves as the silence between them lengthened. Taking her hands in his, he squeezed them gently. "Tessa, tell me something. Do you really want to go to China?"

"It's what's best for my career."

"I didn't ask that. I asked if it's what you want." She didn't answer and he continued. "I don't think it is."

"Why do you say that?"

"For one thing, look at your house." He gestured in that direction. "It's not just a temporary rental to you. It's a home. You planted flowers. Painted the kitchen. I bet you even made the curtains." Her quick flush made him sure he was right.

She pulled her hands away and crossed her arms. "I like to plant flowers. It's therapy for me. I see nothing so unusual about that."

"At a rental?" He felt a surge of irritation at her denial. "Come on, Tessa."

She hunched a shoulder, not giving in.

"Okay, fine, maybe some people like flowers so much they'll plant them at a house they're renting. But what about Goofy and Pepe? They spell permanence. What do you plan to do with them when you go off to China?"

Her shocked gaze met his. "I hadn't thought about the animals." She looked across toward the house, then back to him. "I can't take them with me."

"No, you can't. And I think you knew that when you adopted them. They're your way of saying you want to stay put. You want to put down roots." If ever he'd seen a woman who was crying out for a home, it was Tessa. Why couldn't she see that as easily as he did? Why was she so determined to leave? For China, for God's sake.

Her expression settled into a worried frown. "I'll have to find homes for them."

"Unless you stay." The words emerged before he even thought, but he couldn't regret them. It was the perfect solution. He could work from Uncertain. He wouldn't even have to transfer Ranger companies, since his own company covered Northeast Texas as well North Central Texas. He'd just change his base of operations. He stepped to her, held her face in his hands. "Stay. With me."

Her eyes searched his. "What are you saying?" Her voice dipped, low and husky.

"I love you, Tessa. Marry me." He covered her mouth with his, sliding his tongue inside in slow, deep strokes, hoping to convince her with his actions, since she wouldn't listen to his words. Wrapping his arms around her, he pulled her nearer, content when her body relaxed against his as she responded to his kiss.

Suddenly she pulled out of his arms. "Don't, Will. I can't think when you do that."

Frustrated, he jammed a hand through his hair. "Am I moving too fast? Is that the problem?" She shook her head. "I wouldn't have said anything if you weren't talking about running off to Timbuktu like it was a done deal."

"China."

"Whatever. It's still halfway around the world." How to convince her to give them a chance? A chance, that's all he wanted. "I know it's too soon for you. I realize just because I'm in love with you doesn't mean you feel the same. But I know you care about me, or you wouldn't be with me. If you leave, we won't have the chance to find out what it is you feel. To find out if there can be more for us.''

''Oh, Will. I do love you. That isn't the problem.'' She said it so quietly he almost missed it.

''You love me?''

Her blue eyes sparkling with moisture, she nodded. In two strides he reached her and pulled her into his arms. Ignoring her half-uttered protests, he claimed her mouth. After a long, heartfelt kiss, he drew back and looked down at her. ''If you love me, then what's the problem?''

''The problem is my career. I can't just abandon all my dreams, all my hard work. Even—even for you.''

Stunned at her words, he released her. ''Damn, Tessa, I would never ask you to do that. But anyone can see that you're happy here. That you love teaching.'' She protested, but determined to make her listen, he continued. ''When you talk about China, or Peru, you get all uptight. I can see the worry lines forming. But when you talk about teaching, you shine. When you talk about making a difference to a student, your whole face lights up. Just the other day you went on and on about the student who'd decided to switch majors. Because of you. You said you felt that you'd made a difference.''

She winced, then lifted her chin. ''Teaching isn't my career,'' she insisted. ''I can't waste these opportunities.''

Opportunities. It hit him then, where he'd heard that phrase before. Her mother. God knows what else the woman had drilled into her mind. He'd only heard a minuscule portion of that one conversation, but he didn't need to be Einstein to know the woman was a control freak. "This isn't you talking. It's your mother. The other—that's your mother's career, the one she wants for you. Not the career *you* want."

She stared at him as if he was crazy. As if she'd never even considered that possibility. But how could she not know something so obvious? There had to be a way to open her eyes to the truth.

"Don't you see? You're doing what she wants you to do, and pretending to yourself it's what you want." And he couldn't figure out why. What kind of number had the woman done on her?

"I'm not pretending anything. I've trained for an opportunity like this, worked for it for years. How dare you tell me what I want, what I think?"

"Somebody has to." His voice rose in anger, so frustrated he wanted to curse, or to put his fist through a wall. "You're too busy following your mother's dictates to recognize what you really want. Or what would make you happiest." Damn it, he shouldn't have said it, shouldn't have lost his temper, but he couldn't stand her blind obedience to her mother's commands. Why was it so important to her to please a woman who didn't even love her?

The color had drained from her face. "To claim to be in love with me, you sure don't think much of me."

"Tessa." He stretched out a hand, but let it fall when she shrank from him. "I'm sorry. I shouldn't have said that."

"Only if you didn't mean it. But you meant it, didn't you, Will?"

If he could kick his own butt, he would. *Way to go, McClain. Insult her, that'll help.* "Can you honestly say you want the career your mother has mapped out for you—exactly as she hands it to you—without any doubts?"

"Of course I have doubts. Everyone does. But that doesn't mean I'm willing to throw away everything I've worked for." He made an impatient gesture of denial, but she continued. "What if I asked you to give up your career for me? If I asked you to quit the Rangers and come with me? Would you do it?"

"I'm not asking you to give up your career, damn it! I'm asking you to give us a chance to be together."

"On your terms."

He frowned, wondering how they'd gotten to this point. "The last thing I want to do is argue with you. Can't we talk about this rationally?"

"I don't know. Apparently not." She turned away and spoke softly. Not angry anymore, but resigned. "We want different things, Will. I want a career that will take me all over the world. You want a woman who'll stay in one place and make a home for you."

Will shoved a hand through his hair, tempted to rip it out in frustration. She wanted the same thing he did, only she was too damned stubborn to see it. "Am I supposed to apologize for wanting to marry you? For wanting a wife and family someday?" For wanting a normal life, with a woman he loved. Wanting to have kids and friends, to go fishing early on a Sunday morning or have the luxury of knowing he could roll over in bed and make love to his wife. To be married to a flesh-and-blood woman, and not live only for his work.

"Of course not." She laid a hand on his arm. "But that's your dream, Will. Not mine." Her gaze was soft, compassionate.

"Are you so sure of that?"

"I've known what I— I've known my career path since I was twelve years old."

His point, exactly. She'd known her path ever since she'd been brainwashed into believing that's what she wanted. But Tessa wasn't interested in logic. Maybe emotion would help her see the truth. "You said you loved me."

"I do love you."

"Then why won't you even consider the possibility that you've changed? That what you once wanted isn't necessarily what you want now?"

"Because I haven't changed," she insisted stubbornly. "I didn't—falling in love wasn't in my plans. I have to think of my career."

He couldn't believe their entire relationship had fallen apart in the space of minutes. Infuriated, hurt, he grasped her arms and jerked her up against him. Her eyes widened and she stared at him. "Think about this," he said, and crushed his mouth to hers.

He meant to shock her out of her obstinate refusal to listen. He hadn't counted on the feel of her causing him to go up in flames. And the knowledge that he could lose her turning the flame into a full-blown inferno.

Whatever her words, her body responded to his. She flung her arms around his neck, tightening her hold the longer and harder he kissed her. Her fingers speared through his hair, her breasts rubbed against his chest, tormenting him.

"Do you really want to give this up? The way we make each other feel?" He kissed her again, his hands sliding over her bottom to pull her closer, to push his aching erection between the softness of her thighs.

"Don't talk," she said, breathless. "Just kiss me."

His fingers slid beneath the skimpy shorts she wore, to stroke, to tease. Desperate, he looked around for somewhere besides the splintery wooden dock to lay her down and finish what they'd started. An oak tree stood near the dock, the grass beneath it soft and inviting, the shadows it cast dark and concealing. He urged her over there, his hands fumbling with her shorts, unbuttoning, unzipping, greedy to feel her naked flesh.

"Will. Oh, hurry."

Mouths fused together, they sank into the grass. Her hands were everywhere, then suddenly she was unzipping his shorts, closing her warm fingers around his erection.

The thought hit him as she was poised above him. "No...condom," he panted. Gazes locked, he held her above him. The thought of being inside her with nothing between them made him harder than he'd ever been in his life.

She lowered herself onto him. "It's...all right."
Her eyes closed, her head fell back, she lifted herself
up and slid down slowly, sensuously. "Wrong time,"
she gasped out.

He sure as hell hoped so, because there was no possible way he could stop and she wasn't stopping, either. She rode him, her muscles contracting, tightening
and releasing, until he came in a fierce torrent. She
gave a hoarse cry, sank down on him a final time,
convulsing tightly around him for what seemed like
forever.

Sanity returned gradually. Tessa collapsed on top of
him, her face buried against his neck. He felt moisture,
felt the shudders running through her, and knew she
was crying.

"You're still leaving, aren't you?"

"I have to, Will."

There was nothing left to say, nothing that hadn't
been said already. They dressed in silence and he
walked her to her door.

"Are you—" She cleared her throat and started
over. "Are you staying?"

He gazed at her for a long, intense moment. Though
the tears were gone, traces of them showed on her
cheeks, and in her eyes. "Do you want me to stay?"
For tonight, he thought bleakly.

"Yes."

"Then I will." He laid a hand on her arm to stop
her from going inside. "You could be pregnant."

Her eyes widened. "I'm not. I told you it was all
right."

"But you could be."

"I—yes. It's possible, but not likely."

"If you are, we'll work it out."

"How?" she whispered.

"I don't know," he admitted. "But we'll think of something. Just promise me you'll tell me."

"I wouldn't keep something that important from you."

He nodded and followed her inside. It was a mistake to stay, he thought, but he didn't care. He'd lie in a cold, lonely bed soon enough.

CHAPTER SIXTEEN

AT DAWN, Tessa woke to find Will already gone from her bed. She hadn't slept much during the night, and she knew Will hadn't, either. Neither did they talk. Instead, they made love, hungrily, desperately, and marked with a sorrow that had never before been present between them. But what could she do to change it?

She couldn't abandon a career she'd spent years working toward. No more than Will could be expected to toss his career in law enforcement into the garbage. When she'd made that comment, she hadn't been serious, but had only wanted to show him what he was asking of her. Due to her mother's efforts, she had an opportunity to take part in something most archaeologists would kill to be able to do. How could she ignore that?

Deep inside she wanted to go with her heart, but her heart had betrayed her before. You couldn't trust your heart, Tessa had found, because it saw what it wanted to see, not harsh reality.

A sound from the doorway drew her attention. Will walked in, bringing her a cup of coffee. She accepted it gratefully with a murmured thanks, and sipped it as he sat beside her.

''We need to talk,'' he said.

He looked solemn and heart-stoppingly handsome. He must have been up for a while, for he'd showered and shaved, his blond hair still damp, combed back from his face, with an unruly lock falling over his forehead. He wore his customary work clothes, a pale blue button-down dress shirt, nicely pressed, faded jeans and boots. Sighing, she remembered he'd been wearing something similar the first time she saw him, and she'd been overwhelmed by his sheer presence. Sometimes she still was.

And she was leaving him. It wasn't fair that she had to make this decision. Why couldn't she have met him earlier, or later? Any time but now. ''There's nothing to talk about,'' she said, squeezing the words out through a tight throat. ''Talking won't change anything.''

''I know. That's why...'' His voice trailed off. He leaned forward, propping his forearms on his thighs, and stared straight ahead.

After a long moment, he turned to her and she read the pain and confusion in his eyes. She'd never seen Will so uncertain of himself, hadn't thought he *could* be so unsure. Shaken, she set her coffee mug on the nightstand and waited for him to speak.

''I can't do this, Tessa. I can't be with you, knowing you're counting down the days until you go to China. I can't wonder how many more times I'll kiss you, hold you, make love with you. And I can't put my life on hold while you spend two or three years halfway around the world.''

"I never—I don't expect you to."

He smiled ruefully. "Maybe you don't, but I seem to have different expectations. Falling in love with you made me want things I—I never believed I could have. A home. A family. After Frannie disappeared, I figured that was my last shot at family. And then you came along."

"Will—"

"I wanted those things with you, thought I could have them with you. But you said it yourself, yesterday. We don't want the same things."

"What are you saying?" she asked, forcing the words out. She waited with her heart slamming against her ribs.

His eyes were dark gray, as flat and lifeless as she'd ever seen them. "I'm saying goodbye," he said hoarsely.

"Goodbye?" she echoed. "Now?" Her heart twisted. She'd known it would end, but she had wanted the last weeks, wanted to savor the time they did have together.

Face grim, he nodded. "I thought I could handle it, but last night...after last night I knew I was kidding myself. I'm sorry, but I can't—I can't look at you every day and know I'm losing you." He looked miserable, as miserable as she felt. "I need a clean break. It's the only way I can...deal with things."

"Don't go," she choked out, tears filling her eyes and trickling down her cheeks. "I love you."

He stared at her, his gaze more impenetrable than

the moss hanging from the Caddo cypress. "Maybe you do. But it's not enough, is it?"

"I wish…you don't know how much I wish things could be different."

"Yeah," he said heavily. "So do I." He leaned over, took her face in his hands and gazed at her, as if memorizing every detail. "Be happy," he said, and kissed her.

He put her away from him, roughly, and strode to the door. Once there, he halted and turned to look at her. "You'll call me if you're—if you're pregnant?" Unable to speak, she nodded. "I'll get my stuff when you're not here. It'll be…easier that way." The next moment he was gone.

And Tessa lay down and cried until she had no more tears left.

WILL DID THE ONLY THING he knew to do. He buried himself in his work. Nothing would make him feel better, other than Tessa suddenly changing her mind and staying in Uncertain. But she'd made her choice abundantly clear.

He'd made the right decision to end it cleanly. When your life fell apart, you endured it, you picked up the pieces and you moved on. That lesson had been burned into his soul from the age of eight, when his mother had deserted him. From foster home after foster home. From Frannie's disappearance when he was seventeen and he'd hitchhiked out of Uncertain one step ahead of the foster care system.

Damn straight, he'd learned that lesson.

ARMED WITH a twenty-year-old phone book, which he cross-referenced with a current one, Will spent the next several days slowly wading through the pages, calling the area jewelry stores, starting with the ones closest to Uncertain. First, he culled the ones that had gone into business after 1982, the date of Frannie's death. The ones that had been operating in 1982 and had gone out of business since, he set aside to deal with later, if necessary.

Given his specific criteria, he didn't have a lot of places to try. One morning he paid a visit to a shop in Longview that currently carried silver glasses cases, and had in the past as well. Over the phone, the owner had agreed to look at the police sketch of the object, but Will didn't get his hopes up. He'd found one other store that carried the items and had learned nothing new from them.

Augustus Perdue had owned The Jewel Box, his small but exclusive jewelry store in downtown Longview, for over thirty years. Will glanced around, noticing the quiet elegance of the place. Nice. Must be doing all right to have stayed in business so long.

Dark green plush carpet covered the floor. Queen Anne chairs were scattered around, some in front of brightly lit display cases that stood out in the muted lighting of the store. The wedding set display caught his eye and a sharp pain stabbed his heart. Fortunately, the jeweler came out, so he didn't have to think about Tessa and his broken dreams for long.

To Will's surprise, Perdue greeted him enthusiastically, leading the way to his small office in the back and telling the clerk not to bother him. A small man, Perdue had a mess of untidy gray hair and wore a neat gray suit. His deep brown eyes were as sharp and bright as the diamonds he worked with.

"I'm a big believer in supporting the police," he told Will, closing the door behind him. He pulled a pile of papers from a chair and tossed them aside, offering the chair to Will. "Or the Rangers, or any arm of the law. I'd have been a dead man a few years back if the local cops hadn't shot an armed robber who came in here."

"I appreciate your cooperation. I'll get right to the point," Will said, pulling the sketch out of his pocket. "Do you recognize this design as something you've carried?"

Humming an off-key tune, the jeweler studied the paper for a moment. "Hold on a minute." He left the room, returning a few minutes later brandishing a silver case. "This isn't exactly like the one in the sketch, but it's close. I've carried this line for about ten years now."

Wishing he'd gotten a better look at the one on Ray Jennings's desk, Will studied it, then raised his gaze to Perdue's. "According to my sources, the case in question was only manufactured from 1975 to 1985." He named the manufacturer and asked without a lot of hope, "Do you remember if you carried that brand?"

He nodded briskly. "Sure did. I carried a lot of items from that manufacturer. I don't get a lot of call for these—" he tapped the case in Will's hand

"—but every now and then someone will want one. Good markup. Worth keeping in stock." He scratched his head, clearly pondering. "Matter of fact, one of my regulars goes in for this sort of thing. Don't know if you know him. He's a banker over in Uncertain, name of Ray Jennings. Partial to anything sterling. His wife, though, she leans toward the gold."

Hot damn! Too good to be true, Will thought. "Would you remember if you sold him a case, say, nineteen or twenty years ago, or so?"

Perdue shook his head regretfully. "Sorry. But he has bought several over the years."

Will picked up the paper in preparation to leave. It was a long shot, but he asked anyway. "How long do you keep your sales receipts?"

"Forever. Have them going back to the day I opened," he said proudly. "Martha, that's my wife, she says I'm a pack rat. But I like keeping the information on hand. Never know when it might come in handy. You want to look at them?"

Good thing he didn't have allergies, Will thought a short time later as they began sifting through the files. The dusty files, kept in open cardboard boxes, could trigger a major attack. Even with Perdue helping, it was slow going, but finding a receipt would make any amount of time spent worthwhile. Proof of purchase might not hang Jennings, but it would sure as hell incriminate him.

It took them two hours, but Will left the place armed with Perdue's good wishes and two receipts for sales of silver glasses cases to one Raymond Jennings of

Uncertain, Texas. One dated August of 1981 and another, for an identical case, dated shortly after Frannie's murder. Still circumstantial evidence, but as damning as any of the evidence against Jed.

Now he had to decide how to play this in order to have the best shot of proving Ray Jennings had killed Frannie Granger. Because even though the glasses case placed Ray at the site, and even though Will was becoming more certain by the day that Jennings was indeed the murderer, he still lacked motive. Why would Jennings have killed Frannie?

Still undecided about his best course of action, Will left Longview and headed for the Cypress Bank and Trust. As he crossed the lobby on his way to Jennings's office, he found his way blocked by five feet seven inches of platinum blond bombshell. Amanda. Great, just what he needed.

"Will! Where have you been hiding yourself?" She put her hand on his upper arm and squeezed lightly, brushing herself up against him and fluttering her eyelashes. "Don't you have time for your old friends anymore?"

Will opened his mouth to brush her off with a quick comment, but something in the eyes gazing hopefully at him changed his mind. Amanda must be awfully lonely, he thought, to try so hard to latch on to him when he'd shown so little interest. His pity stirred, he stayed to talk to her a minute, allowing her to pull him aside to a small seating area arranged against one wall. Ray wasn't going anywhere Will couldn't find him.

"I've been around," he said. "Working on Frannie's case."

"You know what they say about all work." Voice husky, eyes sultry, she squeezed his arm again, this time deliberately rubbing her breasts against him.

If they'd been alone she'd have had him down on the floor in no time flat, he thought, grateful they weren't.

"Tell me it's not true."

"What's not true?" he asked, a little dazed by the come-on.

She batted her blue eyes at him and all he could think was that they were nowhere near as pretty as Tessa's.

"I heard a rumor about you and that archaeologist." She laughed, placing her other hand on his chest. "And of course, I couldn't believe it. You're not living with the woman, are you, Will?"

"Not anymore," he said without thinking. *Shit, now he'd done it. Stupid move, McClain.*

"Good," she said, her voice a husky purr. Her fingers walked up his chest, the bracelet on her wrist tracing a trail as they went. "Why don't you come pick me up tonight and we'll go somewhere—" she pursed slick red lips "—private. Very private."

Women had come on to him before, though never quite this blatantly. He gazed down at her. She was pretty, if a bit overdone. There was no reason he couldn't take her up on her offer. No reason he shouldn't lose himself in hot, no-strings-attached sex.

Except that he didn't want Amanda in his bed or in his life. He wanted Tessa.

He heard a stifled shriek and turned around to see Joleen Berber, Frannie's best friend. Her round face drained of color, she stood stone still, staring at them. Her hands curled into fists, her breath came in short, staccato gasps.

"Joleen, are you all right?" he asked, concerned she might be having a heart attack. The older woman had been in poor health for years now, he knew from Emmy and also from seeing her himself when he'd interviewed her several weeks before.

Amanda huffed out an exasperated sigh as Joleen tottered toward them. But she wasn't looking at Will. She was staring straight at Amanda with a ghastly expression on her face.

"Is that— Where did you get that?" she asked, stretching a blue-veined, trembling hand toward Amanda.

"Will, what is wrong with her?" Amanda demanded in an urgent undertone, shrinking against him. "Ooh, she's giving me the creeps."

"Joleen, let me help you," he said, moving out of Amanda's grasp to take the older woman's arm. The woman's whole body quaked, and he grew more alarmed. "Can I get you some water?" Or call a doctor, he thought.

She shook him off with surprising strength. Ignoring him, she addressed Amanda. "Please. Where did you get that—that bracelet?"

Amanda flicked her wrist impatiently. "This?" she

asked, indicating an intricately tooled pearl, emerald and gold bracelet. "From my mother, not that it's any of your concern. It's a family piece, part of a set."

"A family heir—heirloom?" she asked brokenly, then moaned pitifully when Amanda nodded.

"Really, Will," Amanda whispered in another urgent aside, "the woman needs to see a doctor."

"I'm s-sorry," Joleen stammered out. Blinking rapidly, she looked away. "I didn't mean...I have to go." She turned and rushed toward the entrance.

Hampered by the ever-clinging Amanda, Will went after her.

Ray Jennings entered the building just as Joleen, in her haste, crashed into him and cried out. Startled, Ray grabbed her arms, preventing her from toppling backward. Will reached them just as Joleen, staring up at the man, her expression one of sheer terror, crumpled into a dead faint. Jennings caught her before she hit the ground, thank God, preventing no telling how many broken bones.

"What the hell?" Jennings said, supporting the limp form whether he wanted to or not. "Someone call the paramedics. This woman is ill."

A short time later, Joleen had recovered enough to sit on the couch and sip a glass of water. After being assured of the older woman's well-being, Jennings went to his office, obviously irritated by the scene she'd caused.

Amanda, fuming at the interruption, left after tucking a note into Will's shirt pocket and whispering a highly erotic suggestion in his ear. He blessed Joleen for her timing, if nothing else.

In spite of Joleen's protests that she didn't need medical attention, the paramedics checked her out to be safe. "Her blood pressure's low, and her respiration's a bit shallow, but she seems all right," the medic told Will after examining her. "She refuses to come to the hospital, but it might be better if she had someone to watch her at home for a little while. Bring her in if she does it again. You a relative?"

"No, just a friend. But I'll take her home." Because he meant to get to the bottom of Joleen's behavior. She'd been frightened to the point of fainting at the sight of Raymond Jennings.

Will intended to find out why.

CHAPTER SEVENTEEN

BY THE TIME Will drove Joleen home, she'd regained her color and looked much better. Good thing, because he couldn't see badgering her for an answer to her strange behavior if she'd continued to look ill.

Besides, he had a few fond memories of the older woman, dating back to the first time he'd met her. Joleen had still been nursing then, and since Will refused to go to the hospital, Frannie had asked her to treat his injuries, courtesy of the bastard from his most recent foster home. Even though she obviously hadn't approved of him, Joleen had been kind and gentle to the scared kid he'd been.

Emmy had told him Joleen had changed. He'd thought her odd himself, he remembered, when he'd interviewed her. But not as weird as she'd been at the bank.

Joleen knew something. Something important, if his hunch was right.

"You don't need to stay, Will," she said nervously. "I'm fine. Had a touch of flu the other day and I'm sure that's what it was. Why, I fainted right out, here at home, too. You just can't tell with that flu bug, what's going to happen."

Will took a seat beside her on her drab brown twill

sofa. Everything about the place was drab, including its owner. The strong odor of stale cigarettes permeated everything, including the air. "Good, I'm glad you're feeling better. Because I need to ask you some more questions."

"Questions?" Her faded blue eyes widened in alarm behind her glasses. Lanky gray hair surrounded her face, half-hiding her jaw. The soft, aged skin of her round face wrinkled in concern. "I already told you what I remembered about the day—the day Frannie disappeared."

"Not that day. I'm talking about today." He asked the question softly, keeping his eyes on her face. "Why does Ray Jennings scare you, Joleen?"

Her pupils dilated. Her breath came faster. "He doesn't. I told you, I've been sick."

"You weren't sick. You were scared to death when you realized who he was. I know, I've seen that look before. Remember, I'm a cop."

"You're mis-mistaken," she stammered. "I just fainted because I've been sick. That's all."

Right, and he was the tooth fairy. "If you're frightened of him I can help. I can protect you if you need it." She didn't speak and he continued, "Did it have something to do with the bracelet?" That little episode had been as weird as Joleen fainting in Ray Jennings's arms.

Joleen compressed her lips, her normally cherubic expression hardening. She started to rock, a slight swaying of her body, staring ahead of her as if she saw something. A memory?

Finally she whispered, "You'll think I'm terrible. But I didn't steal it. Not really. She owed it to me. She owed me, I tell you. I paid for the funeral." She turned to Will, eyes suddenly crafty. "Cost me money I couldn't afford. And I took good care of her. Tried my best to help her. It wasn't my fault she…died."

Totally confused, Will asked, "Who died?"

"Emmy's mother. Ginny Owens, her name was."

To say he was rocked didn't even touch it. "Emmy Monday? You're talking about Emmy Monday's mother? You knew her?"

Twisting her hands together, Joleen nodded. "I met her when I was working at the free clinic in Tyler. She was such a sweet thing. Some slick-talking man had left her pregnant, and she was alone, like so many of the girls. Parents kicked her out when she turned up pregnant." She sniffed, dismissing the parents. "Can you imagine, just turning your daughter out to fend for herself at a time like that? Girl wouldn't hear of going to a home. Said she didn't intend to give the child up. Besides, she was afraid the father of the child would find her if she did."

"And that would have been bad?"

Joleen snorted and rolled her eyes. "The dirty bum had given her money for an abortion, but she wouldn't do it. She didn't know when she let him talk her into bed, but he was married—scared to death Ginny would make a mess of things for him."

Still floundering but beginning to see light, Will said, "This married man who fathered Emmy is…"

"Raymond Jennings," Joleen pronounced without hesitation. "The bank president himself."

Given Joleen's reaction, he'd suspected that, but to have it confirmed sent adrenaline rushing through his bloodstream. He started to ask for confirmation, but once she'd begun, Joleen didn't stop.

"I never liked him. No, never. Why I swear, he always looked right through me, even though I've been banking there all my life. Thinks he's too good for the likes of me." She snorted, obviously miffed at the shoddy treatment Jennings had given her.

Attempting to get back to the point, Will asked, "Do you know this for a fact? That Raymond Jennings is Emmy's father?" If she did, why hadn't she ever told Emmy? And why hadn't she told Emmy of her mother?

"Not for a fact. But who else could it be when his daughter, his *legitimate* daughter, is sporting that gold, pearl and emerald bracelet? The bracelet that goes with the brooch."

Will resisted the urge to rub his temples or ask Joleen just what the hell bracelets and brooches had to do with anything. Mustering patience, he said, "Joleen, I'm still mystified. Can you start from the beginning and tell me the story?"

"All right. But let me get something first." She disappeared into another room, returning a few moments later clutching something in her hand. "Here. Take it. I could never do anything with it, anyway, what with Frannie talking on so about losing it."

She dropped it in his palm. Will stared at a piece

of jewelry. A brooch in the shape of a gold tree, a big pearl at its base, emeralds dotting the branches. Amanda's bracelet had pearls and emeralds, he remembered. And according to her, it had been part of a set. No wonder Joleen had been struck speechless at the sight of it.

"That's a Caddo pearl there," Joleen said, pointing to the lustrous white gem. "Just like the ones in the bracelet that Amanda Jennings was wearing today. Ginny Owens pinned this brooch in the basket the day she died giving birth to Emmy."

Defiantly she raised her chin and repeated her earlier words. "Ginny owed me something for taking care of her funeral. And for taking care of her baby like she begged me to. That's why I took the baby to Canton. To make sure Frannie got her. Emmy never suffered not having her mother, not while Frannie lived. I did right by her, and by Frannie, too, giving her a child she could love like one of her own."

"How did Frannie know about the brooch, if you've had it all this time?" He remembered the stories, of course, that Frannie had told Emmy. About a beautiful pearl and emerald brooch that had belonged to her mother. Emmy's legacy, Frannie had called it. Except it had disappeared a few weeks after Emmy had been found at the Canton First Monday trade fair and had come to live with Frannie.

"You didn't know it was there, did you? When you put Emmy in that basket, you didn't realize the brooch was in there, too."

Looking ashamed, Joleen nodded. "But when I saw

it, when Frannie showed it to me, I—I couldn't help it. It was so beautiful, and it didn't seem right I should have nothing.'' Indignation strengthened her voice. ''Not after all I did for the pair of them. What did a little baby need with something like that anyway?''

Will didn't respond to her attempts at self-justification, but she continued regardless.

''Even then, I wouldn't have done it if Frannie hadn't kept talking of tracing the parents through the brooch. Ginny was scared of the father, I tell you, and I was afraid what would happen if Frannie ever found him. So I took it. To protect them, that's all I wanted,'' she said virtuously.

Nice rationalization, Will thought. ''So when you saw Amanda's bracelet, and especially when she told you it was a family heirloom, you knew Ray Jennings was the father. The man Ginny Owens had been afraid of.''

''And I was right to be afraid. Look what happened to Frannie.''

''But Frannie didn't know, did she? About Ray?''

''No, at least... The day before she disappeared, Frannie was upset about something. She never would say what, though. Even to me, her best friend.'' She leaned forward and grasped Will's hand. ''But she cleaned house for the Jennings. If she'd seen that set, she would have known Ray Jennings was Emmy's father.''

Will frowned. ''But if that's true, why did she never see the set before then?''

Joleen tossed her head in disgust. ''People like that

have so much jewelry, they can't wear all of it. Maybe Mrs. Jennings just never kept it out for Frannie to see. Or maybe she kept it in the bank and only took it out for special occasions. Besides, Frannie hadn't worked for the Jennings but for three or four years. Could be Mrs. Jennings never wore it much.''

True, Will thought. And it wasn't the sort of jewelry a woman would wear every day. Unless you were Amanda, he amended, and flaunted your jewelry. But Catherine Jennings wasn't like her daughter.

''Frannie would have confronted him,'' Will said. Not a doubt of that. Frannie had always had a strong sense of right and wrong. She'd have demanded Ray own up to his obligations, and she wouldn't have cared that the banker would lose Catherine Jennings and her family fortune if the truth came out.

So Raymond Jennings had reason to protect his marriage, to keep the truth about his illegitimate daughter from coming out. A hell of a motive for murder.

WILL TRIED NOT TO THINK about how this turn of events would affect Emmy. She'd told him she wanted to know her birth parents, had even searched for them, before quitting because someone—Ray Jennings, he'd bet—had threatened Riley and Alanna. Will didn't think the knowledge that her father was a murderer would comfort her much. But he couldn't focus on Emmy now. He'd consider how to tell her later. Right now he had to concentrate on the case. On the law and how to proceed to catch a killer.

Once again, he had circumstantial evidence. Strong evidence, but was it enough to convince the D.A. to proceed? And if the D.A. did proceed, what then? With a good lawyer, Jennings might get off. Will meant to see he paid for his crime. The only way to insure that he did would be to obtain a court admissible confession from the suspect himself.

It didn't take him long to realize Catherine Jennings was the weak link. Ray would deny everything. But if Will surprised Catherine with the brooch, that could provoke a spontaneous response. He'd bet Catherine Jennings wouldn't be any too pleased to discover the proof of Ray's infidelity, in the form of one Emerald Monday Gray Wolf.

He needed to show Catherine the brooch with Ray present. But they couldn't be forewarned, because his plan would only work if a surprise. Fielder, that's who he needed to bring in on this. For one thing, it was his case, too. For another, Will looked forward to proving to the old man that he'd been wrong about Jed's guilt all along.

As always, he found Fielder in his office. And just as Will had expected, the sheriff was skeptical of his theory. Until Will filled him in on the details of his morning. The older man's frown grew heavier as Will showed him the receipts for the glasses cases, then told him the events at the bank, followed by Joleen's confession.

"Let me see this brooch," Fielder said, rising to face Will. "I don't see how you or Joleen Berber can be so sure it's from the set of jewelry that belongs to

Catherine Jennings. And as for Frannie Granger discovering it in Emmy Monday's basket and then the thing being stolen—'' he snorted in disbelief ''—it all sounds pretty danged far-fetched to me.''

''Far-fetched, maybe. But logical, when you think about it,'' Will said, handing the piece over to the sheriff. Fielder studied it a long moment.

''She—she wore this set to the last Anglers' Ball, just a few weeks ago,'' he said slowly, naming an annual charity event all of Uncertain and most of East Texas attended. ''The department is in charge of security for it, and I was standing by the front door when she came in.'' His gaze met Will's, the surprise in it evident. ''Joleen Berber is right. This brooch looks just like the necklace and earrings Catherine Jennings wore that night. Even at a ball like that, those pieces stood out. Never seen the like of them.''

''So you agree it would be worthwhile to see Mrs. Jennings's reaction to this brooch?''

''I'm not saying I buy the whole thing,'' Fielder warned, ''but yeah, it's worth a shot.''

''Great. I want to show this to Catherine. I'll call and ask to see her at home, as soon as we finish up here. I want Jennings to show up while I'm doing it. Can you manage to get him there?''

Fielder nodded. ''I reckon.''

''Obviously, you can't tell him anything about the brooch. If you just let him know I'm at the house questioning his wife, that will probably be enough to bring him home fast.''

''I'm coming with him,'' Fielder said. ''Because if

this cockamamie story is true, then there's no telling what he'll do when his wife finds out.''

Will grimaced. ''He's no threat to her. He needs the family money too much.''

''Oh, I'm not worried about what he'll do to his wife. But you're another matter. You need backup.''

''I can handle Ray Jennings,'' Will said. And it would be a pleasure. ''But if you feel the need to be there, that's your privilege. It's your case, too.''

''And don't you forget it.'' He stared at Will a moment, flinty eyes unreadable. ''About Louis, if it turns out I was wrong, I'm sorry for it. I know it caused you a lot of grief. Him, too.''

Surprised at the gruff apology, Will nodded. ''You had cause to suspect him. I never denied that. I just never agreed that he was your only suspect.'' It shamed him that he'd suspected Jed at all, but that wasn't something he'd admit to Fielder. ''But Jed's the one you'll need to apologize to, not me.''

And Will wanted to be there to see it.

USHERED INTO A coldly formal sitting room at the Jennings mansion, Will crossed the Aubusson carpet covering the hardwood floor to the woman seated like a queen awaiting peons. Decorated in shades of gold and white, antique silk Louis XIV chairs flanked a white damask sofa. The sitting room was about as welcoming as the ice queen expression on Catherine Jennings's expensively maintained face.

Catherine inclined her head, her smooth blond hair glinting in the light. No brassy dyes for Amanda's mother, Will thought, wondering how much money she spent to maintain her classic, youthful image.

"What is it you want, Ranger McClain?"

He hoped his timing was right and that Fielder would bring Ray Jennings home from the bank shortly. "I believe I have something that belongs to you, Mrs. Jennings."

"My missing flat silver?" Her eyebrow arched. "I reported that loss to Logan Fielder six months ago. Four spoons and three forks. Sterling, of course. Francis I. Don't tell me he's finally found it. Was it that maid I told him to question?"

"No, ma'am. Not silver." Hearing a racket outside the room, he smiled to himself. He hadn't wanted Catherine to have to wait too long before her husband's arrival. He and the sheriff had coordinated their movements as closely as possible, but some of it had to be left to chance.

Will reached into his pocket and pulled out the pearl and emerald brooch, silently handing it to her. "Is this yours, Mrs. Jennings?"

Catherine stared blankly down at the piece of jewelry. "What—where did you get this? It's part of a set made for my grandmother. I don't understand. How can that be?"

"You recognize this piece of jewelry, then?"

"Of course I do." She looked up at Will just as Ray Jennings burst through the open doorway with Fielder on his heels. "It's the missing piece to my set. My grandmother's set. Where on earth did you find it?"

"What the hell do you mean, invading our privacy? You dare come here and question my wife?" Ray thundered from the doorway. "Catherine, my dear, you don't have to answer any questions."

Will smiled. "I'm not here to ask questions, Mr. Jennings. I'm returning something that belongs to your wife."

Catherine stared at the brooch in her hands as if she couldn't believe her eyes, then slowly raised her gaze to meet Will's. "I haven't seen this piece in more than thirty years."

Ray paled, stepping forward to go to his wife. She held out her hand, the brooch lying in her open palm. "It appears Ranger McClain found something that belongs to me."

"I don't know what kind of trick you're pulling, McClain, but you can get the hell out of my house!"

Catherine ignored his outburst. "The last time I saw this brooch, Raymond, was just before you took it to have it cleaned as a surprise for me. You told me it was stolen from the jeweler's."

"Catherine, I can explain."

She turned to Will. "You didn't answer me, Ranger McClain. Where did you get this?"

"The brooch was pinned to the lining of the basket Emerald Monday was found in, thirty-two years ago. Her mother, Ginny Owens, gave it to her as the only token she had from the child's father."

"You don't know what you're talking about," Ray shouted. "The damn jeweler was a thief! He must have sold my wife's brooch to this woman."

Catherine spared him one annihilating glance. "Go on, Ranger McClain. Why is this only now coming to light? Has this Emerald Monday had my brooch in her possession all this time?"

"No. It was stolen when she was only a few weeks old. From Frances Granger's house," Will said, looking at Ray. "But she told Emmy about the brooch, and that it was a legacy from her mother."

"This is ludicrous," Ray blustered. "I'll have your goddamn badge for this, McClain!" Fielder took a step closer to him. "I didn't even know this woman. Ginny, whatever he said her name was. He's lying, Catherine."

"Someone is lying, Raymond. I think we all know who that is," Catherine said, her voice colder than a glacier. She walked over to him. Fielder stood aside, shooting a warning glance at Will.

Catherine stared at her husband for a long moment. Suddenly she slapped his face with a sharp crack. His head jerked back, but otherwise he didn't move. Didn't speak.

But Catherine did. "How dare you? How dare you give my jewelry, my family heirloom, to that little floozy? Did you think I would have forgotten her name? You swore to me the affair was over."

"It was over." His head came up and he glared at his wife. "I had to do something, had to give her something to pacify her. She was supposed to have an abortion. It was never supposed to come to this."

"So you gave her my jewelry, to pay her off for having your illegitimate child."

''Damn it, there was never supposed to be a child! I told the little bitch to have an abortion! How was I to know she hadn't done it?''

''But you found out, didn't you, Ray?'' Motioning to Fielder to watch Catherine, Will crossed to the banker's side. ''Nineteen years ago you discovered Ginny Owens had never had the abortion you paid her to have. When Frannie told you that you were Emerald Monday's father.''

''Snoopy, interfering old bitch!'' Ray said, his face contorted with rage. ''She wouldn't listen, wouldn't agree not to expose it all. I offered her money and she laughed in my face. Spouted insanities about integrity and doing what was right.''

''So she had to die.'' Will said it quietly, careful not to accuse the man of the crime, but leaving him plenty of rope to hang himself.

Eyes bulging wildly, he gazed at his wife, standing stone cold in shock. ''I didn't mean to, I was only trying to keep her quiet! For us, for you and me.''

''Raymond.'' Catherine's face drained of color. ''You killed that woman?'' she whispered. ''You— murdered her?''

''No! She fell and hit her head. Goddamn it, it was an accident! Not murder! I didn't mean to hurt her, I swear, I only meant to scare her. To make her shut up, but she just kept on.'' He grabbed his wife's arms and shook her. ''The bitch wouldn't listen to reason. Kept saying I had to do the right thing. She would have ruined everything, made me a laughingstock, made me own up to fathering that trashy little nobody.''

"Let go of me." Her voice shook. Her skin, already pale, looked bloodless now. "Let go of me, right now."

His hands dropped away. The flush died as well, leaving his skin an ashen hue. He looked old, defeated. Scared shitless.

"Surely you don't think... It was an accident, I tell you! I made a mistake! I'm not a killer, Catherine. You know I'm not."

"I don't know you at all," Catherine Jennings said, and walked out of the room.

"I'll see if I can find someone to be with her," Fielder said. "You take care of him." He jerked his head toward Jennings, staring vacantly at the empty doorway. "I guess you earned this one, McClain."

"Raymond Jennings," Will said, stepping forward and taking his arm, "you are under arrest for the murder of Frances Granger."

CHAPTER EIGHTEEN

THANKS TO DEPUTY MASTERS thinking Tessa and Will were still together, he allowed her to wait for Will in his office. Tessa had debated calling him, but in the end decided a phone call was too impersonal for her news.

After all, a man deserved to be told in person he wasn't going to be a father.

Or maybe, she admitted, she just couldn't stand to give up the chance to see him again. Talk to him. Touch him. To see if his eyes still lit up when he saw her, or if he'd already forgotten her and put her behind him like a bad dream. *Get a grip,* she told herself. *You're only here to tell him the news. Nothing has changed, nothing is going to change.*

She seated herself at his desk, taking the only chair in the tiny room. Glancing around, she noted the bareness of the cubicle. A desk, a chair, a wastebasket. Nothing on the walls but a water stain, nothing to brighten up the drab beige color. Not much on the desk except a black cordless phone, a paper clip and an old phone book. She wondered how Will worked in so small an area, especially considering his own size. She'd be claustrophobic after ten minutes in the place. But Will probably didn't even notice the spartan surroundings, or the limited size, because when he was there, he gave his full attention to his work.

His career, which he couldn't leave any more than she could leave hers. Tessa sighed deeply and rubbed her temples. She couldn't say why, but she hadn't yet told the college her decision. Hoping for a miracle?

The door opened just then and Will strode inside, halting abruptly when he saw her. "Tessa?" He looked like he'd seen a hallucination, and not a particularly pleasant one. "What are you doing here? Are you all right?"

"I'm fine." She stood, tucking her hands into her skirt pockets, for lack of anything better to do with them. "I—needed to talk to you. I know I could have called but I—I thought—" She halted, thinking she ought to simply spit it out, but she couldn't. Just as—starved for the sight—she couldn't stop staring at him.

He stepped forward and grasped her upper arms gently, gazing into her eyes intently. "I can think of two reasons you'd be here. One is that you've changed your mind. Have you?"

Her throat closed, tears stung her eyes and she hastily blinked them away. "I haven't changed my mind," she said in a choked whisper. "I'm sorry." If only it were that easy. If she only had love to consider...

His gaze became shuttered. "So you're pregnant."

She shook her head. "No, I'm not. That's what—I thought I should tell you in person. I guess it was a stupid idea. I should have called."

His fingers tightened on her arms. "Yeah, you should have. But I'm glad you didn't." Their gazes locked. His head lowered, her heart began to pound. She could feel his breath on her lips, could almost taste him. Wanted to taste him, hold him…love him. Then his hands dropped and he turned away.

Bereft, she stood staring at his back. "You look…tired," she finally said, aching to touch him, to soothe the tiredness away.

He shrugged, taking a seat in the single chair. Propping his arms on the desk and his head in his hands, he muttered, "God."

"I'm sorry. This was a mistake. I'll go."

"Stay," he said harshly. He looked up at her, completely expressionless. "I arrested Frannie's killer today. A couple of hours ago. He gave a full confession."

"You arrested him?" If he'd arrested someone today, that meant it couldn't be Jed. He would have phrased it differently. "You cleared Jed?" Her heart leaped in happiness for him. "Will, that's wonderful."

"Yeah." He laughed without humor. "Wonderful. I'm sure Jed and Gwyn will be happy. As happy as they'll be to never have to look at my face again."

"You were doing your job. Don't you think they'll understa—"

He cut her off with a savage oath, all the more shocking since she rarely heard him curse, and never so violently or crudely.

"Jed will always think I betrayed him. Which I did. I was so goddamn focused on finding Frannie's killer, I didn't consider anything—or anyone—else." His hand curled into a fist, he pounded it once on his desk, so hard it rattled. "I knew Jed hadn't done it, but I arrested him anyway. I knew that evidence was circumstantial, and couldn't be trusted. Goddamn it, I knew he was innocent!"

Wanting to comfort, she stepped closer, laid her hand on his shoulder and squeezed. "You had no choice, given the evidence. You know you didn't. You said it yourself, if you hadn't arrested Jed, Sheriff Fielder would have."

His eyes flashed, dark gray with anger. "Do you think that's going to matter a damn to Jed? All he'll see is that I doubted him. That I didn't believe wholeheartedly in his innocence." He closed his eyes and swore. "I flat out told him I thought he could have killed her accidentally."

"I think you're doing Jed a disservice. And yourself."

He shook her off, buried his head in his hands for another long moment. Finally he looked up. "I'll find out soon enough. When I tell him he's cleared of all charges because Raymond Jennings confessed to Frannie's murder."

"Ray Jennings?" That pompous old goat? "The bank president? Why would he have killed her?"

Will smiled, grimly and without humor. "Because he didn't want Frannie to tell his wife that he had an illegitimate daughter. Living right here in Uncertain."

Frannie. Illegitimate children. A daughter. "Oh, my God. Not Emmy..."

He nodded sharply. "You got it. Emmy Monday. Frannie's foster child. My foster sister. As soon as I tell Jed he's off the hook for murder, I get to tell Emmy that the man who killed Frannie, who killed the woman she loved like her mother, was her own father.''

Tessa didn't know what to say. What to do to comfort him. But if ever a man needed unconditional support, Will needed it now. So she did the only thing she could think, the only thing that felt right. She put her arms around him, pulled his head against her breast. Ran a soothing hand over his hair, his face, patted his shoulder. "Oh, Will, I'm so sorry. It's all right. You'll find a way through this.''

His arms came around her slowly, reluctantly. Then he was holding her tightly, so tightly she had trouble drawing breath. Or was that because of the heaviness in her heart, the sorrow crushing her chest?

"How?'' he asked, his voice an agonized rumble. "How do I tell Emmy her father is Frannie's murderer?''

The sound of someone clearing his throat came from the doorway. "Sorry, I, uh, knocked.''

Slowly Will released her. Uncertain what to do, Tessa stood awkwardly beside his chair, watching as Kyle Masters entered the room with a sheaf of papers. "Sorry to interrupt, but we need your signature on this, Will.''

"No problem,'' Will said, in control once again.

Tessa marveled at how quickly the change came over him. The lawman took the place of the grieving brother, in the time it took to clear a throat. He reached into his pocket for a pen and, when he pulled it out, a piece of paper came with it, fluttering to the floor.

Tessa leaned down to pick it up, intending to hand it to him, but her hand stopped in midmotion. The words jumped out, bright as the crimson lipstick the author of the note habitually wore. "Tonight. My place. Amanda."

Deputy Masters left the room with another muttered apology. Silently Tessa handed the paper over to Will, her heart twisting as the meaning of the note hit home. She meant to ignore it, should have ignored it, but instead she said, "You didn't waste any time, did you?"

A look of chagrin crossed his face. "Tessa, it's not what you think."

"Isn't it?"

They stared at each other, then he shrugged, tossing the note down onto his desk. "Does it matter?"

"No, I guess it doesn't," she said slowly. "I have no hold—" She hesitated, wishing it weren't true. "I have no hold over you. No right to question you. You're perfectly free to date whoever you want."

"I'm not dating her." His jaw tightened, a muscle ticked in it.

"Oh, sorry." She arched an eyebrow, to appear cool even though she was dying inside. "I chose the more euphemistic term for what I'm sure Amanda has planned."

He swore, low and furiously. Then he reached for her, jerking her into his arms. Her head falling back, she gaped at him in astonishment.

"What do you want from me?" he demanded. "Do you want me to tell you it's killing me? Thinking about never seeing you again, never talking to you, never kissing you or making love to you?" His mouth came down on hers, roughly, a kiss of despair and longing.

"Then I'll tell you. It's killing me," he said again, his mouth an inch from hers, his eyes boring into hers. "It's eating me alive and there's not one goddamn thing I can do to change it."

Abruptly he released her, turned away. His voice emerged, harsh and gritty. "Go, Tessa. Just go."

And coward that she was, she fled.

FOR A MAN WHO DIDN'T LIKE emotional scenes, Will thought, he was racking them up in record numbers. He wanted to put off seeing Jed and Emmy, but they deserved to know the truth, as soon as possible. At least, Jed did. Emmy didn't deserve what was coming, but someone had to tell her. He prayed Riley would be there to comfort her, someone she could count on to love her unconditionally.

Will left his office with Tessa's sweet taste still lingering in his mouth, the feel of her in his arms a sharper pain than the bullet that had plowed through his arm during a drug raid years before. But he couldn't think about Tessa now, couldn't afford any more fragile memories or feelings or regrets.

June showed him into the parlor, the room Will was coming to think of as the place where he'd killed Jed's trust for him. Killed his belief in him. Not once but again and again. He took a deep breath and squared his shoulders. He would tell Jed what had happened and then he'd get the hell out of his brother's life.

"Why are you here? To take me back to jail?" Jed asked from the doorway. Gwyn stood behind him, a tall, beautiful woman with auburn hair and worried eyes, her hand on his shoulder in a silent show of support. Jed's mouth looked grim, his demeanor weary. He seemed older than he had even a few weeks before. Being suspected of a murder you hadn't committed would do that to a man, Will thought.

He didn't know how to fancy it up, so he gave Jed the words straight out. "We arrested Frannie's killer today. He gave a full confession."

Stunned, Jed stepped forward. "Someone…confessed? Confessed to killing Frannie?"

Will nodded. "You're completely exonerated."

"I—I don't know what to say." He turned to Gwyn. "Did you hear? Gwyn, do you know what that means?"

Her eyes brimmed with unshed tears. "Oh, Jed, it's over. The nightmare is over." A moment later she was in his arms.

Wanting to give them a moment of privacy, Will looked away. Jed and Gwyn deserved to celebrate, deserved the happiness that would come. Once he was gone for good.

Long moments later, Jed cleared his throat and spoke, his voice suspiciously husky. "Who is it? Who killed Frannie?"

"Raymond Jennings."

"Ray?" Jed simply stared at him. "Why?" he finally asked. "Why would Ray kill Frannie?"

"It's a long story." And even though Jed hadn't been close to the man, he'd said he still felt gratitude toward Ray for his help years before. "You might want to sit down."

Jed pulled himself together. "Come to the library. I want to know everything you can tell me."

Though Gwyn tried to leave them alone, Jed insisted she come along. Half an hour later, Will had finished the basic story, including Joleen's part in Ray's downfall. Jed shook his head in wonder. "How did you get him to confess? It doesn't sound like you had anything but circumstantial evidence, just like you had on me. Thorny said a conviction would be rare, given those circumstances."

"Surprise, and a lot of luck."

"I think there's more to it than that," Jed said shrewdly. "You orchestrated that whole confession, didn't you?"

"I got lucky," Will repeated. Then the words burst out, pulled from him, though he hadn't meant to say them. "I owed you, Jed. It was the least I could do after—after what I put you through. And I swore I'd make damn sure Frannie's murderer paid for his crime."

"I should go," Gwyn murmured.

"No, don't," Will said. "I owe you an apology, too. My actions hurt both of you." He paced the room, trying to marshal his thoughts.

"Will—" Jed began.

"No, let me finish. Let me say my piece and then I won't—I won't bother you again. I know it's too much to expect you to forgive me, but I'd like to explain, anyway."

Jed nodded, not speaking, and Will continued. "I had to find Frannie's killer. It was the most important thing I'd ever done with my career, with my life. I couldn't afford to let you matter. To let our relationship matter. I couldn't afford to believe in you like Emmy did. Like Gwyn did. Without any doubts, any doubts at all. No matter how much I wanted to, I couldn't allow it. Not when...not when all the evidence pointed toward you. And especially not when—" he stopped pacing and met Jed's gaze "—I believed you could have killed her accidentally.

"But, Jed, I have to tell you no one ever tried harder to find something, anything, that would implicate someone else. Even if I couldn't say it, I was doing everything I could to find the real killer."

"I know that, Will. I never doubted your motives. And I know what you felt for Frannie. Remember, I loved her, too."

"I know it's not much, considering what I did, but I'm sorry. More than I can say." He added the only thing left. "I won't bother you again."

"What are you saying?"

Surprised at the sharp question, Will looked at him. "I won't stick around. I'll be back for the trial, of course, but I'll be leaving town as soon as we get things squared away."

"You're leaving?" Gwyn asked. "Why?"

"There's nothing for me here. Not now that I've alienated the only family I had. Jed and Emmy don't need me here, not as a reminder of what I did. Frannie's gone and—there's nothing left."

"What about Tessa?"

"That's…over." As dead as his relationship with Jed and Emmy.

"What about your family?" Gwyn asked. "Are you just going to go off and desert them? Just when they need you? What's Emmy going to do when she hears the truth? Don't you think she'll need all her family around her? Supporting her? Loving her?"

"I—she'll have Riley. And you and Jed. I'm not family anymore. I lost that right the day I arrested an innocent man. My brother."

Jed crossed the room to him. "You're wrong, Will. We're still your family, no matter what mistakes fall between us."

Will stared at him, unable to believe what he'd heard. His heart stuttered in hope.

"I won't deny I was hurt when you arrested me. That you even suspected me just about killed me. And I was angry." He shot Gwyn a glance and smiled. "Okay, I was furious. But I think I can understand what drove you. I can even understand that a lot of what you did came from feeling you had no choice. You acted from loyalty to Frannie, and that's not a bad thing, even if it did hurt me."

"You should hate my guts, not forgive me."

"Why? Because you did what you had to do to find

the murderer of as fine a woman as ever lived? Sorry.''
He shook his head and put a hand on Will's shoulder.
''Remember what Frannie always said? We're a family, and families stick together. No matter what.''

Will looked him in the eye and saw nothing but understanding. And love. He could only manage to say, ''Why?''

''You're my brother, Will. You always will be.''

''I...don't know what to say to you.'' He wanted to tell Jed what his forgiveness meant to him, but he was too damn choked up to speak much more.

''Say you'll stay. Let us all learn to be a family again. Gwyn's right. Emmy's going to need us all.''

CHAPTER NINETEEN

TESSA SAT IN HER OFFICE, fingers poised over the telephone. Her two weeks would be up soon. She needed to tell the science department chair her decision. There was no point putting it off, no point dwelling on that last scene she'd had with Will. Yet it played endlessly in her mind, reminding her every time she shut her eyes just exactly what she would be giving up to go to China.

And if she were honest with herself, she had to question how much she really wanted to go. She didn't like going to exotic locations. From the age of twelve, she'd been dragged from pillar to post with her parents, and she'd detested it. Living conditions at the best digs were not very comfortable, and some of them were downright miserable. Somehow, she'd blocked a lot of those feelings in her drive to get first her master's, then her Ph.D. She'd come to accept that she would have to deal with the discomforts in order to have the career she wanted. The career she *thought* she wanted.

Then Will had entered her life and she'd begun to question everything. What did she want? What would make her happy? If she didn't have to consider anything beyond doing what she really wanted to do with her life and career, what would she choose?

"Ms. Lang, can I talk to you?"

Tessa looked up to see one of her students standing in her office doorway, a couple of books tucked under his arm. Jonathon Andrews, she realized, the boy who'd told her he was changing his major to archaeology because he'd liked her class so much. "Of course, Jonathon. Come in."

"Thanks." He shuffled in, taking the chair she offered. He wore the standard student uniform of jeans and a T-shirt with a heavy metal rock group logo emblazoned on the front. Funny, Tessa wouldn't have pegged him as a heavy metal fan. She'd have thought him more conservative.

"I know I don't have an appointment but I—I really need to talk to you."

He was a shy, rather earnest young man who hadn't grown into his gangly body yet. His brown hair was cut short, and stuck up in spikes; she couldn't tell if the style was deliberate or not. A late bloomer who seemed more at ease with his books and his computer than with people. In the short time she had taught him, Tessa found that he had an analytical and innovative mind she thought well suited to archaeology. She hoped he found what he needed from Caddo Lake College, and knew she'd miss him when she left.

"What's wrong? Don't tell me you're worried about the final."

He smiled weakly. "No, it's not that. It's my father. He doesn't want me to change majors. He wants me to stay in business. I declared for business as a freshman, because—'' he shifted uneasily in his chair ''—well, I wasn't sure and it seemed so important to him. Now he's dead set on me staying put.''

Uh-oh. She'd have to tread carefully. It wasn't her place to encourage a student to defy his parents. ''Does he say why he doesn't support the change?''

Jonathon shot her a shrewd glance that suddenly made him seem older. ''He says archaeology is a dead end and I'll never make any money in it.''

Tessa had to smile at that. ''Well, to be honest, you're not likely to get rich going into archaeology. It's possible to make a living, but if money is your goal, then you're in the wrong profession.''

He waved his hand impatiently. ''I know that, and I don't care. But my father does. He's like the ultimate in corporate America. He wants me to go into business and won't even talk about anything else. It's like, he wants me to be his clone or something.''

''I don't think it's unusual for a parent to want his child to follow in his footsteps.'' God knows, a lot of them did. Hers included. ''And it isn't necessarily a bad thing.''

''Yeah, but he doesn't care what *I* want.'' He began to fidget. ''What's the point of making a living doing something you hate? I've told him and told him I can't take business anymore. It's not for me. But my father, he doesn't see that. He's only interested in how it affects him.'' Eyes blazing with emotion, he halted in front of her. ''He wanted me to go to a different school, one that had more prestige. The only reason

I'm at CLC is because they gave me a full scholarship, tuition and living expenses." He waited a beat and added, "In the business school. He wasn't about to turn down a free ride."

"Oh. That does make it tougher. So you need his financial assistance if you're going to transfer to the science department."

Stuffing his hands into his pockets, he shrugged. "It would help, but I don't have to have it. I can work. And I might be able to get some sort of scholarship or student loan. That's why I came to you. I thought maybe…" He looked at her eagerly. "Could you help me, Ms. Lang? If you could put in a good word for me, it might make a difference to the scholarship committee."

"Of course I will, if that's what you really want." She put her hand on his arm, looking at him intently. She didn't see a speck of confusion or doubt in his gaze. "Jonathon, you're taking a huge step. Shouldn't you discuss it with your father again before you make this decision? You're talking about something that will affect the rest of your life."

His gaze turned cynical, odd in one so young. "I know, that's why I have to change." He pulled away, sat in the chair again, dejected. "It won't make any difference, my talking to him. I've talked and talked and talked and he never hears what I'm saying. He thinks refusing to pay for it is going to change my mind. Or threatening to disown me. But he doesn't understand that it's my life, my future." His gaze caught Tessa's, locked on it. "I have to be the one to make the decision. He can't make it for me."

Struck, Tessa stared at him. Wasn't that what she was doing? Letting her mother make decisions for her? But they were talking of Jonathon, not her. "I hate to see you estranged from your parents. Can your mother help?"

"She's dead," he said matter-of-factly. "Died when I was a baby."

"I'm sorry."

"It's okay. But it just makes my dad more… focused on getting me to do what he wants."

"Would you like me to talk to your father? I can't say it will help, but I'd be glad to try." *Oh, that's good, Tessa. You can't stand up to your own mother, but you're going to stand up to this man?*

"Thanks, but he won't listen to you, either. My teachers in high school used to try to talk to him, but it never did any good." He drew in a breath, blew it out, his brown eyes full of determination. "My father will either get over it or he won't. But at least I'll be on the career path I want in the meantime."

"You're very determined."

"I know what I want. And I'm going to get it."

The gangly boy she'd pictured was gone, replaced by a young man who knew his own mind, a man who would succeed, whatever his chosen field. Tessa wished she had a tenth of his self-possession. A tenth of his certainty.

She leaned back against her desk. "What if—what

if you find out you made the wrong decision? What if archaeology isn't for you, either?''

"It is. But even if it isn't, it'll be my mistake, not my father's. It's my life, not his.''

Tessa gazed at him as Will's words came back to her. *"It's your life, your career. Not your mother's."*

This twenty-year-old boy was willing to risk financial hardship and disinheritance by his family in order to have the career—the life—he wanted. And she was afraid to risk—what? Her mother's anger and disapproval? Why was that so important, when she'd never managed to gain her mother's approval in her life?

Here she was, on the brink of throwing away not only a career she'd discovered she truly enjoyed, but the man she loved because she couldn't admit what she really wanted was right before her. Not because she didn't know what she wanted, but because, out of some misguided sense of loyalty to her mother, she couldn't admit to wanting it.

"Ms. Lang? Are you all right?'' Jonathon stood beside her, eyebrows drawn together in a frown of concern.

With an effort, Tessa smiled. "Sorry, you've given me lots of food for thought. I'll do whatever I can to help. With your grades it shouldn't be a problem to get you at least a partial scholarship. I can't guarantee it, of course, but I'll do my best. And Jonathon, you're welcome to work at my Caddo dig and any future ones I have in the area.''

His face lit up. "Wow, thanks, Ms. Lang. I really appreciate that.''

''The pay isn't great,'' she warned. ''But the experience will help you.''

He shook her hand, pumping it up and down enthusiastically, and thanked her again. Finally he started to leave, but turned at the door and looked back at her. ''About those digs, I thought you said you were only here for the summer?''

Tessa gave him a brilliant smile. ''My plans have changed. I'm staying.''

''Great! I know a lot of kids who'll be happy to hear that. A lot of them think you're the best teacher they've had. And some of them don't even like archaeology. They took it to fulfill their sciences requirement, and they thought it would be easy. But you made them like it. Even glad they had to take it.''

Unexpectedly touched, Tessa laughed. ''High praise, indeed. Thank you, Jonathon. You've helped me, more than you can imagine.''

Tessa waited until he left, then picked up the phone and punched in a number. ''Dean Salazar, please,'' she said, asking for the head of the sciences department. He came on the line a moment later. ''Dean Salazar, this is Tessa Lang. About that offer for the professorship, I accept. I'm thrilled to be a part of your faculty.''

She hung up a few minutes later, grinning from ear to ear. Her grin faltered when she thought about the next call. She was on a roll, though, so why put it off? A short time later her mother's ice-cold voice sounded in her ear. ''Theresa, finally. I've been waiting for your call. I can't put the China expedition off forever. Now, you'll depart for San Francisco—''

Tessa interrupted. ''I'm not going, Mother. I've been offered a full professorship of Archaeology with Caddo Lake College. I accepted today.''

A stunned silence greeted her announcement. ''Wh-what?'' Olivia finally said. ''You must be joking.''

''No, I'm very serious. I'm sorry, I know it's not what you wanted for me, but it's what I want. What I need to do to be happy.''

Total silence.

''Mother? Are you still there?''

''You've lost your mind. It's that man, isn't it? He's the one who's behind this. You're ruining your life because of a fleeting sexual attraction.''

Tessa gave a gurgle of laughter. ''Will's part of it, yes. The attraction isn't fleeting, though. You really shouldn't talk that way about your future son-in-law.'' Unless he'd gotten so fed up with her he no longer wanted to marry her.

Her mother moaned but didn't speak, so Tessa continued. ''I'm doing this for me. Not for Will, or you, or anyone else. For me. Because I want to teach. I want to see those faces light up when they discover that they want a career in archaeology. Or even when they discover that archaeology class is a lot more fun than they'd expected. And I want to try to reach the ones who are bored, who don't know what they want and aren't sure they even want to be in college. I want that challenge, and that joy.''

''Teaching isn't all challenge and joy. You've got

some ridiculous Pollyanna view of it. It's drudgery, ninety percent of the time.''

"Not for me. Oh, I know I'll have failures, kids I won't be able to reach. But I can handle that, as long as I have the others, too.''

"You're throwing away the chance of a lifetime to teach at a backwater country college. Why?'' For once, Tessa heard true emotion in her mother's voice.

"I have the chance of my lifetime right here, Mother. Don't you see, I want a home. A family. I want kids and dogs and cats and birds and a husband who loves me.'' Glancing out her window, she saw two students walking hand in hand. She smiled, thinking how much she wanted that with Will, the time to walk through the woods, simply holding hands.

"I want to go to work and know I'll be coming home to the same place, day after day, year after year. To know that I can make friends and not have to leave them after six months or a year. I want to plant flowers and trees at a place that's mine. I want roots and permanence, and all those things you never seemed to miss. With grandmother, I had those things, and I've missed them ever since. I want them now, Mother, and I intend to have them.''

"I—I don't know what to say to you.'' Olivia sounded uncertain, another first in Tessa's memory.

"Say you wish me happiness. Say you'll try to understand.'' Say you love me, Tessa thought, but she knew that wouldn't happen.

After a long silence, Olivia spoke. "I...sometimes wonder what my life would have been like had I made different choices. Perhaps your way is better. For you.''

It was a concession she'd never expected to hear from her mother. A concession she hadn't thought her capable of making. Could she possibly have misjudged her mother for all these years? Or was it because she'd finally stood up for herself and actually told her mother what she wanted? ''It is, Mother. Believe me, it is.''

''Are you really going to marry that man? It's that serious?''

''Yes. If he'll still have me.''

''If he'll have you? Why wouldn't he?''

''I—I hurt him. I'm not sure how he feels about me right now.''

''He'll come around. You are, after all, a Lang,'' her mother said loftily, sounding more like her old self. ''If he's the man you want, then you'll just have to convince him.''

Tessa laughed. ''Oh, I intend to. And Mother—'' She hesitated, choosing her words carefully. ''Thank you. I didn't expect you to take my announcement so well.''

''I'm disappointed, of course. I may not agree with you, but I—I want you to be happy. It may not have seemed that way to you, but I do.''

Tessa hung up the phone feeling like the weight of Tut's tomb had been lifted from her chest. In shock, she sat and stared at the phone. Had that really been her mother? Speaking as if she cared about her—cared about her feelings, not just her career? Maybe the thing lacking in their relationship for so many years had been Tessa's backbone. They might establish some kind of connection after all.

If only her talk with Will would go as well. Now she had to find him and convince him he still wanted to marry her.

CHAPTER TWENTY

AT NINE THE NEXT MORNING, Will met Jed at the Gray Wolfs' house. Jed had wanted to be there when Will told Emmy the news, and Will had agreed he should be. Emmy would definitely need all the support she could get.

They had hoped to take care of it the night before, but when Will had called, Emmy had already gone to sleep. Instead, he set up a meeting time for this morning with Emmy's husband, Riley. Riley was too well mannered to ask what the hell Will wanted, and Will didn't fill him in. It wasn't a conversation for the phone.

He still didn't know how to tell her. But he knew she had to be told, and by someone who cared about her.

"Will, are you going to ring the bell or do you intend to stand there all day?" Jed finally asked.

"Stand here all day," he muttered, but he rang it.

The door opened a couple of seconds after he rang. Emmy's gaze fastened on his. "Okay, Will, what's the big mystery? Riley said you wouldn't tell him what this was about." The words tumbled out before she finished opening the door. Then she saw Jed standing behind him and her eyes rounded. "Jed? What— I didn't think you two— Why are you both here?"

Her eyes darted between them, her expression worried. She looked cautious, unsure. And why wouldn't she be? Will thought. After all, he'd arrested Jed.

"We have some news we thought we should tell you together," Will said. "Why don't you let us in and we'll talk?"

"Oh. All right." Emmy stood back to let them enter. She hugged Jed, started to hug Will, but then she backed off, settling on patting his arm. It hurt him, to think of Emmy too scared—or too angry—to hug him.

"Can I get you some coffee?" she said, her confusion evidently growing.

"Yeah, thanks." She left the room quickly, after shooting another puzzled glance at them. Will glanced around the living room and frowned. To Jed he said, "I hope Riley's here. I asked him if he would be."

"Riley's just getting back from taking Alanna to preschool," Emmy said, reentering the room carrying a tray with four mugs. "I hear his car now."

"We'll wait, then," Will said. "You'll want Riley here." He looked around at the living room of the house Emmy shared with Riley and his daughter. Emmy's adopted daughter now, he reminded himself. A nice room, a comfortable room. The oak and leather furniture showed signs of wear and tear, though the room was tidy, with newspapers stacked neatly and Alanna's toys in bins in the corner of the room. Not Emmy's doing, he suspected, unless she'd changed drastically from her childhood. But Riley had always been neat.

Riley entered just then, greeting the two men and taking a seat on the couch beside Emmy.

"Why are you being so mysterious?" Emmy asked, impatient as always. "You're making me nervous. And Jed hasn't said two words."

Jed smiled. "Hard to get more than two words in with you here, Emmy."

She returned the smile, then sobering, turned to Will. "What is it? Is it—is it more bad news? Why are you two here together? I thought—I thought you weren't even speaking."

Will took a deep breath, fumbling for a way to begin. "I'll get to that. I know you've been…upset with me lately, Emmy, and I'm sorry for it."

Candid green eyes met his. "Well, I still don't really understand how you could suspect Jed." Her gaze flitted to Jed, then back to him. "But Riley tried to explain that part of it is your job. He says it's understandable, you being in law enforcement, that you would have to approach the case the way you did." She shot Riley a glance that implied she didn't agree with him, either. "But just because I was upset with you didn't mean you had to quit seeing me. I've missed you, Will, and so has Riley."

"Given the circumstances, I thought it was best. But I missed you, too." He hadn't realized how much, though, until just this minute. He looked at Jed and nodded.

"Speaking of those circumstances," Jed said, "the

charges against me have been dropped. I'm no longer a suspect in Frannie's murder.''

Emmy jumped up from the couch and crossed the room to hug Jed enthusiastically. "Oh, that's wonderful, Jed. When did you find out?''

"Last night. Will brought me the news." He patted her back and smiled, but Will could see his eyes looked worried.

"We arrested the murderer yesterday," Will said. "He gave a full confession.''

She sat beside Riley once again, barely containing her excitement. "But this is wonderful news!" She looked from one foster brother to the other. "Isn't it? Why don't you two look happier? What's wrong? I don't understand.''

Will cleared his throat, wishing he knew an easy way to break the news to her. "It's great for Jed. But it isn't so great for you.''

Riley spoke up for the first time. "I'm confused, too. Why isn't it good for Emmy? Who killed Frannie?''

"Ray Jennings.''

Still confused, Emmy frowned. "Why? Why would he kill her? And what does that have to do with me? I barely even know the man.''

Will moved to the couch to sit on Emmy's other side. "Frannie found out a secret that Ray didn't want told. Emmy," he grasped her hand and squeezed gently, wishing he didn't have to be the one to make those pretty green eyes widen with horror. "Emmy,

I'm sorry, but it turns out Ray Jennings is your father. He killed Frannie so it wouldn't come out.''

Dumbstruck, she stared at him. ''My...my father?'' she faltered. ''Raymond Jennings is my father?'' She shivered, the thought obviously unnerving her.

Will nodded. ''Yes. He's admitted it. And he admitted writing those anonymous letters, so you and Riley would call off the search for your birth parents.''

''How—how can he be my father? How is that possible?'' She turned imploring eyes to Jed. ''Did you know?''

Jed shook his head. ''Not until last night. When Will came to tell me the charges had been dropped.''

''And you, Will. How long have you known?''

''Not much longer than Jed. Let me tell you the whole story.'' So Will told her, glossing over some of the worst parts in the hope she'd never have to know the full extent of her father's perfidy. Absorbing it fact by fact, she didn't talk much, only asking a question now and then. Riley sat with his arm around her, also interjecting a sharp question or two. When Will finished, a prolonged silence fell.

''I can't believe this,'' Emmy finally said. ''I wanted—I wanted to know who I came from, but I never expected...this. My father is Ray Jennings. And he killed Mom Fran.'' She choked. Tears welled in her eyes, then trickled down her cheeks. Turning into Riley's shoulder, she threw her arms around his neck and sobbed.

Will and Jed exchanged helpless glances and listened to her cry. Finally Emmy sat up, wiping her eyes. Jed handed her a handkerchief and she gave him a wan smile.

"It's not all bad," he said gently. "You know who your mother was now, too. And you know she loved you and wanted you."

"And this time Joleen is going to give us some answers," Riley said grimly. "It's the least she can do after all her lies."

"I think Joleen will be happy to share what she knows about your mother now, Emmy. She really regrets keeping it from you." Will ached for her, but he didn't know what to say to comfort her.

Emmy gave a hollow laugh. "I guess I should be grateful my mother didn't hate me. Unlike my father." She was silent a moment, then burst out, "He hated me. I bet he wanted her to have an abortion. Didn't he? Didn't he, Will?"

Damn it, why was he always the one who had to hurt people? Why did he have to tell Emmy something that would only cause her pain?

"Tell her the truth," Riley said. "She deserves to know the whole truth."

"Don't make me spend my life wondering," Emmy said. "Just tell me."

His job, his responsibility, Will thought. He told her the truth, as gently as he could. "Ray thought your mother had had an abortion. That's why Frannie's finding out and confronting him about you was such a shock. Remember, he said he was trying to reason with her and things got out of hand. He says Frannie died accidentally, that he never intended to kill her."

''What do you think?'' Emmy asked.

''It's possible. But I think that's for the jury to decide. Even if it's true, and it was an accident, that doesn't make up for his hiding her and letting Jed take the blame for her death. Or anything else he's done.'' Such as denying his daughter's existence.

''And that's who I came from. A murderer.''

''You also came from your mother, who loved you,'' Will said. ''Don't forget that.''

''Oh, how can you understa—'' She broke off, her gaze locking with his. ''You do understand, don't you? You and Jed both.''

Will nodded. ''I'll never know who my father was. And my mother, well, she was a pretty sorry excuse for a mother. Nobody would want to claim her. But it doesn't have to rule your life, Emmy. Only if you let it.''

Jed squatted in front of her, taking her hands between his. ''My father was no prize, either. But he didn't do anything more for me than contribute some genes. He didn't make me who I am. And neither did your father make you who you are.''

''I don't know what to think. What to say. I'm— stunned. I never expected this.''

Jed released her hands and rose. ''We're all here for you, Emmy. Gwyn and I, and Will, too. Whenever you want to talk, whatever we can do, just say the word.''

''Emmy,'' Riley said, ''you're still the same person you were before you knew. Don't forget that.''

She smiled at her husband ruefully. ''So it makes

no difference to you? To know your wife has a murderer's blood running through her veins?''

"Not one bit of difference." He smiled back lovingly. "I love you, Emmy. I always will." She went into his arms and he held her tightly.

Swept by conflicting emotions, Will looked away. Emmy would be all right, he thought, especially with Riley beside her. But seeing that unconditional love made him think about losing Tessa. And wonder if there was any way they could be together. To have a chance at what Emmy and Riley, and Jed and Gwyn had.

There had to be a way he and Tessa could be together. Some way, somehow. He just had to find it.

IN THE END it was simple, Will thought. He could spend his life wishing he hadn't let Tessa go, or he could find a compromise they could both live with. So what if he didn't know anything about compromising? He could learn.

Of course, first he had to find her. She wasn't at the college, or the Caddo burial site. Her friend Ellen hadn't seen her, and neither had anyone at Bubba's or the Caddo Kitchen. Finally he went to her house and waited there. Though he had a key, he didn't use it, waiting instead on the porch. And since Goofy was barking nonstop, he let the dog out of the backyard and brought him around front.

He sat on the swing, Goofy lying in blissful abandon at his feet. The dog would never be a beauty, but something about those adoring brown eyes really got to him. He still couldn't see Tessa leaving him behind, but he knew he'd offer to take him—and the damn cat, too. Pepe, he had a feeling, wouldn't make life easy for him.

He heard the car a half mile away. Choking and sputtering, the ancient Subaru wagon pulled into her driveway. Tessa got out and started toward him, but he couldn't read her expression. She wore one of those sleeveless summer dresses she liked so much. This one was white, which gave her fair skin a luminous glow, and made her red hair that much brighter. She looked beautiful, he thought, and wondered how long it had been since he looked at Tessa and merely thought her pretty.

Goofy ran to meet her, but to Will's surprise, the dog didn't jump on her. She must have been training him.

She stopped a couple of feet in front of him. "I've been looking for you. I came back here to call you."

"Yeah, I've been looking for you, too. We have to talk," he said. He wanted to kiss her, and knew he shouldn't. He didn't know how she'd react. Instead, he waved a hand at the porch swing, and she sat beside him, smoothing her dress down.

"I know," she said. "I have some things I need to tell you."

Focused on what he wanted to say to her, he didn't really hear her. Now that the moment had arrived, he felt a flash of insecurity. What if she didn't really want him with her? What if the job was just an excuse, and she didn't love him as much as he'd thought? Well, he'd know soon enough.

"I'm glad you're here," she said. "I've missed you."

Will plunged right in. "I hate being without you. I thought I'd get used to it, thought I could deal with it, but I realized I don't want to. It doesn't matter what I have to do, it will be worth it if we can be together."

"Will, that's what I wanted—"

"No, let me finish. I have some things I need to get off my chest." She seemed about to speak, but then she nodded. Will propped his forearms on his knees. "I told Emmy this morning. About her father."

"How did she take it?"

"About like you'd expect. It was rough. She's going to have a hard time, but she'll be all right. She's got a lot of support from her family. Riley and Alanna. Jed and Gwyn."

"And you."

"Yeah. And me. Emmy and Jed want me to... They say we're family."

She laid a hand over his and squeezed. "I'm so glad for you, Will. I hoped the three of you would work things out. You deserve it."

"I don't know about that, but I do know I'm happy to have them back in my life." He turned his hand over to hold hers. "But seeing them together, Emmy and Riley and Jed and Gwyn, seeing how they've handled all the crap that's been happening, has made me realize a few things." He looked at her then, gazing into those beautiful blue eyes. "I want to be with you,

Tessa, and I don't care what I have to do. You were right. You have just as much right to ask me to give up my career as I do to ask you to give up yours.''

Her mouth fell open. She closed it and asked, ''What are you saying?''

''I'll go with you. To China. Or wherever you think you need to go.''

''What? Will, are you crazy? You can't give up your work.''

''Why not?'' he asked quietly. ''I asked you to do it. Why shouldn't you ask me the same thing?''

''But—but what would you do? In China?''

''Security or something.'' He shrugged. ''It doesn't matter, I'd find something. I could be a hell of a security consultant for some of those big digs.''

''I can't believe you'd give up your job for me. Your career.'' She pulled her hands loose and parked them on her hips, glaring at him. ''Have you lost your mind? You love your career! It's everything to you.''

''No, not anymore. You're everything to me.''

Her gaze softened. ''What about being so sure I was making a mistake? You're willing to give up your career so I can make a mistake?''

''Who am I to say it's a mistake? I kept saying you were letting your mother make your decisions, and that you were making a mistake to let her run your life. And here I was trying to do the same thing.''

''No, you weren't. You were just trying to get me to see things clearly.''

''Yeah, but I wanted you to see things the way *I* saw them. And it isn't my decision, or my career. It

has to be yours. As for it being a mistake—'' He
paused, trying to think how to present his thoughts. ''I
wasn't thinking of joining you right away. I thought—
if you stay in China for several months, you'll know
whether it's a mistake, won't you?'' She didn't answer
and he rushed on. ''If you decide that's what you
want, then obviously, I was wrong. I'll quit the Rangers then, and come over there to be with you.''

She grasped his hand and squeezed. ''I can't have
you giving up a career you love for me. You'd resent
me after two weeks. If not before. And I wouldn't
blame you.''

He stared at her for a long time before he released
her hand and stood. ''You're trying to let me down
easy. You don't want me with you, do you? Just tell
me the truth, Tessa, and I'll leave you alone. Don't
drag it out.''

She jumped up and threw her arms around his neck.
''I don't want you with me in China. Oh, Will, I can't
believe you'd do something so crazy for me.''

''It's not crazy. If you want to be with me. But since
you don't—''

She drew back and smiled, a dazzling smile of happiness. ''Who said I didn't want you? I want you right
here in Uncertain.''

Cheeks flushed, eyes bright, she looked like a kid
on Christmas morning. ''What the hell does that
mean?''

''It's what I was coming to tell you. I accepted the
job here.''

"You—you did what?" His hold on her loosened, but she only held on tighter.

"I took the job here. The professorship at CLC. Today."

"Because of me." He frowned. "That's not what I wanted, either. Then you'll resent me, and I won't do that to you."

"No, I took the job because of me. I asked myself what I would do if I could do anything I wanted. If I could have any career I wanted. And in my heart, I knew I wanted to teach."

He couldn't quite buy it, much as he wanted to. "What about China?"

"I finally admitted that China is the last place I want to go. Or anywhere else. I'm tired of traveling. I've been doing it since I was twelve, and haven't ever enjoyed it. The thought of living in China for two or three years makes me shudder. But the thought of staying here, researching the Caddo Indians as much as I want, teaching, being with you— Oh, all those things make me want to sing. What's the point of doing something you hate the rest of your life?" She laughed. "Someone very wise asked me that today. I had to admit he was right."

"You're serious. You've thought this through."

"Not only thought it through, but acted on it. I told you, I accepted the teaching position. I also told my mother to forget China. I told her I was staying here."

"Bet she was happy about that." Oh, man, she'd probably take after him with a machete.

"She took it better than I'd expected. But that's not

important. What's important is what you and I want. And I want you, Will. So much.''

He still couldn't believe she'd changed her mind. Couldn't believe he wasn't dreaming. ''You're sure?''

She pulled his head down and kissed him. A kiss brimming with love and happiness. ''Positive,'' she murmured against his lips.

Will gathered her to him and took the kiss deeper. Long moments later he came up for air, aware that her front porch wasn't the most private of places. ''I want to make love to you. Right now.''

She smiled, taking his hand to draw him inside. Goofy rushed past them, and Tessa shut the door, backing Will up against it.

He raised an eyebrow. ''You look like a woman with a purpose in mind.''

''Oh, I am. I'm in charge this time. And I'm seducing you.''

''Yeah?'' Smiling, he reached for her. ''Is that a threat or a promise?''

''A promise,'' she said.

The look that accompanied her words raised his blood pressure sky-high. ''I can live with that.''

''Good, because you're going to have to.'' She kissed him, plunging her tongue into his mouth.

He returned the kiss, sliding his hands beneath her dress, pulling it up, and finding nothing underneath but the incredibly soft, bare skin of her bottom. He couldn't help a heartfelt groan as his body instantly hardened. ''You don't believe in wasting time, do you?''

"Don't you think we've wasted enough time?"

"Yeah. Way too much."

Her smile was wide and sweet. "I love you, Will. I guess I should have said that first thing."

"As long as you say it, and keep saying it for the rest of our lives. I love you, Tessa." He kissed her, long and deeply.

And Tessa made good on her promise.

EPILOGUE

One week later

WILL HADN'T BEEN SURE what to expect from Frannie's memorial service, but he was glad they had it. It had given him a sense of closure and he thought it might have done the same for Jed and Emmy.

From the French doors of Jed's morning room, he watched Alanna wielding a croquet mallet on the lawn. June's husband, Josiah, was out there with her, looking a little dazed by her energy. The little girl was a female version of Riley.

They had all returned to Beaumarais after the memorial service and people had been dropping by all afternoon to pay their respects. Jed was just now taking leave of one of the last, lingering guests, while Will and Tessa talked with Gwyn.

"I hadn't realized how many people knew Frannie," Will said. "I think all of Uncertain showed up at the graveside service."

"A lot of them came for Jed and Emmy and you," Gwyn said.

Emmy came over to them just then. "Have you seen Alanna?"

"She's out on the lawn, and I can't swear to it, but it looks like she's hitting a croquet ball," Tessa said, looking out the French doors. "In fact, I think she's hitting it this way."

"Last I saw, she was swinging the mallet like a baseball bat," Will added.

Emmy paled. "Wooden balls? With all this glass? Oh, no, I'd better go out there and—"

Her words were interrupted by the sound of glass shattering. "Stop her," Emmy finished with an exasperated sigh.

Riley came up behind her. "No, you stay here. I'll handle it. I told Gwyn it probably wasn't a good idea, but it was too late. Once Alanna heard about croquet—" He shrugged. "She wasn't supposed to face the house, but..."

"...she didn't mean to," he and Emmy both finished and laughed. "I hope Jed will forgive us."

"Forgive you what?" Jed asked, returning to the morning room just then.

"I'm afraid Alanna had a little accident," Emmy said guiltily, motioning out the window. "Croquet balls and my daughter don't mix with all that glass," she murmured.

Jed smiled. "Glass can be replaced. Don't worry about it." He peered outside, as well. "Looks like she got the greenhouse, anyway. June and Josiah are dealing with it. They've got four kids of their own, so don't worry about leaving Alanna with them, either. Don't go, Riley. Gwyn and I have something we'd like to share with all of you."

Will looked at him curiously, waiting for him to go on.

"This seemed like an appropriate time, after Frannie's memorial," Jed said, putting his arm around Gwyn. "Because it's something I want to share with the family I wouldn't have if not for Frannie."

"Don't keep us in suspense, Jed," Emmy said. "What is it?"

"I'm getting to it, Emmy." He turned to his wife and smiled before speaking to the rest of them. "I don't think this is out of place, because this is news Frannie would have rejoiced in, too. Gwyn and I are having a baby."

"How wonderful!" Emmy said, and promptly threw her arms around both of them.

Will shook hands with Jed and kissed Gwyn on the cheek. "That's great news. Jed will be a terrific father, you know."

"I know," she said, smiling mistily.

"I have a feeling you'll be a terrific mother, too."

"Thanks, Will." She smiled and accepted a hug from Tessa. Tessa approached Jed much more gingerly, but Will was glad to see him accept her congratulations with no strain. Tessa had told him she was still afraid Jed didn't like her, but Will thought he'd forgiven her for taking him to court long ago.

Will decided to wait a while to make his own announcement. Instead, he turned to Emmy. "I don't like to bring up touchy subjects, but I saw Joleen come up to you at the service. Are things okay with her?"

Emmy's expression sobered. "Poor Joleen. I really

don't think she meant to act maliciously. And after all, she did make sure that I went to live with Frannie. I owe her a lot just for that.''

''I still think she should have told you the truth long before now,'' Riley said, putting his arm around Emmy and giving her a hug.

''She was afraid,'' Emmy said. ''And she's trying to make up for it. She says I'm a carbon copy of my mother, and that's why she was so shocked that first time we went to see her. We're going to talk more about my mother soon. Joleen even offered to do what she could to help me trace my mother's family, but I told her not to bother. Anybody who would abandon their pregnant teenage daughter isn't someone I'm interested in knowing.''

Though he didn't want to hurt her any further, Will still needed to know if she'd come to grips with the truth about Ray Jennings. ''You're okay about the— other side of your family?''

Her expression hardened. ''My natural father, you mean. As okay as anyone would be, I guess. I saw him.''

''When?'' Jed asked. ''We would have come with you if you'd asked us.''

''I know you would have, but Riley was with me. It was...strange.'' Her eyes clouded with memory. ''I thought I'd feel something, some kind of connection to him, since I knew the truth. But I didn't.'' She included all of them in her announcement. ''I didn't feel a thing, except regret and anger that he killed

Mom Fran. It was like looking at a stranger, because he is a stranger to me. And I don't see that changing.''

''Did Ray say anything? About his treatment of you?'' Will asked.

''Not much. He tried to justify what he did a little, you know, about totally denying my existence.'' Her eyes sparkled now. ''But he shut up pretty fast when I told him what I thought of him. And I know he was glad Riley was on the other side of the glass,'' she said with a laugh. ''I can't blame Ray—Riley looked like he wanted to take him apart.''

''He's not the only one,'' Will said. But since Will hadn't wanted to do anything to compromise the case, he'd had to settle for arresting him. Tessa slipped her hand in his and squeezed. He smiled down at her, reminded that he had an announcement of his own to make. But first, he had some unfinished business with Jed.

''I've been trying to find the right moment to return something of yours to you. Seems like this is it.'' Will pulled Jed's high school ring out of his pocket and handed it to him. ''The prosecution doesn't need it anymore. I told Fielder I wanted to return it to you.''

Palm open, Jed stared at the ring. ''Thanks. I still can't figure out how it got there, you know. I remember losing it, and looking everywhere for it.''

''Is that your senior ring, Jed?'' Emmy asked, peering at the object in his hand.

''Sure is.'' He turned it over, his eyes taking on a faraway expression. ''Tessa found it on Beaumarais, where Frannie…'' His voice trailed off and he cleared his throat. "Where Frannie was. It's what led to my arrest."

"I'm sorry, Jed," Will said, unable to halt the feeling of guilt.

"Water under the bridge," Jed told him.

"This was the evidence you couldn't tell me about? The reason you arrested Jed?" Emmy asked Will. He nodded and she held out her hand to Jed.

"Can I see it, please?" Jed handed it over and Emmy studied the inside of the band. "She didn't have time to get it engraved," she murmured. "How ironic that something Mom Fran intended as a loving gesture was what almost got Jed convicted."

"What are you talking about, Emmy?" Jed and Will asked at once.

"Mom Fran told me—I guess it was a few days before, when you were searching for it, Jed. She told me she had the ring safe and that she planned on having it inscribed as a surprise for your graduation."

"It might have saved us a lot of trouble if we'd known that," Will said. "But I couldn't tell you and I guess Jed and Gwyn never thought to."

Jed shook his head. "No, we didn't. Did Frannie tell you what inscription she intended to put there?"

Emmy nodded, her eyes bright with unshed tears. "'The future's yours, F,'" she said softly, and gave the ring back to Jed.

Jed didn't speak for a moment, then cleared his throat. His voice was husky when he said, "That sounds just like something Frannie would have said."

Emmy covered his hand with hers. "I think we

should have it inscribed now. She would have wanted us to.''

Will noticed Jed simply nodded, without speaking. He didn't blame him. He was choked up, too.

''Something weird happened the other day,'' Emmy said after a long pause. ''Amanda came to see me.''

''Lucky you,'' Tessa murmured.

''I think Ray's revelations really shook her. And I hear her mother isn't doing too well. She's holed up in that house like a recluse, refusing to see anyone except Amanda.''

''Did Amanda actually acknowledge your relationship?'' Gwyn asked. ''Somehow I can't see her doing that.''

Emmy nodded. ''Sort of. She admitted that we're technically half sisters, but she wanted to assure me that she didn't expect us to have a real relationship, and she hoped I didn't expect it, either.''

''Not much loss,'' Tessa said.

''I understand why you don't like her, Tessa, but you know, I felt sorry for her. And the funny thing was, I think she was lying. I think she'd like to have a sister, someone she could count on. She's not lucky, like I am, to have two brothers and a sister-in-law.''

The perfect opening, Will thought. ''What would you say to having another sister-in-law? Tessa and I are getting married in two weeks.''

''Wonderful!'' She turned to Jed. ''I told you they'd work things out.''

''Tessa's taken a teaching position with Caddo Lake College and I'm transferring to the East Texas division of my Ranger company. We're going to stay in Uncertain.''

While congratulations abounded, he pulled Jed to the side. ''I need a best man. I know it's—if you'd rather not, I understand. But I wanted to ask you.''

''I thought we'd put our differences in the past, Will. I'd be honored to be your best man.''

''Will wanted to have it next weekend,'' he heard Tessa telling Gwyn, Riley and Emmy. ''But my mother intends to come, and she asked us to put it off another week.''

She still looked stunned that her mother was coming. Will was glad for her sake, though he didn't fully trust the woman. But it meant a lot to Tessa to have her mother there.

''The wedding will be at the Methodist church,'' Tessa added. ''At three o'clock.''

''Do you have a place for the reception?'' Jed asked. ''Gwyn and I would be happy to have it here.''

''Thanks, but it's going to be at Santiago's,'' Will said, and grinned at Tessa, remembering their conversation with Carlita. ''Carlita's already told me that if we don't have it there, she won't stop at boxing my ears.''

Everyone laughed and the six of them continued to talk and plan. Eventually Alanna came in, eyelids drooping, and Riley and Emmy left to put her to bed. Tessa and Will left shortly thereafter.

At home, Will pitched his coat and tie, and he and Tessa went out to the dock. ''It's hard to believe it's over,'' he said, standing behind Tessa and wrapping his arms around her. The water lapped at the dock. An owl hooted. "Frannie's finally at peace." And so was he.

"It's not over, though," Tessa said, turning in his arms. "Our life together is just beginning." She kissed him and added, "Here's to beginnings."

"Beginnings," he said, kissing her in return. "Frannie would like that."

HARLEQUIN *Super***ROMANCE**

CREATURE COMFORT

A heartwarming new series by

Carolyn McSparren

**Creature Comfort, the largest veterinary
clinic in Tennessee, treats animals of all
sizes—horses and cattle as well as family
pets. Meet the patients—and their owners.
And share the laughter and the tears with
the men and women who love and care
for all creatures great and small.**

#996 THE MONEY MAN
(July 2001)

#1011 THE PAYBACK MAN
(September 2001)

*Look for these Harlequin Superromance titles
coming soon to your favorite retail outlet.*

HARLEQUIN®
Makes any time special ®

Visit us at www.eHarlequin.com   HSRCC